BODY
AND
SOUL FOOD

Abby Collette

BERKLEY PRIME CRIME
New York

BERKLEY PRIME CRIME
Published by Berkley
An imprint of Penguin Random House LLC
penguinrandomhouse.com

Copyright © 2021 by Shondra C. Longino
Excerpt from *A Deadly Inside Scoop* by
Abby Collette copyright © 2020 by Shondra C. Longino
ISBN: 9780593336175

First Edition: November 2021

Printed in the United States of America
1 3 5 7 9 10 8 6 4 2

Book design by George Towne

*Love and support to all the friends
and family in foster and kinship care,
the adoptees, adoptive parents and birth parents.
God's got you.*

Chapter One

"HE PUT HIS foot in those greens."

Reef stopped and looked at me. Hand hovering midway between bowl and open mouth. A forkful of collards dangling. Juice dripping. His eyes went from mine to Koby's flip-flop-clad feet to the dark, limp greens in front of him. "You mean like they do with grapes?" Scraping his teeth across the surface of his tongue, he stuck it out and scrunched up his face. "Ugh! Is that how you make 'em?"

A bright, sun-filled afternoon, we were out back of our soon-to-be bookstore and café. We'd put out three umbrellaed wooden tables with our logo in the bricked alleyway and scattered brightly colored potted plants around.

"No." Koby pursed his lips and shook his head at me. "That's not how I make them. She just learned that term," he said, and chuckled. "It's just a saying, Reef. You know. You say it about the person who cooked something that's really good."

"So you didn't actually *stick* your feet in 'em?" Not mov-

ing his head although talking to Koby, Reef rolled his eyes
my way.

"Nope." Koby was sitting on one of the benches with the
head of his yellow Labrador retriever, Remy, resting on his
lap. "Not literally." He grinned and scratched Remy's head
and around his torn ear. "My feet"—he held up a hand like
he was swearing—"at no time during the cooking of those
collard greens were anywhere near them."

Satisfied, Reef slurped the greens from his fork and covered his mouthful of food with his fist. "Man! These are
good." He smacked his lips before shoveling in more, letting
everyone in earshot know how much he liked them.

"You've mentioned that with each mouthful," I said, and
laughed.

"Because they are." He chewed while he talked. The grin
on his face matched the one Koby was wearing. "Even if you
did try to sabotage my enjoyment." He narrowed his eyes at
me. "Bad sister."

Koby laughed. "Don't call my sister bad."

"Koby," Reef said, swallowing his food, his laugh almost
causing him to choke. "You know Keaton's my girl." He
winked at me. "But what I don't get is why haven't you ever
made these for me before?"

"I'm not in the habit of cooking for you, Reef."

"Well, you should, bro. Even if you need to stick your feet
in them. I mean, even the juice is good."

"Guess what the juice is called," I said.

Reef looked down in his bowl and swirled the brownish-
green liquid around. "Okay, I'll bite. What is it called,
Keaton?"

"Pot liquor," I said.

Reef mouthed the words as he sat on the picnic bench next
to my brother. "Didn't you cook 'em in water? I thought you
said you put them in a pot of water. You know I don't drink
anymore."

"I did cook them in water," Koby said. "It's just another

word that Keaton's learned. You'd think as a librarian, her vocabulary would be broader."

Reef laughed.

"Gotcha," I said. As much as Reef teased me, it was fun to get him.

"Koby Hill and Keaton Rutledge." Reef held up his plastic bowl and winked at me. "Here's to your new venture together. If all the food is as good as what I've sampled so far, it is definitely going to be a success." He turned up his bowl and downed the juice.

Koby Hill was my twin brother. Fraternal. Of course. But there's a story to why we have different last names. One that tends to tug on the heartstrings of whomever we tell.

Born July 2, twenty-five years ago. As far as we know, the only two children of one Morie Hill, age twenty-two.

And as it was to be our fate, on July 3, two years later, we were separated after having our last birthday together the day before. Abandoned, maybe orphaned, I was soon adopted. Koby wasn't. That's how he still got to keep our biological mother's last name. Or our father's. We weren't sure about that either because we knew nothing about him. Yet.

Koby had grown up in foster care. I didn't find out about him until he showed up at my door, a DNA kit in hand. "Just to make sure," he'd said. But standing there looking at each other, neither one of us had any doubt. We knew right then that there was an incontrovertible bond between us. And the resemblance was obvious. We had no idea whom we looked like, but we definitely looked like each other. Light skin, full lips, big eyes and long lashes. He was taller than me by nearly a half a foot, one of our few differences. Our hair was sandy brown, and it had Koby questioning if we were biracial. Then his DNA came back, knocking that idea down. According to our countries of origin, we were Black.

We found each other shortly after my dad died. Koby's appearance in my life was just what I needed to pull me through my grief.

My father had left me a little nest egg, and with Koby's help, we found my house in Timber Lake after I landed the library job. That was when I first found out that my twin brother was a phenomenal chef. He'd come over and hang out, cook me food and borrow from my bookshelf as if it were part of the county's library system.

It was a late-fall evening, over a big bowl of creamy, cheesy grits with big juicy blackened shrimp, that I found out about his dream. I had told him he should open a restaurant.

"You could clean up!" I said. "Everyone would come and eat your food."

"I've been thinking about doing that. With you," he'd said. "Ever since I was thirteen. That's when I first went to Mama Zola's, and she let me hang out in the kitchen with her."

"Doing it with me?" I placed an open palm on my chest. "You didn't know me when you were thirteen. How did you think you would have a business with me?"

"I knew I would find you."

"And did you think I would be able to help you cook? Because I can't cook."

"You wouldn't cook."

"What would I do?"

That was when he pulled out a tattered folded picture from his wallet. He must have found it in a magazine. The color had started to rub off.

"It's a bookstore and café." He gently passed the picture over to me. "A soul food café."

"A bookstore café?"

"No. A bookstore *and* a café. One business, two sides. You would run the bookstore. Which is perfect for you. I would run the restaurant."

I stared down at the picture. An archway separated the two sides, but books were everywhere. "And did you know at thirteen I was going to be a librarian?"

"I *learned* to cook, but my love of books was innate." He touched his heart. "I was sure you'd have that same love, too."

And he was right. My love of books came from deep inside. Going to the library was one of my first memories.

Koby had had a clear vision for Books & Biscuits. It had been his idea in the first place. And even though I had just started my first job as a librarian, it didn't take much for him to talk me into it. I could hear my father, who, at the time, hadn't too long before become my guardian angel, telling me to go ahead, spread my wings, because he knew I was ready to take on the world.

Koby had known about me all along, and after that conversation, I found that once he learned about me, he'd made plans for our lives to be spent together. Sure, he didn't know my name, but he knew I was somewhere out there.

That was thanks to Reef Jeffries. The man who'd been stopping by to help us get our new soul food and book café up and running. Yep, I decided to partner with my brother to fulfill the dream he had for the two of us. The money my dad left helped us to do that.

But anyone who stopped by while we were getting the bookstore and café up and running would have thought that Reef was in on the deal. He was always dropping by, and usually, like now, it ended with him eating up whatever Koby was working on in the kitchen.

Six years older than us, Reef had remembered that when Koby came to the group home, he hadn't come alone. A sister had been with him. Koby decided to find me. Starting at thirteen, he tracked down people who might have known us, dug through county records that might have documented our hazy history and Googled whatever information he'd come up with to find any links that might lead him to me. And thanks to all his sleuthing, eventually, somehow, he did.

Unfortunately, the only branches popping up on that genealogy website after I got my results back for us were the ones that linked us to each other. That was enough for me. But not Koby.

Koby wanted to find our biological mother. I didn't care

about it. About her. I figured I just had two mothers. One I knew. One I didn't. I couldn't imagine my life any different or any better by knowing about the one who'd given birth to us. The one who'd given us away. I had Imogene Rutledge. The best mother anyone could ask for. Adoptive or otherwise. I didn't have any need to find out more. But for Koby, Morie Hill was the only mother he'd ever had, and he needed to know what had happened to her.

A beeping sound interrupted my thoughts.

"What's the alarm for?" It had gotten Koby's attention, too, but he needed to know what it was about.

"Man, mind your business." Reef laughed. He pulled his cell phone out of his pocket and silenced the alarm.

"You got an appointment?" Koby raised his eyebrows. "Maybe you need a reminder not to eat up all our food? I'm all for that." Koby was enjoying ribbing his friend.

"Always trying to be a detective," Reef said. Shaking his head, he stuffed the phone back in his pocket.

"You hiding something?"

"It's a reminder to take my pill. You know, my vitamin. I am so absentminded lately that I forgot to bring the vitamins with me," Reef said. He dismissed the alarm and dug into his pocket. He pulled out a red and white round peppermint candy and popped it into his mouth. He was always sucking on those minty hard candies. "Now you know all my flaws. I stopped drinking. I'm taking vitamins. My short-term memory is shot. But I'm trying to be healthier."

"Koby, come and see what I've done."

Our attention was drawn away from Koby and Reef's banter to the back door. Georgie was standing in it. Our only employee so far, she'd come to report her progress in the kitchen.

Georgie Tsai had pale skin and black hair, and her entire left arm and right lower leg were covered in colorful tattoos. Green. Red. Blue. Her body said more than she did.

After she'd worked for us for a few weeks, I wasn't sure

she'd work out, and I was ready to let her go. Her nose was always stuck in the books we'd ordered when she should have been placing them on the refurbished bookshelves we'd painted white. I didn't want to have the headache she was sure to cause after we opened. But my softhearted brother took her hand, literally, led her to the kitchen and put her to work. "We've already hired her," he said to me later. "She's counting on us, just like we're counting on her. How about if we give her another chance?"

Koby had Georgie learning recipes, helping him pick out plates and flatware, painting walls, setting up tables and putting up groceries. She hadn't missed a beat with him.

"Something to show me?" Koby said, standing up. He walked over to the door "Okay. Let's see what you've done." He placed a hand on her shoulder and turned her around. "Lead the way." Remy followed right behind him. Koby stopped and patted Remy on the head. "You know you can't come in the kitchen." He held out a hand for him to sniff. "Stay." He lowered his hand and Remy sat. "You stay here. Okay?"

I followed. I hadn't been given any commands to the contrary. Plus, butterflies took flight in my belly whenever I was alone with Reef. But I was doing my best to calm all the nerves because I liked him hanging around.

Inside, I looked at the stack of boxes and books scattered everywhere and let out a huff. I needed to get to work.

The bookstore and the eatery were separated by a wide, curved archway. Each of us in charge of one side. My side was the bookstore. I had books to shelve and cozy little corners and nooks to fashion for browsing and reading. Koby had the kitchen and café seating area.

Our first tasting party and the official opening was fast approaching, and I wasn't ready. I had grand ideas that took a lot longer to execute than it did for Koby to put up groceries and set up the tables and chairs. His motto was to keep it simple. I could learn a thing or two from him.

The new furniture I'd ordered was still covered in plastic. The new wood floor was covered in drop cloths because we still needed to finish painting the walls and crown molding I had added to create ambience.

"I'm going to head out," Reef said. He'd come in behind me, threw his disposable plastic bowl into the big trash can we kept in the middle of the room. He brushed his hands together, then stuck them down in the pockets of his blue jeans. Walking over to me, his eyes locked with mine. He came and stood right next to me, brushing his bare arm against me. I could feel his warm breath on my face and the smell of peppermint when he turned to talk to me.

"Tell Koby," he said, "if he needs me to try any more dishes you guys are thinking of adding to the menu, to call me." Then he leaned in closer. "But *you* can call me anytime. For anything."

I wasn't able to speak until he had moved away from me. And then I wasn't sure if my voice was even audible.

He stood at the door. Hand on knob and a grin on his face.

"I—I thought you were going to help me . . ." I cleared my throat. "You know, finish unpacking books," I said, and gestured to the stacked boxes.

"I thought you were going to come hear me play my sax. I'm going to be at the Hemlock Jazz Club Friday."

"The one on Lake Street?"

"Yup." He smiled. Tilting his head, he gave me another wink. "But don't bring your brother when you come. I don't want him coming and messing up us having a good time."

"I don't . . . I don't know if . . ." Blushing, I lowered my head, lifting my eyes, looking toward the kitchen to make sure Koby hadn't heard him. He didn't like Reef flirting with me. He'd just started doing it, or maybe I just started noticing it.

But I didn't mind it at all.

"Okay." I finally stopped stumbling over my words and gave him an answer. I wondered, did he consider this meetup a *date* . . .

"Good. I'll come pick you up. Friday," he said, and nodded to confirm before he flipped the lock and left.

Swinging my eyes away from the door, I caught sight of a man out the corner of my eye. Bent over one of the low bookcases, he stood up, three or four books in his hand he'd evidently taken from the ones I'd already shelved. He placed them on top of a pile of books I'd just taken out of a box. He looked surprised to see me.

I felt the same way about him. *Where had he come from?*

"Who are you?" I asked. I wasn't frightened. I always felt safe when my brother was around.

"Pete."

Pete had on a trench coat, and when he raised a hand up to cover the cough that erupted when he told me his name, I saw he was holding a Totes umbrella. Unusual for these parts. Timber Lake hadn't seen anything but blue skies for the last week and a half, not a drop of rain in sight. But I guess it was always good to be prepared.

Everything about Pete was odd. From his lopsided haircut to his ruddy complexion, Hello Kitty book bag hanging off one shoulder, to the misbuttoned blue shirt he wore underneath his open coat.

Cocking my head to the side, I blew out a breath. "Pete," I said, making my voice even and calm. "We're not open yet." I waved my hand around. "Not for another week. Maybe you can come back then?" I let my eyes rest on the books he'd put down.

"I'm here for a job," he said. "To help get everything, you know, in order and then afterward, too."

"A job?" I hadn't listed anywhere that we were hiring. I shook my head, trying to understand. "How did you get in?" I asked. Which, in hindsight, should have been my first question. I knew the double front doors had been locked. We'd just finished painting them and cleaning the windowpane inserts with Windex and newspaper that morning. No one had been in or out. At least not through that door.

"The girl with the tattoos." Pete gestured with his head toward the front door. "She let me in."

"Georgie?" I frowned. She hadn't said one word to us about anyone else coming here.

"I don't know her name."

"So who is this?" Koby was standing in the archway. He was drying his hands with a red-and-white-checkered tea towel. He smiled at the stranger.

"I'm Pete." The man said his name again for Koby.

"You got a last name, Pete?" Koby asked.

"Only if I'm getting hired."

At that, an impromptu interview with Pete commenced with everyone still standing in the middle of the floor. Koby did all the talking, including me only at the end to ask if I had something to add. Twenty minutes after I'd found him loitering in our yet-to-be-open bookshop café, Pete, last name Howers, was hired and helping me put books on the shelves.

My brother was always picking up strays, like that rescue dog that he took everywhere with him. He said that's what we were—strays—and that I should be more flexible about helping out others like us find their place in this world, especially seeing that someone had been kind enough to give me a home.

Chapter Two

"I DON'T LIKE you going anywhere with Reef," Koby said. "He's always . . ." Not finishing his sentence, my brother curled up his lips and wrinkled his nose like he'd just smelled something bad.

"Flirting?" I finished his sentence for him.

Koby snorted.

I smiled.

We were standing on the underground platform at the Westlake Station in Seattle, where Koby lived, Timber Lake's closest big city, waiting for the 6:44 p.m. southbound. It would take me to the International District Station, one stop away. From there, I'd have to catch the Sounder out of the city. And that train's closest station to Timber Lake still left me with a fifteen-minute walk home.

Koby hadn't liked that idea at all.

My brother now slash business partner and I had been out on a last-minute shopping trip. Picking up cloth napkins, checking on our lighting that hadn't arrived, getting yet another crate of the mason jars he wanted to serve our signature sweet tea in. Spending the last of our budget, we had just enough to ensure next-day delivery to Timber Lake on the items we purchased.

We'd also stopped at the Seattle Central Library to search recent newspapers for obituaries and old records that might give us a lead on where we could find Morie Hill, our biological mother. Koby went often. So I thought, while I was hanging out in Seattle, I would help him with his research.

After a meal at Tacos Chukis on Broadway—a messy plate piled high with tender slices of seasoned grilled pork, holy green chunky guacamole, sweet onions and juicy pineapple—and a whole, long conversation about him rethinking the decision to hire Pete Howers, we found the day had gotten away from us. Koby worried about me getting home. He wanted to be the big brother, although we had yet to find out which of us had been born first.

"There was a mugging last week in Capitol Hill," he said. "A woman got her purse snatched."

"I'm not even going that way." I raised an eyebrow. "Remember? I live in the opposite direction."

"Still . . ."

"Koby, you act like someone got murdered. It was a purse. And it didn't even happen on the train."

Koby had a car. An old, usually out-of-commission, car that he said he wouldn't let me ride around in because he never knew when it would break down. So the most inexpensive way for me to get home was public transportation.

There really wasn't any need for him to worry. I had lived in Seattle for most of my life before going off to college and then moving to Timber Lake. I knew every light rail and Sounder station, and probably every streetcar route there was. And then there were fare enforcement officers always lurking around.

My town was too small and my trips to the big city too infrequent for me to own a car. Once in Seattle, the trains on the Red Line of the light rail came often and ran late. The platforms were well lit. I had walked the neighborhoods of Seattle since I'd learned to put one foot in front of the other. It was easy to get around. And if that failed, I had the Uber app on my phone.

Plus, Timber Lake was probably the safest place I could be. It was practically crime-free. Located in the Pacific Northwest, it was sparsely populated and was situated on a spit of land nestled between Bishop Creek and the ravine our town was named for.

Connecting green space and trails to community, Timber Lake was burrowed in the midst of cottonwood trees and weeping willows, their leaves rustling in the wind that carried sweet birdsong. Surrounded by sweeping meadows of native grass, the views from most vantage points were calm, blue lake waters. We prided ourselves in keeping our waterways pollution-free from runoffs.

And on a clear day, in the far skyline standing anywhere in Timber Lake, shrouded in a thin layer of white mist, you could see the majestic Cascade Mountains.

I loved the area so much. It was where I'd insisted we have our bookstore and café.

"I worry. I just found you, Keaton. I don't want to lose you again." We were leaving the restaurant, and I'd guessed the dwindling sunlight of the day made him realize that it would be dark before I made the forty-five-minute trek home.

"You're the only family I have," he said.

"You have more family than anyone I know," I said. "Reef. Miss Zola. Your Captain Hook. I could go on and on." I sucked my tongue. "All over the state of Washington."

"It's not the same. My foster family means a lot to me, you know that. But I mean *real* family. Blood."

"I'm sure we do have real family somewhere, Koby. And we'll find them," I said, although I hadn't ever really thought about doing that until Koby and I had been reunited.

"You know what I mean," he said. "And even if we do, I don't have another *twin* sister."

"Okay. You got me on that one." I smiled to reassure him. "C'mon." I gave him a light punch in the arm. "Nothing is going to happen to me. I'll be fine."

"Maybe you should get an Uber," he said in that voice he gets when there's no talking him out of something. The same voice he had when he insisted we hire Pete.

Luckily, that was when Reef had called.

Reef was heading to Timber Lake, although he wouldn't tell us why, and when Koby told him where we were, he said he'd be happy to escort me home. He was at the UW Station, two stops away, waiting for his train to arrive.

"The train'll be here in a few minutes," I heard Reef say. Koby had put him on speaker. "What station are you at?"

Koby looked up at me from his phone. I think he wanted me to tell Reef that I'd rather have my brother take me home. But to do that, Koby would have to catch two trains with me, walk me home and then turn around and trace his steps back to get to his apartment. That was a lot. And a waste of time. Plus, I wanted to stop by the bookstore café and check on what Pete had done. And I didn't want my brother to know I was keeping an eye on our newest employee.

Pete had been there all day, a key to the place in his possession, painting trim and shelving the last of the books. He was supposed to have locked up when he left. I wanted to make sure all that had happened.

But more than that, I had gotten up the nerve, I hoped, to spend some time with Reef when my brother wasn't around—without getting tongue-tied.

"We can meet you at the Westlake Station," I said, leaning down into the phone.

"Or she could just take an Uber."

I looked up at Koby and he locked eyes with me.

"Takes six minutes to get there from here." Reef's voice came through the phone. "I'll text you when I get to Capitol Hill so you'll know I'm a stop away. Once she's on the train, Koby, she'll be safe with me."

The Westlake Station was only a couple minutes' walk from where we were, and the thought of hanging out with Reef put a little pep in my step.

"You're walking fast," Koby said.

I shrugged. "I just don't wanna miss the train."

"The one Reef is on."

"Yes. The one Reef is on." I reached into my purse and pulled out a debit card. Tapping it on the screen of the yellow card reader, I heard the familiar single beep signaling the start of a ride. Rail stations were on the honor system (with the help of the enforcement officers) and passengers were expected to go into the Fare-Paid Zone only if they had paid. But before I could turn around to bid farewell to my brother, I heard another beep.

"Did you just pay for the train?"

"Yeah." He waved his blue ORCA card at me.

"Koby!" I tilted my head. "Really?"

"I'm just gonna wait on the platform until you get on the train."

"Koby."

"What?"

"So, you're just gonna pay for a ride that you're not taking?"

"As long as you leave within five minutes, I can reswipe and my money'll be refunded."

"Oh, brother." I rolled my eyes.

He smiled. "Yes, sister?"

His phone buzzed before I could say anything else.

He pulled his phone out of his back pants pocket. "It's Reef," he said, looking down at the screen. "He texted that his train is pulling out of Capitol Hill."

"See, he'll be here in a couple of minutes."

"More like a minute and a half."

"So you can go!"

"I can wait."

That deadpan look on his face told me to just go with it.

Happy when the train arrived, I stood close to the edge, waited until the door opened and boarded without looking back at my brother.

I had to walk through to the other end of the train car to find Reef. He didn't even turn around to greet me or wave me over.

"You could have come to the door or let me know where you were sitting," I said once I got to his seat. "Move over." I gave him a nudge with my hip. I smelled the peppermint coming from his breath. I felt a little bolder than I usually was around him. I was looking forward to this ride.

But with that bump, his phone dropped out of his hand and onto the floor. I reached down, ready to pick it up, but the train jerked as it started to pull away, and instead I bumped into Reef again. This time, it made him fall over across the seat.

That's when I saw the blood coming from his nose.

And then his blank eyes staring back at me.

I reached up and pulled the emergency cord. The screech of the wheels against the metal rail and my shrill scream could have cracked glass. With the jerk of the train coming to a halt, his body rolled over and hit the floor with a *thud*.

Wringing my hands, I noticed all eyes of the five or so passengers on me. Hadn't they seen what I saw? I didn't think I'd even heard a gasp from them. Or maybe I was in shock, and I couldn't sense anything.

I let out a small groan and wished now that I'd let my brother take me home. I really wanted him right here with me.

I looked out the window of the train's door, back where I'd left him. A light rain had started and was beating down on the glass. But through it, I could see my brother, running down the tracks, headed my way.

Chapter Three

KOBY REACHED THE train before the conductor made his way into the car. Climbing up the back of the cab, he pulled the door open and his eyes searched for mine. When they locked on, I turned my gaze to where Reef lay.

Koby's mouth opened, seemingly in slow motion, but no words came out. His chest heaved and a look of anguish crossed his face. I could feel his pain.

He glanced around the car, seemingly stopping to take in each of the passengers, before starting toward me. His steps exaggerated and awkward, as if he were wading in a rock-filled creek. It was like he was unsure how to move forward, afraid he might stumble. I reached out my hand to him.

But he brushed past me and knelt beside his friend's limp body. By this time, a few of the passengers had come over to take a look as well.

I was kneeled down next to him. Not knowing what to do and keeping an eye on Koby, seeing if he knew what to do to help. One passenger stooped down on the other side of me to get close, her hair falling in her face. She leaned in and reached out. I hoped she might be a nurse or medical professional, but she didn't do anything.

Koby shook Reef's shoulder as if trying to wake him, but when there was no response, he put his hand over Reef's nose, then he looked up at me. I already knew the answer to what he was trying to determine, but knowing my brother, he would need to find out those answers for himself. Needing more, he leaned down and placed an ear over Reef's heart before reeling back on his legs. "What happened?"

"I don't know." My voice was hoarse after the shriek that came with my discovery. "He just fell over." I felt the tears well up in my eyes, and my hands started to shake. I decided to answer out loud what he was questioning in his head. "He's d-dead." My words came out strained.

Koby ran his hand over Reef's face, closing his eyes before he stood up. He put his arms around me. "Yeah. I think so." He rubbed a hand over the top of his head. I could hear his breathing. Short. Quick. Labored. "This is crazy." He tugged at the corner of his eye as if he was trying to stop a tear from falling. "We just talked to him."

"What is going on in here!" The driver of the train burst through the door. His eyes were glaring, easy to tell he was angered by having to respond to a pull cord. I wondered how many kids had pulled it as a joke before.

I glanced at Koby before directing the driver's attention to Reef. "It's our friend. He. Uhm. He needs help."

Although I knew there wasn't any help for Reef.

"Oh. Good Lord. What happened?" He looked at us standing over him. "What did you two do?" He came closer to take a look at Reef.

"We didn't do—"

Before I could finish my sentence, Koby, holding on to my arm, squeezed it tight. I tried to pull away, but he held on to it. "You need to call 911," he said, answering the driver with a directive.

"What happened?" the driver repeated. This time he looked around at the other passengers.

"We don't know," Koby said, looking at me, then back at the driver. "But you need to get the police here. Now."

"I'm calling the transit police." The driver pulled a two-way radio from his belt, his eyes landing back on us. "Nobody leave!"

"You need to call the Seattle PD," Koby said.

The driver walked past us and I saw his ID. He walked to each of the sliding doors, putting a key in a hole above them and giving it a hard twist. I guess locking us in.

His ID read, "Lance Bender. Driver."

And, with his actions, it seemed that Driver Lance Bender didn't want to listen to us either. Well, Koby. I hadn't said anything else after being cut off. Which was fine with me. I'd let Koby do all the talking because I wasn't sure if I had regained control of my voice yet.

Koby must have noticed the driver's name tag, too.

"Mr. Bender," Koby said. "I think someone killed him." He pointed to Reef's lifeless body. "You're going to need more help than you can get from ORCA's security detail."

Koby was throwing shade. Being snarky. The Metro Transit Police weren't just security guards, they were certificated just like the Seattle police and had the same powers. Still, I understood what he meant. I wasn't sure if a homicide detective was among their ranks.

If a homicide really had been committed.

I looked at Koby. Clenching and unclenching his jaw and staring down the driver as he made the call over his radio. That just wasn't like Koby to say mean words. But I was sure his attitude was only because he was upset about Reef.

He was strong, but me? I knew the only reason I wasn't breaking down right then was because Koby was there. Even in the time I'd known him (that I could remember), I'd always felt better (and safe) when he was around.

But, according to Koby's assessment, what little he'd done, this was even more serious than I thought.

Well, you know, I mean, death is serious. But murder? That was much worse and ratcheted things up—I looked around at the people in the train with me—to a whole other level.

I don't think that I was ever unsure that Reef was dead, but it never even crossed my mind that he'd been killed.

IT WASN'T LONG before a swarm of Metro Transit and Seattle police and EMTs crowded into the one train car with us and . . . the body.

Creepy.

And sad. At least for the two of us.

I listened intently as a man who introduced himself as Homicide Detective Daniel Chow said he would send an officer around to get our names and addresses. Koby and I tried to relay to him that we were friends of Reef's, but he held up a hand. "Please wait until I ask the questions," was his response. Then he relayed he wanted to question all of us before we could be released to go home. In another car. One at a time.

"I didn't see anything," the girl with the phone said.

"And meanwhile," he said, finishing up his little spiel, "please do not share any thoughts with each other about what happened." He looked over at the one passenger on the other side of the aisle from us, pushed up against the window, her leg stretched across the seat. "And no phones until you're off the train."

She let out a huff.

"Thank you," he said, a weak smile on his face.

His talk made me think that he, evidently, had the same mind-set as Koby—something sinister had happened to Reef. Why else would he tell us not to share? Why else question us somewhere else?

Then I wondered if he'd be able to figure out the guilty party that quickly. In the span of a train conversation.

Or was this detective's plan to release a murderer out into the city after only a brief conversation? A person who had seen all of our faces and who might not want to leave any witnesses.

I looked around the train car and sighed. There were five other people in our car besides us. Not one of them looked like a murderer to me.

Although, I couldn't be quite sure what one actually looked like.

Koby and I, sitting next to each other, didn't say much while we waited for our turn to be questioned. I was nervous, my hands folded in my lap to keep me from fidgeting, but nothing could stop my leg from shaking a million miles a minute. I was surprised Koby hadn't asked me to stop, I wasn't sure if my actions, involuntary but definitely necessary, weren't causing the entire train to rock.

Koby was quiet. The only muscle he moved was the one in his jaw. He kept it so tight, I was convinced his face must be sore. He seemed intent on watching every movement made by the EMTs and police from the moment they first approached Reef until the time they wheeled him out stuffed inside of a black bag.

I didn't once glance that way. I cared about Reef, maybe even liked him a little more than that, even though I hadn't known him long. And I knew how much he meant to my brother. But I couldn't watch or listen to what they were doing to him. Around him. I purposely focused my attention on everything else. All the other commotion and conversations. I already had my ID out when Officer Mateo (I'd heard his name when Detective Chow tasked him with the assignment) came to get our information. I had kept my attention on him as he had rounded the car. We were the last ones he came to.

Koby didn't even look away from where Reef was when the officer got to us.

"Koby"—I gave him a little nudge to get his attention—"he needs you to tell him your name and show your ID."

He moved like he was in a trance. "Koby Hill," he said, reaching into his back pocket without taking his eyes off the spot where Reef had been. "Spelled with a 'K.'"

The officer left, leaving all of us alone.

The car was quiet, and it seemed even quieter after all of what had happened. There I was, sitting next to someone I knew and not talking. But I didn't know what to say to Koby, how to comfort him. I hadn't had a brother long, but I felt so close, like somehow he'd always been there with me. But there were still so many things I didn't know about him yet. Like how I could make him not so sad.

They say twins can feel each other's emotions. I swear I could feel his, but that feeling left me with no clue on what to do about them.

"Calliope Pussett." The first of us was called to the next car.

She sat with her husband all the way at the end of the car. The only seats that faced opposite all the other ones. I watched as the middle-aged couple, probably in their forties, stood up. Their names sounded European—Calliope and Basil Pussett—although I hadn't heard an accent when they'd given their names.

Calliope Pussett wore a lavender sweater set. Fuzzy and soft-looking, it was one I'd have in my closet. Her pants fit snugly over her skinny frame, although they weren't nearly long enough. Her legs and ankles were pale. Her fingers long and her pink glossy-tinged lips thin.

I thought perhaps her lipstick should have been a shade of orange to match better with her carrot-colored hair.

Although it was Mrs. Pussett who was called, both she and her husband got up and walked to the door to where Driver Lance Bender had been stationed. He had been told, I assumed per his actions, to let one person out of our car at a time, being sure no one else could leave. Then they'd have to wait on the platform for Driver Bender to let them into the attached car where Detective Daniel Chow was waiting to do his questioning.

"Only her," Driver Bender said. "You'll have to wait."

"I'll be fine," she said, and gave a slight smile and a nod of her head. Her husband took a seat next to the door and waited. Worried, I guessed.

I was worried, too. If the two of them had done something to Reef, I'd rather they both left. I would have felt much safer. But looking around the car, I didn't really think I could feel safe left with any of them.

It took about fifteen or twenty minutes for Calliope Pussett to reemerge. When she came through the door, Basil stood up and together they walked back to the seat they had previously occupied.

"Aubriol Meijer." The next name called.

"It's pronounced 'Meyer,'" she said. "The 'j' is silent." The twentysomething popped up out of her seat, pulling her earbuds out and wrapping the cord around her phone. "And I didn't see anything."

"Tell the detective that when you go in to talk to him," Lance Bender said, his face conveying he didn't care about the "j" in her last name or the lack of information she knew.

She stomped her way out of the car and stood on the platform, waiting for the driver to lock us back in and open the door to the other car.

Second one in. Five more of us to go. I did the math in my head: Fifteen minutes (at least) spent with the detective in the other car times the ones who hadn't yet spoken with him, including Aubriol Meijer with the silent "j," would come out to having one hour and thirty minutes left. Ninety minutes. Five thousand four hundred seconds . . .

It seemed like we'd already been there for days.

And then I wasn't sure if there were other people on the train. In other cars.

I wondered when I'd ever get back home.

Chapter Four

THE LEG SHAKING had calmed down a bit and now it was just the tapping of my foot as I waited my turn. Miss Aubriol Meijer, who had nothing to say, had taken nearly twenty minutes to tell the detective that.

"Tessa, uhm, Chai . . ." Driver Bender was back. He looked up, then back at his paper. I guessed he did care about calling out people's names wrong.

"Chaiken," the owner of the name offered.

Tessa Chaiken nearly bumped shoulders with Aubriol as she made her way out. They couldn't have looked more different. Aubriol short and thick, saggy jeans, fingernails painted different colors. Tessa, shoulders back, strode more than walked. Her hair cut even to her jawline, her nails short and well manicured and tons of eye makeup. Eyeliner. Thick mascara. Lip liner and gloss. Her jeans were low-riders with a bootleg cut. She had on a green stretchy tee, fitting over her curves, that read **Find a Way or Fade Away**, the words going vertical, getting lighter as they went down.

Cute, I thought. And it gave me a feeling of déjà vu. Seemed like I'd seen that T-shirt somewhere before . . .

Aubriol rolled her eyes as the two women just missed colliding. Tessa didn't seem to notice. I watched the door close after her and then Bender locking it.

At least one hour, ten minutes left . . .

My mind wandering, in a loop, back to the last time I'd seen Reef—alive—and the last time I had talked to him. I could still hear his voice.

I couldn't wait to get back to Timber Lake. Nothing ever happened there. Plus, the initial shock was wearing off, and that loop of Reef playing in my head was making me sad. Really sad. I didn't know how much longer I was going to be able to hold back the rush of tears that were banking up inside.

"This all seems so surreal." Koby was talking. Finally.

"Unbelievable." My voice low and unsteady.

"And what a coincidence we were here." He shook his head. "Right when this happened." He puffed out his cheeks, filling them with air, then blew it out. "What were the chances of that?"

"Astronomical."

I had been waiting for him to come out of his zombielike state, and now that he was, I had only one-word responses to add to the conversation.

"And I wonder if any one of these people saw anything, would they tell?" I saw his eyes scan the car.

I cleared my throat and turned to him. "This reminds me of *Murder on the Orient Express*."

My go-to, whenever I felt uneasy, had always been books. Agatha Christie was one of my favorite murder mystery authors. *Murder.* Ugh.

I shook the word off before finishing my thought. "If," I emphasized, "there was a murder, maybe they're all guilty." Lowering my voice, I leaned in closer to Koby. "They're all in it together."

"Together in what?" He looked at me, for probably the first time since they'd taken Reef out. "You're talking about a movie?"

"A book." I nodded. "Made into a movie, though." Koby was a reader, but not like me. It's all I did. I'd pick a book over television anytime. And I hardly ever watched a movie made from a book I'd read and enjoyed.

"I should have known you were talking about a book." I thought I saw a weak smile cross his face. "I think I saw that movie," he said. "Is it the one where the couple that plotted the first victim's death end up killing other people to keep them from telling on them?"

"No." I swallowed, wanting to keep my voice low. But I'd had that thought earlier, although *that* book hadn't come to mind. "That one is called *Death on the Nile*. Took place on a big ship. The one I'm talking about took place on a train."

"Oh."

"In it, the victim was stabbed twelve times. Once by each of the passengers on the train. Well, in the car they were assigned to. All in it together, so no one told."

"And why would they do that?"

"He, the murder victim, had killed someone near and dear to them. They all wanted to exact their revenge."

Koby drew back and looked at me, one eyebrow going up higher than the other. "Reef didn't kill anyone."

"I know," I said, grabbing his arm, tugging it to bring him back closer to me. "The point I was making is that everyone was involved."

I saw the muscles tighten in Koby's jaw as he scanned the car. Tessa Chaiken still hadn't finished with the detective.

"That couple didn't have anything to do with what happened." He pointed to the Pussetts.

"You don't think?"

"I'm sure of it."

"And why aren't the Pussetts on your who's-the-killer radar?"

"I don't have a *killer* radar." He made a face. "And why do you remember their names?"

I chuckled and shrugged. "I just do. Calliope and Basil Pussett. Not too common a name. Easy to remember."

He chuckled. "Okay." He adjusted himself in his seat. "She's wearing those dark glasses on the train."

"She's sitting by the window." I gave a head nod her way. "Maybe the sun is in her eyes."

"She wasn't sitting there when I got on the train," Koby noted. "She was sitting in the aisle seat. But"—he stuck up a finger—"even so, there isn't any sun out. It's raining. No need for sunglasses."

"It only started raining after I'd gotten on the train," I said. "She was already here. She hadn't been outside when it started raining." I held out my hands. "Maybe she just kept them on from when she boarded."

"True." He nodded like he was processing what I'd said. "But most people take sunglasses off when they go inside. Or flip them up over their head. But more than that, those don't look like regular sunglasses."

"As opposed to *irregular* sunglasses?"

"Look at them."

I did. "Okay. They're a little clunky-looking." I thought about my earlier observation of her. "They don't really match her style."

He licked his lips and nodded his head like he was adding up something in his mind. "And did you notice how she's been trying to make up to her husband about something? Clearly they've had some kind of disagreement."

I took another gander at the couple. I looked and tried to notice things like Koby had. I mean, I had remembered their names—maybe I was more observant than I gave myself credit for.

Calliope had on pearl earrings. Small balls, but none of her jewelry had pearls. So maybe they'd been a gift? If they were real, they might be expensive. Did that mean they were a well-off, power kind of couple?

I scrunched up my face.

Koby was right, her sunglasses weren't the kind you'd buy at Nordstrom. He wore glasses, too. But his weren't dark, and he evidently needed them to see. But none of those things told me the things that Koby had seen in the two of them. I tilted my head to one side. Had they been arguing?

I didn't know what Koby was seeing or how it could mean they weren't involved because of it. How did sunglasses and an argument between the two of them stop them from being the ones who killed Reef?

"You wanna explain this to me?" I asked.

"Sure. When the driver called her to go and talk to that detective, her husband walked with her, remember?"

"Yeah, I remember that. It was like he wanted to go in with her, even after Detective Chow had said one at a time."

"Exactly. Driver Bender had to stop him."

"That could mean they had something to hide. He wanted to keep an eye on her."

"Maybe. But didn't you notice how he was holding on to her arm? Like helping her." I frowned up, trying to remember that part of it. Koby must have noticed my grimace. "You know, guiding her."

"What are you getting at, Koby?"

"Something's wrong with her eyes. Maybe she's been to the eye doctor?" He hunched his shoulders. "Had her eyes dilated?" He held up his hands. "Maybe just her eyesight isn't good. Something."

"Yeah." I nodded. "Those are the kind of glasses you get from the eye doctor. Shield your eyes from the sun after they've been dilated." I licked my lips. "They're not the flimsy rolled-up ones."

"Right."

"Okay. So what?"

"So, who goes to get their eyes dilated when they're planning to commit murder?"

"Hmm. I don't know." I thought about his conclusions.

"Maybe they saw Reef and knew this was the only chance they'd have to do it. Planning it for a while, they saw the opportunity."

His one eyebrow arched again, letting me know my deduction skills weren't as good as he thought his were.

"Okay," I said, moving on. "How do you know they'd been arguing?"

"Because he walks and guides her when necessary, like he did to the door. But when she tried to hold his hand once they got back to their seats, he pulled away from her. And whenever she talks to him, he keeps his eyes straight ahead. Not looking at her."

"Maybe she's the one who did it and he now has to cover for her." I smirked. "That would make *me* mad."

But Koby had moved on, showing me my Agatha Christie connection wasn't holding water. He turned his attention from the Pussetts and settled his eyes on another passenger while finishing his summation of the couple. "Yep. He's definitely simmering about something."

"And let me guess. They wouldn't kill Reef because they're arguing?"

"When people argue, they kill each other, not some random third person."

"Maybe Reef intervened. Got in the way of a fight they were having."

"Their argument wasn't loud or out of control," Koby said. "It was between the two of them." He gave an inconspicuous point of his finger to the girl with the phone. "She said she hadn't seen anything." He looked at me. "You remember her name?"

"Aubriol."

"Oh yeah. With the silent 'j.'"

I smiled. He remembered, or else he had been reading my thoughts.

Twin telepathy.

"Right," I said.

"When the detective first got on the train, Aubriol volunteered that, without anybody asking what she'd heard."

"Yeah." I remembered. "She said that to the driver when he called for her to go and talk to the detective in the other car."

"Right."

"You heard her say that?" I hadn't thought he was paying any attention to anything.

"And I heard it when she said it to whoever she's been texting with."

I sucked my tongue. "You can't read her texts from here, I know."

"She was talking to them before she got the eye from Detective Chow. Whenever he wasn't looking at her, she'd text."

"And you know she was texting the same person she was talking to?"

"I don't *know*," he said. "But she needed to finish telling them the story, whoever it was she hung up on." He shrugged. "You gotta figure if the Pussetts had been fighting and Reef got involved, Aubriol wouldn't have said she hadn't heard anything."

"I think she said she hadn't *seen* anything."

"Same difference. She is glued to that phone. I'd bet it had all her attention."

"Maybe she's lying?"

"Look around," Koby said. "Look at them." He placed a hand on mine. "Does anyone look like they've been in a fight?" He looked at me. "No. They don't. And the way she's holding on to that phone, I'm thinking if it was something that serious, somebody getting killed, she would have videoed it."

Now, that observation I agreed with.

"And," he said, "who would want to be on the train with a murderer if they knew?"

"I don't know, maybe *she's* the murderer."

Koby shook his head. "She is too self-involved. Nothing about her is calculating. And she looks uninterested."

"Uninterested?" That made me chuckle. He was right. It

was how she looked. "Maybe she was threatened and now is acting all aloof to save herself."

"She doesn't look that savvy either."

I chuckled. I didn't know why my brother thought he could know so much about people he hadn't ever spoken to and had been around only in the hour or so we'd been stuck on the train.

"Like I said"—he continued his assessment—"she's not interested in anything but that phone." He cocked his head to the side. "Plus, that's a lot to have happen—a killing and a plan for the cover-up in the two minutes it took for the train to get here after Reef texted me."

"Actually, a minute and a half."

"See."

The doors slid open and Tessa Chaiken walked back in. Koby's eyes traveled along with her. She took a seat opposite the one where she'd originally sat. Keeping her eyes straight ahead.

"If anyone is lying, it's those two."

"Who? Tessa?"

"Yep. And that guy." He was talking about the last person from our car, other than us, who still needed to speak to the detective.

"Are they together?" I glanced between them. I was confused. I hadn't even seen them interact. "They haven't even said anything. Not that I've heard."

Now what was he using for his deductions?

"They haven't said anything to each other, but their eyes."

"What about their eyes?"

I looked at them and didn't see anything.

"What, Koby?"

"Jason Holiday." Driver Bender was calling the next suspect—uh, witness. Person.

Jason reminded me of a nerd. Nerd's not a bad thing, I'm a nerd. But it made me think he probably wouldn't be a good witness or have much to add about what happened to Reef.

Lots of times we tend to be always thinking and not paying much attention to our surroundings. He wore jeans torn at the knee and canvas tennis shoes. His reddish hair looked like he ran his fingers through it when he got out of bed and nothing more.

"You think they did something?"

"I just think . . ." Koby narrowed his eyes and watched as the guy walked past us. "They look suspicious."

"Like they're the murderers?"

"Like they are up to something."

"How can you tell?" I asked.

"Just a hunch," he said. His mouth opened to say something else, but nothing came out.

"Something in their eyes?" I asked, wondering what it was he saw in them.

"Shh." He watched as Jason got up. Then he looked back at Tessa. "Those two, in my opinion, are the ones to watch." He pointed to his eye with a finger, then used the same one to wag between the two of them.

Jason walked past us and out the door.

To do what, I wasn't sure, but Koby certainly was.

I had thought I was the one keeping an eye on all that was going on. Listening to the detective when he spoke, paying attention when everyone gave their names, noticing how they looked and what they were wearing when Driver Lance Bender called each one out to be interrogated.

I thought that Koby had paid attention only to what was going on with his friend.

But he had seen, without me even noticing, things about the other passengers that actually had something to do with the reason we were all sitting in the car.

Every day, it seemed, I learned something more about my brother. Today, I learned he was a lot more observant than I knew. And, after today's incident, I'd discovered he just might be a real-life Hercule Poirot.

Chapter Five

I TOLD THE detective exactly what I knew, which wasn't much.

And I didn't take as long as Aubriol to do it either.

I was called in after Jason Holiday came back. I knew I was going to be next, something just told me. So, when I saw the driver reappear in the windows of the train door, butterflies started to flutter in my stomach even before he called my name.

I don't know why I thought the "interrogation" car would be any different from the one we'd been stored in. There were a couple of police standing around inside and outside both doors. (Just in case one of us decided to bolt and try to make a getaway?) But other than that, it was the same. When I walked in, one of the police officers gave a directional nod toward the counter in front of the built-in booth where the driver sat.

"Sign and print your name. Then put down your address and telephone number." He pointed to the pen.

I did as told. As I was writing, I noticed a stack of business cards. They belonged to the detective.

"Take one," the officer said.

My hand was a little shaky, so it wasn't an easy task to complete. The cards were sticking together. But I got one and headed down the aisle toward Detective Chow.

He was seated in the front-facing seats, the same ones that the Pussetts were in, in the other car. He smiled as I approached.

"Hi, Keaton." He pointed to the bench opposite him. "Take a seat."

"Thank you," I said.

He bit his nails. That was the first thing I noticed. And he wore a pinky ring. Silver. His shoes were black. His pants were black. His white shirt had black stripes. The tan-colored trench coat he'd donned earlier was folded in half on the seat next to him. Now I could see his shiny coppery badge on his black belt.

He wasn't a suspect, of course, but I wondered, using his superpower of reading people, what Koby would make of him. It had made me realize something not so interesting about myself: The only thing I noticed about people was what they were wearing.

I was going to have to do better to keep up with Koby.

"I heard you were the one who pulled the emergency cord." The interrogation was beginning.

"That would be me." I smiled, not to show I was a truthful and helpful interviewee, but to mask my jitteriness.

"Why did you pull it?"

"Because my friend was hurt." I pushed my lips together tightly and closed my eyes momentarily. "Dead. My friend was dead."

"How did you know he was dead?"

My eyes met the detective's. He was trying to make his eyes soft and friendly without letting his lips turn into a full-fledged smile. And his questions were nonaccusatory—they were like he was just interested in what happened and not investigating a murder.

Murder. Ugh. That word again.

How did I know? I thought about Reef falling over with just the nudge I'd given. His empty eyes open, staring at nothing. There was no other answer to that question. But I knew exactly what Chow was trying to do.

But he wasn't going to goad me and make me talk myself into a hole. My mother, Imogene, was a clinical psychologist. I hadn't lived with her my entire adopted life and not learned a trick or two.

"Because they took him out of here in a black bag," I said, answering his question without him being able to accuse me of knowing anything that could be interpreted as guilt.

"Ah." He nodded. I think he liked my answer. "Do you know how he died?"

"Do you?" I asked. "I'd like to know because he's my friend. I was meeting him on the train so he could accompany me home."

"Your friend?" He looked down at a small notebook he had, seemingly reading over something he'd written. Then he scribbled something more into it. "You knew him?"

"Yes. He's a friend of mine and my twin brother's." I pointed toward the other car. "Koby Hill. They grew up in foster care together."

"Mr. Hill is your brother." It wasn't a question. He wrote it down, at least that's what I thought he was writing. I definitely was no Koby.

"Twin. Brother." I corrected.

"And you grew up in foster care?"

"Not me," I said, not knowing how that would help his investigation. But I had been the one to bring it up, so I just went with it. "Just him. I was adopted."

Then I decided to answer his next questions before he asked and before he got too personal. I wanted to help with what happened to Reef, not have Detective Chow delve into my life (although it wasn't very interesting).

"My brother and I had spent the day together here in Seattle, and it had gotten late. He didn't want me riding out to Timber Lake, where I live, alone. Reef was already on the train. He offered to ride there with me." I watched the detective write. "And no," I said just as he looked up from his notebook. "I don't know why he was going there."

"He doesn't live there?"

I hunched a shoulder. "Actually"—which surprised even me—"I'm not sure where he lives."

"Do you—"

"Know where he was coming from?" I didn't let him finish the question, not because I was trying to be flippant. Just helpful. And expeditious. I didn't want to get in the way or hinder the detective from doing his job. "No. I don't know that either."

"Let me ask the questions," he said, looking at me like he was disappointed in me.

"Sorry," I said. I wrapped a hand around the card I was holding and folded the other one overtop and placed them both in my lap.

"I take it since you pulled the cord at this station, it's where you boarded?"

"Yes, it is."

"And that's what we'll see when we check the security cameras?"

"Yes. It is."

"Had you prearranged your meetup with Mr. Jeffries?"

"No." I shook my head. "As far as I know, he just happened to call."

"How fortunate for you."

"Or serendipitous for him," I said. "In a beneficial way, I mean. Otherwise, our friend might have ridden around all night on this train and you wouldn't have known that he had died for a while. Or *when* he died."

"True." He swiped a finger along his eye, like he had something in it. "But even with that, we still don't know the when."

"We talked to him when he was at the UW Station, right before he got on." I knew I could help fill in that timeline. "And he texted us when he was passing the Capitol Station."

I wondered, hadn't any of the other passengers noticed when he had stopped moving?

"Can I see that text?" He held out his hand, waiting for me to hand over my phone.

"He texted Koby."

"Did anyone get on or off at the Capitol Station?"

He was looking down at his notebook when he asked me the question. It could have been a rhetorical one, but I answered anyway.

"You'd have to ask Lance Bender that question."

"Lance?" He let out an abbreviated chuckle. "Do you know him, too?"

"Only his name."

"You're quite calm to have lost a friend."

I didn't have anything to say about that, because as soon as those words left his mouth, I could feel all the emotions that come with a loved one dying come rushing up from my toes, through my stomach and into my chest.

I knew that feeling well. My father had only been dead three years. It seemed like it had happened yesterday. He had died not even four weeks after he was diagnosed. We didn't have any time to wrestle with how our life was *going* to change, when quite abruptly it did.

"Everyone," I said quietly, "doesn't deal with grief the same."

It was all I could say.

He stared at me for a long moment. I didn't know what he was thinking, and I didn't even try to figure it out. I had to use all my strength not to start blubbering.

Yes. I was prone to blubbering. But not in public or around people I didn't know.

"We have your contact information, right?"

I nodded my answer.

"If we need anything else," he said, dismissing me, "we'll be in touch."

I gave a curt nod, got up and started to walk toward the police officer to go out the door. But I only made it halfway down the aisle before I turned around and went back.

The detective watched me head toward him without a word.

"Detective Chow," I said, sliding back into the seat I had just vacated. I drew in a breath, trying to calm my nerves and keep the blubbering at bay. "Was Reef murdered?"

It wasn't that I didn't believe my brother's assessment, it was just that I wanted to hear it officially. From someone official.

"What do you think?" he asked me.

That psychology thing again. He sounded just like my mother.

"It's not what I think, it's what I hope."

"What?"

"That he wasn't. He was a good friend to my brother. And me. And I wouldn't want that to have happened to him."

We locked eyes. Me not moving. Him not answering. But I was good at the staring game. I'd had to stare down my analytical mother plenty of times as a teenager while she waited for the answer she wanted and that she thought would help me see the errors of my ways.

"We'll have to wait for the autopsy, Miss Rutledge." He relented.

"How long does that take?"

"A few days."

I held up his card. "I'll call you then."

Chapter Six

NO MORE THAN five or ten minutes after my brother, Koby, the last interviewee, came back, we were told we could leave.

That put my mind in a swirl.

What did that mean? That Reef hadn't been murdered? Because Detective Daniel Chow letting everyone leave had to have meant he'd come to that conclusion. He wouldn't have done that if a homicide had been committed, would he?

Or did it mean that there *had* been a murder and there *was* a murderer among us, but he just couldn't figure out who it was?

I didn't know if what Koby thought about Tessa Chaiken and Jason Holiday ever crossed Detective Chow's mind. But he must not have pinned any one of us for the deed, and it appeared that none of us, including Koby, had said anything in the interview to make him think any one of us was involved.

I think that was good, though. No need to jump to conclusions. Best to wait until after the autopsy.

When we left the train, Koby kept walking out of the station. Knowing that I needed to catch the next one to get home, I wanted to stick close to him. My brain was foggy, and I needed time to reset, so I followed him. He walked two blocks to a bus shelter and sat down. We had passed a few bus stops along the way. Wasn't sure why he'd picked that one.

He probably needed to clear his head, too.

"I'm going to call for an Uber," he said after we had sat quietly for a few moments.

"Okay," I said, and paused. I pulled out my phone and showed it to him as a gesture. "I could do it from my app."

"It's okay. I gotta get back home after I drop you off. I don't want you to have to pay for that."

"Get back home? You going to Timber Lake?"

"I have to get you home."

"I don't think you can do that in an Uber," I said.

"You can be one of my stops. You get three stops."

"Oh wow," I said. "That will be an out-of-the-way stop, going all the way to my house." I shook my head. "Really. You don't have to do that. I'm good once I get in the car, Koby."

"Just lost Reef."

He didn't say anything else and neither did I. It was probably going to cost him fifty bucks round-trip. But I knew he was feeling he needed to protect those he loved, and right now, that was me.

"What did you say to Detective Chow?" I asked. I wanted to let him know I wasn't going to fight him wanting to see me home. That I understood.

"I don't trust the police," he said.

"Uhm. Captain Hook is your friend."

"He's different. He was always there to help." He turned and looked at me. "I told you that."

He had.

While I was growing up, I lived in the family-friendly, upper-middle-class neighborhood of Wallingford. There I spent afternoons practicing the violin and reading. I spent my weekends either in the air with my father, who owned and piloted a Cessna 414, or among the stacks of books at the University of Washington library, where he worked. When my mother could pull me away from my dad's shirttails, she and I would go to the symphony or have lunch in trendy South Lake Union. And as a family, we traveled all over the world.

My brother, he had told me, spent his childhood getting into trouble with other boys from the group home or whatever foster family he was in at the time. Not any trouble that landed him in the care and custody of the legal system, thank goodness, and he attributed that to one Seattle police officer, Avery Moran.

Officer Moran, so the story went, had a mission to make sure those kinds of kids didn't get "lost in the system." Because of that term, Koby and his band of foster brothers started describing themselves as the Lost Boys. Moran became their Captain Hook.

After I heard the story from Koby with admiration in his eyes, I asked my brother if he realized that Captain Hook was the Lost Boys' enemy. They wanted to kill each other. There was nothing helpful or good in that relationship.

He told me not to "kill his vibe."

I had respect for Detective Chow and his approach. He wasn't accusatory and he seemed to be methodical. Maybe because his questions reminded me of ones that my mother would ask her patients.

But then again, he hadn't made an arrest . . .

Maybe Reef died because he'd had a cerebral hemorrhage. Or a heart attack? He had just told us that he'd stopped drinking. He had set an alarm on his phone to remind him to take vitamins.

But was it for vitamins?

I thought about it. At first, he had said *pills*. Then he had changed to the word *vitamin*. My mother would say that was a Freudian slip.

Maybe Reef was already sick? He did say he was trying to be healthier. Maybe what was wrong with him was what killed him and not someone on the train.

Our Uber ride pulled up, and I got up and followed Koby over to the car. His shoulders were slumped, and he wasn't moving with the energy he usually did. Koby held the door open for me. I climbed in and confirmed my address with the driver.

I wasn't sure if it was a good idea to bring up all what had happened, but I couldn't get it out of my brain why Koby had jumped to murder. And how did he decide who was involved in it and who wasn't?

Only I didn't know how to start the conversation questioning his thought process. So, I decided to ask about the latter.

"How did you make those assumptions about the people in the train?" I sucked my tongue. "You know, how you said who was or wasn't involved."

"I never said any of them were involved. Because I don't know."

"Well, you said who wasn't."

"When you have to move from house to house, person to person, and have to live in the streets, you learn how to read people, you know?" He turned his head to look out of the window. "And you have to make that assessment pretty quickly if you don't want to run into trouble."

"Oh," was all I could say.

I had no idea how that was. I'd had such a good childhood. And it hurt me to know my brother had had such a hard time growing up. Although with his good heart and caring spirit, he had learned not to let those times define him.

I decided not to talk about what happened to Reef anymore. Not until we got more information, because at this point, it was all speculation. I didn't like to jump to conclusions without all the facts anyway (although I had let Koby's comment about murder earlier do just that). I was going to wait until I had a conversation with Detective Chow after the autopsy. I knew, though, I wasn't going to be able to keep how sad I was about losing a friend intact much longer.

I was looking forward to getting home and curling up in a ball.

We didn't say much while riding, but as we got closer to home, I looked out of the window in anticipation of seeing the store.

Books & Biscuits was mostly dark with one or two interior lights on. The place looked quiet, settled and locked up tight. I couldn't see if Pete had gotten everything on the list I had left him completed, but from what I could see, it didn't make me worry that he'd done something detrimental to our new business.

We pulled up to my small Craftsman bungalow, and Koby told the driver to wait for him. I thought he was only going to get me to my door. Nope. When I pushed the door open, he stepped in first.

Roo, my Siamese cat, leapt off a bookshelf on the back wall. It didn't faze Koby. It made me jump, though. Luckily, I composed myself in time to catch her before she got out of the door.

Koby went through each room, turned on the lights and opened closets, cabinets and room doors. I followed behind him, questions all over my face. I didn't have time to voice them, he was moving too fast. What exactly he was looking for, I didn't know, and after a second thought, I was afraid to ask. I didn't want anything more to think about after I was left at home by myself.

After he left the kitchen, I cuddled with Roo, leaning against the sink.

"Is this how brothers act?" I asked her.

"Eeeoww."

"Do you have any brothers?" I cradled her in my arms, stroking her fur. "Aww. I guess if you do, you were separated from them when you were young, too."

I gave her a hug. "I'm glad I found mine."

A few minutes later, Koby came back into the kitchen.

"You find what you were looking for?"

"I need some water," was his answer.

He grabbed a glass from the cabinet, and I watched as he filled it from the faucet and guzzled it down.

"You want some ice?" I asked, although it was a little late for that.

"Nope, I'm good," he said, setting the glass in the sink.

"How about an orange or something? I for one am hungry." I let Roo spill out of my arms and went to the fridge. Opening it, I bent down to look into it to see if I had any food I could offer that he could take with him. We'd eaten a mess of tacos, but that had been a long time ago.

"I've got a car waiting for me, remember?"

"Yep. I remember."

"Unless you want me to stay over?" He came over to the fridge and looked at me. "I can do that if you don't want to be alone."

That surprised me. He didn't like staying too long at my place because I didn't have a TV. He didn't know how people could get along without them. He loved that I had a backyard for Remy, but an hour or so romp for exercise for his favorite pal was about the longest he stayed.

"Nope. I'm good." I turned back to looking in the fridge. I felt tears coming and didn't want him to see them. "See you in the morning?"

"I'll be there." He bent down to stroke Roo. "I gotta see about Remy. He's been home by himself a long time."

"I'm sure he needs to go out," I said, still pretending to search the fridge for food.

Koby stood up straight and put his hand on my back. I looked up at him, eyes widened, asking was it something else he wanted to say.

Instead he blew out a breath. "Later," he said, and walked out of the room. I didn't hear the front door close right away. Maybe he did another sweep . . .

But I was sure he turned the lock and checked it before he got back into his Uber.

I turned back to the refrigerator and pulled out a covered plastic bowl of blueberries and strawberries and a container of Greek yogurt. I found thinly sliced almonds in one cabinet and got a spoon and a bowl.

I sat down at the table and spooned out some yogurt and berries into my bowl, and that was all it took for the tears to come spilling out. I pushed the bowl out of the way and put my head down on the table and I just let the grief pour out.

I missed Reef. He made me laugh. He made my heart race and my cheeks blush. It was because of him that my brother was led to looking for me. He had been part of Koby's family for a long time. And now he had been part of mine. He had been the first one of Koby's extended family I'd met.

Even though Koby stayed cool from the time he burst through the back door of the train car until now when he brought me home, I knew he had to be hurting.

After I felt like I couldn't cry anymore, I got up, went to the bathroom and unraveled at least a yard of toilet paper, balling it up. I blew my nose and wiped my face. Then I dug my phone out of my purse and called my mother.

The consummate psychologist, I knew exactly what she was going to do. She was going to ask how Reef's death made me feel. The wad of tissue I was holding on to should give the answer to that question. That evidence wouldn't matter, though. She'd feel it necessary to inundate me with a plethora of open-ended questions so I could "work" through my feelings.

That was going to drive me crazy, but I was going to suffer through because I needed to speak to my mother. She and Koby were my best friends (and so was Roo), which probably didn't say much about my sociability scale.

"What's happened?" she asked as soon as she picked up. I had FaceTimed her, and seeing her face made me feel a little better. She moved toward the screen and squinted. "You look awful."

Okay. Maybe not.

"Thank you, Mother." I knew she'd comment on my sarcasm.

"Don't hide what you're feeling behind sarcasm."

I inhaled.

"What is going on with you?"

"Reef died today."

"Reef? Koby's friend?"

"My friend, too."

"I'm sorry to hear that. Is that what has gotten you looking like you do?"

"Yes," I said. I felt a tear roll down my cheek.

"Do you think you may be projecting Koby's friendship with Reef onto yourself? Overexaggerating your reaction to what has happened?"

"No."

I didn't tell her that I had been thinking that Reef could be more than a friend. She would have, I'm sure, a whole other set of questions for that.

"How did he die?"

"We don't know," I said. "I found him on the train. Koby thinks it was murder."

"What do you think?"

There she went. Her questions posed to clinically evaluate my emotions instead of valuing them. What I needed—wanted—was sympathy. A little empathy. What I was getting was the benefit of her seven years of formal education and nearly thirty years of practice. I was going to have to wade through that to get through to her twenty-three years of mothering.

"I am reserving my decision until after the autopsy." I swiped the tissue across my eyes. I was sure she'd like that answer.

And I knew I probably did need to talk about what happened. To help me get through the grief I was feeling. "There were five people in the car with him when it happened," I continued. "The police questioned us but didn't arrest anyone."

"Do you feel someone should have been arrested?"

I shrugged. "I don't know. Wasn't sure if he'd even been murdered by any of them. Or maybe he had been by all of them."

"All of them?" She seemed momentarily taken aback. But she reacquired her doctor demeanor and continued. "How does that make you feel?"

"Sad."

"Sad because no arrests were made or because you were not able to ascertain exactly what happened?"

Putting my head down, I started crying again. "Both" came out between sobs.

"What can I do to make you feel better?" Her voice softened.

I looked into the camera on my phone and smiled at my mother. Psychologists ask their patients what they *themselves* can do to make them feel different. Better. Because, ultimately, only you can do what it takes. But now she was asking what *she* could do.

Now she was being a momma*cologist*.

"I'll be okay," I said.

"I know you will." She gave a curt nod. "But I'll bring you some of your favorite cookies."

"I'm going to bed," I said. I was happy she'd taken on the mom role, but if she came over, I couldn't be sure that her Dr. Rutledge persona wouldn't reappear.

"Not tonight," she said. "Tomorrow. You're going into the store?"

"Yes. I'm going. Store is opening in five days." I looked at the time on my phone. Almost midnight. That meant four more days. "I have to be there to get it ready."

"Then I'll bring them there." I saw her reach for her calendar. She still kept a paper one. Flipping through pages and landing on the one she needed, she said, "I have an appointment at ten and not another one until two." She started writing something down, just like Detective Chow had. "I'll bake them tonight and bring them to you between appointments." She looked back up at me. "That'll make you feel better, I'm sure. And a hug. I have one of those for you, too."

"Thanks, Mom." I chuckled. "I gotta go. See you tomorrow." I blew her a kiss. "I love you."

"Love you more."

I looked at the bowl of yogurt and fruit that I'd made. "Ugh." I'd forgotten all about it. I grabbed it and stuck it in the refrigerator, getting a saucer first to cover it, otherwise it wouldn't be any good tomorrow.

I was tired and decided to just call it a night. Only I wasn't sure if I could fall asleep after all the things that had happened today. We hadn't gotten off that train until nearly ten p.m. I wasn't one to routinely stay up late unless it was to finish a book. But I felt I might just toss and turn the night away if I turned in.

I wandered into the living room, thinking that reading might just be what I needed. All the lights were still on from when Koby had gone through the house.

The shiny, honey-colored wood floor felt cool under my feet as I ambled over to the built-in bookcase. It covered an entire long wall in my living room, broken up only by the archway that led into the dining room.

I ran my fingers across the spines of the books. I knew just which one I was looking for. Agatha Christie's *Murder on the Orient Express*.

Along one row, then down another, and I couldn't find what I was looking for. I usually could put my finger right on the book I wanted. I had a system. Not the Dewey decimal kind I'd been taught while getting my master's in library science. It was my own homemade one, the same one I was using in my bookstore. But tonight, it was failing me.

Roo slunk into the room and did a figure eight around my

legs. "Have you seen my book?" I asked her. She had, after all, been on the bookshelf when we came in.

"Erreow."

"I'm going to take that as a no," I said, stooping down to pick her up. "Because I wouldn't want to think you're pilfering my stuff." I blew out a breath. "I guess it's for the best. Shouldn't fill up my brain with any more thoughts of murder. I'll end up having nightmares."

I walked to the other side of the bookcase. "This one," I said to Roo, "is one of my favorites." I pulled *Little Fires Everywhere* by Celeste Ng from the shelf, tucked Roo under my arm and headed up the stairs to my bedroom.

"Instead of murder, I'll read about a kid burning down her family's house." I held my cat up to my face and gave her a kiss. "I wonder what my mother would say about that."

Chapter Seven

I FELL ASLEEP before I even finished the first chapter. I found the book rolled up in the covers that I must have been fighting with sometime during the night.

I unraveled myself and the book and checked the time on my phone. 7:15 a.m. I had gotten about seven hours of sleep. That was enough. I swung my legs around, planted my feet on the floor and took a minute to assess how I was feeling.

It was the last Friday before we were opening up the bookstore café. The morning sun was streaming through my sheer curtains. Roo was still sleeping, her favorite pastime. I was feeling a bit hazy, but it wasn't something a quick shower wouldn't cure.

I wanted to be at the store by eight. We were getting deliveries of some of the things we'd shopped for yesterday. If I didn't get a move on, I was going to be late. It would take me ten minutes to walk to the bookstore, and that was leaving me only thirty minutes to get washed, dressed, do my hair and feed me and the cat.

I brushed my teeth, parted my hair down the middle and

did a French braid down each side. I pulled the bowl of berries and yogurt from the fridge, sprinkled the sliced almonds
I'd taken from the cabinet the night before over the top and
opened a can of Purina's Seafood Stew for Roo.

I checked my bookshelf one more time for the murder
mystery I wanted when I went to reshelve Celest Ng's book.
Thinking maybe I had accidentally misshelved it the last
time I had it out or that my brain was so foggy, I just didn't
see it. But it wasn't there. I couldn't figure out what could
have happened to it.

"Roo!" I called out. "I'm leaving. Your meal awaits!"

I waited for a moment to see if I could hear her scampering into the kitchen. Nothing.

"Must be nice to be able to sleep in," I muttered as I
pulled the door closed. But after the first step down, I turned
right back around, opened it back up, reached inside and
grabbed an umbrella. "Looks like I might need this."

Despite the rain the area got, being outside in Timber
Lake was beautiful and couldn't help but make anyone feel
better. My street, like the town in general, was quaint and
cozy. Rows of colorful houses, short blocks, great walkabil-
ity and lots of green spaces. And being on the water was
probably the best amenity of all.

"Hi, Keaton!" My neighbor waved a gloved hand.

And the neighbors. Most friendly and willing to give a
neighborly hand. And then some who were always ready to
make the community even smaller by sharing everything
they knew about everyone else. Including Joyce Grayson.

"Hi, Mrs. Grayson." I smiled and waved back, although I
knew I probably wouldn't get away with just that.

"Looks like it might rain," she said. She glanced upward,
pushing back her khaki-colored gardening hat so she could
see the sky.

"I'm ready for it." I held up my umbrella.

"Good for my flowers," she said, "but not for my joints.
I'll be smelling like ointment by noon."

I hadn't ever really smelled anything medicinal coming from her way. It was the floral and fresh scent from her roses with undertones of wine and berries, the heavy sweet fragrance of her trumpet lilies and the buttery, honey-like vapors from the huge almond tree in her front yard when it was in bloom that caught everyone's attention.

Mrs. Grayson had so many flowers, shrubs and trees, they covered nearly every square inch of her property. And as she often reminded me, she knew the name and particulars about each of them. They were just as colorful as the houses up and down the road. And from anywhere up or down the road, you could smell what she grew.

"Your flowers are starting to bloom," I said, just making polite conversation.

"Yes, they're coming up nicely." She pointed her shears to the side of her house. "Looks like I'm going to have to cut back my western mock orange bushes so they'll attract more butterflies."

I nodded, feigning interest, but she looked past me. "Looks like someone is having trouble this year, though," she said.

I turned to look behind me. Memphis Jones. My neighbor on the other side. He and Mrs. Grayson were garden rivals and often tried to bring me into their contest, although his garden wasn't as extensive as hers.

"If you got started, you probably can get him beat."

She was all about green space. I found that out about her even before I found out about her intrusive nature. She liked to gossip about everyone, including herself.

I gave her a polite smile. I definitely didn't want to get in their mix of rivalry. My house was sandwiched in between theirs, so I'd be right in the middle of whatever they decided to sling at each other. "We're opening up Books & Biscuits soon," I told her. "I don't think I'll have time."

"Oh! Yes!" She clapped her gloved hands together, never letting the shears go, and gave me a wide smile. "When is opening day?"

"Tuesday," I said.

"Oh. That's close."

"Yep. On my way there now to take care of last-minute things."

"Good to see new shops going up downtown. I so worry about Timber Lake." She calmly waved a bee from her face. "But I will be sure to stop by to congratulate you."

I'd be surprised to see her. I didn't think she'd even ventured downtown.

"Why do you worry about Timber Lake?" I asked.

"So many bad things going on here."

I hadn't noticed anything bad.

"I think we'll be okay," I said.

"For now. But we've got all these new people coming in. Changing things. Not following the rules." She shook her head. "No telling what trouble they'll bring. And they're all renters!" she said, waving her garden shears, seemingly insinuating that that meant they were bad people. "We'll have people moving in and out all the time. Slum landlords who don't care about property upkeep! About our green spaces!"

"I have to go," I said in a sweet, understanding voice. I'd found since I'd moved in how excitable Mrs. Grayson could be. And paranoid. I guessed it was why she never ventured out much past her garden.

"Okay, but you don't forget to be careful," she said, pointing those shears at me, I guess telling me to be wary of renters. Or whatever else was lurking around Timber Lake as of late. I chuckled at the thought.

Timber Lake had been where I'd wanted to be while I'd been sitting on that train yesterday. It was the safest place I knew.

No. I hadn't forgotten about what had happened the day before and how, per Koby, it might be murder. But it hadn't happened in Timber Lake.

I had, though, managed, while getting ready, to store it in a temporarily inaccessible part of my brain, which my mother would say wasn't healthy. She'd want me to deal with it.

And Mrs. Grayson's comments had seemingly jarred me into agreement. As soon as I headed out from talking with my neighbor, thoughts of Reef came bursting into my psyche like fireworks on the Fourth of July.

I thought about the last time I saw him, how he winked at me and got close, whispering in my ear. How he smiled at me and how that made me feel.

I passed the breezy waterfront, clear waters underneath bleached-out wooden docks, shepherded over by the glaucous-winged gulls, with their gray wings, red spots and yellow bills. My surroundings were calm and quiet as I took the walking trail that cut across the Timber Lake ravine, but I couldn't seem to take my mind off Reef. Even the weeping willow trees, brushing their leaves against the ground, seemed to utter his name.

Reef . . .

I swiped a couple of fingers across my eyelids and swallowed back any other tears that were threatening to fall as I stepped onto the paved road from the wooded shortcut. The morning rush–time noise and activity of the town smacked me in the face and changed my mood. Timber Lake had a population of about three thousand folks, and it seemed like half of them were out.

Downtown Timber Lake was all bustle, well, as much bustle as we could muster for our size. Right on Cedar Street, at the edge of downtown, were a few residential houses, usually rented out seasonally (ah, perhaps those were Mrs. Grayson's culprits). But most of the center of town was retail.

More than a few cars were still on the road as I walked down Sixth Street, probably owned by people who either worked in town or stayed at home, for those who commuted to Seattle had long been on their way.

And then there were walkers and bikers out with dogs and kids. In town there was a small library where I had once worked, a bank and more independent small stores like the one my twin and I had started. The tree-lined streets were filled with friendly faces smiling their morning salutations.

"Hi."

It was Pete.

Enjoying the walk, before I knew it, I was at the store. He stood outside of it, his hands stuffed inside his rumpled trench coat.

"Good morning," I said, putting on a smile. "You're right on time."

"I'm early," he said. "Being tardy is a firing offense."

I guess it was. I wished someone would tell Georgie that. She was always late.

"I got everything finished last night that you asked." He gave me the update as I unlocked the door. "There was a box that came in, I signed your name for it."

"Oh. Okay. What was in it."

"Didn't look. Wasn't on my to-do list."

I tried to hide my chuckle.

"It's looking good in here," I said, taking the room in as I stood by the door. I let my eyes roam around. There weren't any more boxes left on the floor, no trash from unpacking and everything looked shiny, dusted and new. From the shelves to the three crystal chandeliers that hung throughout to the freshly vacuumed carpet that was in the author area, where I hoped to have readings and book signings.

On some of the bookshelves that covered the walls, separated by reading nooks, Pete had set up to showcase the books by having their covers face forward. Then some were shelved with only the spine showing. I walked alongside the shelves and scrutinized Pete's work. His displays looked beautiful, and he seemed to have my classification system down pat. And I had shown him only once.

The shorter shelves in the middle of the room were stuffed with books, too. Thick and thin, colorful and bright with signs along the top indicating their genre.

"Wow," I finally said as I bent over to get a closer look in the classic-mystery section. Thinking my missing book might have gotten there somehow. "You've really done a good job."

"And you were worried about how he would do here all by himself."

I stood up and saw my twin standing next to Pete. Both had grins on their faces. Pete's as lopsided as his appearance with his unkempt hair and Hello Kitty bag slung across his shoulder.

"Koby! When did you get here?" I looked at the door, wondering how I hadn't heard him or his dog enter. Remy scampered over to me after hearing my voice. I gave him a hug and kiss. "And I wasn't worried."

That statement wasn't true—I had been worried. Even had planned on stopping by to check on Pete's work when I thought I was coming straight home after my day out with Koby.

But I had never told Koby that. How did he know?

I waved a hand to dismiss the conversation. Turned out Pete had been a good hire.

"Looks like you're about done in here," Koby said.

"I am," I said, pleased. "Just some back-office inventory, accounting kind of stuff left to do."

"So, you don't mind if I borrow Pete?" Koby gave Pete a pat on the back. "I've got lots more things to do and a couple of deliveries coming in."

"Oh, Pete said something came in yesterday. You may want to check that out."

"Mind giving me a hand, Pete?" Koby spoke to our new hire. "I don't think Georgie will be coming in until this afternoon."

Pete nodded his agreement to help and followed Koby through the archway that led to the café side of our little enterprise. I knew he'd stop out back first and drop off Remy, his dog.

My first thoughts went to Georgie not being in the shop

and not coming in until later in the afternoon. Because she was slacking, Koby had to borrow my help. But looking around the place, I knew I didn't need to get anything else done that Pete could help me with.

Still . . .

But then I realized that my brother was acting normal. Like he hadn't just lost his best friend. And channeling my mother, I determined that that wasn't good, and I probably needed him to talk about that.

So, I traced their steps and pulled my brother aside. But before I could say anything, he said, "A leaf popped up last night."

"What?"

"On the Ancestry website. We got a DNA connection."

"For us? A relative."

"Yep." His eyes twinkled. "A cousin." His phone dinged. A few times in succession. He pulled it out, and I saw a few notifications that I couldn't read upside down. He silenced the phone.

"Does our cousin know anything?" I asked after he'd stuck his phone back in his pocket. "Anything about Morie? Oh wait. Which side?"

"I don't know. We're going to get together tomorrow and talk. He's still building his family tree, but he thinks he remembers Hill being a name mentioned in his family."

"Really? Wow . . ."

"You wanna go with me? To meet him?"

"You know I do," I said, and smiled. Then I remembered why I'd come to talk to him. "Hey. Are you okay?" I asked in a whisper.

"Yeah. I'm good." I could see his eyes light up a little. "We just got good news."

"I mean about the bad news we had yesterday."

"Oh," he said. I knew he hadn't forgotten, but like I had that morning, in order to push myself and get the day going, he had tucked Reef's death into the back of his mind.

His smile was weaker, but he still gave me one. "I'm good. Just need to get back to work. Gotta be ready to open on Tuesday."

"If you need to take some time, I can help out in here."

"No need."

"What will happen next?"

"With what?"

"You know. Funeral stuff." I flitted my fingers. "And. Other. Stuff." I didn't want to spell it out.

I knew burying someone was a lot. My father had died right when I was finishing my master's. And it was almost more than I could take—getting through my finals and helping my mother, who was beside herself, make the arrangements.

"I'm his only family," he said, and I saw then his countenance change. "I'm going to take care of everything. You know, I'll figure it all out."

"I can help you," I said. "I did it for my father."

"I got it."

My brother was used to having to do things for himself. Until he found me, he was pretty much on his own and didn't ever have family kind of stuff to deal with. But he wasn't alone anymore.

"And I got you," I said. "We're doing this together."

"Thank you, sister." I thought I saw a tear in his eye, but he put his arms around me and hugged me tightly, then turned away before I could see for sure. "Now let's get back to work," he said. "We have a business to run."

Chapter Eight

AFTER MY CHAT with my brother, I decided to go out and get food for the three of us. My fruit-and-dairy breakfast wasn't cutting it.

I didn't mention where I was going to Koby, just told him I'd be back in a minute. If he knew I was going out for food, he'd insist on cooking some up himself.

What? he'd say. *I have plenty of food here. Just give me a minute.*

But he was working out his recipes for opening day and the first author event I had planned for the week following. And that was important. I didn't want to distract him just for a plate of bacon and eggs.

He had had enough distractions.

Our shop was the first floor of the corner building on the intersection of Park and Second Streets. Two half-moon steps were outside our front door. Above the shop were apartments, with, so far, tenants who were pretty quiet. We hadn't heard a peep from them.

On the Second Street side, Books & Biscuits was attached

to the Attic, an antiques store that was attached to the Mane Attraction, a hair salon, and that was attached to the last store in the block, the Second Street Farmers Market. It was where I was headed.

"Morning!" I said to the proprietor of the market as I entered.

"Keaton! Good morning to you! I've got something for you."

The market was an open-air kind of place. With fresh fruits and vegetables and fresh-cut flowers. A deli that sold all kinds of sandwiches, cuts of lunchmeats and sides, like potato and macaroni and antipasto salads. There was a cheese section and a wine section and an artisan bread section. But the fresh herbs growing in the back of the store were what caught your senses from the time you opened the door and were what drew you in.

Mr. Al, the owner and longtime resident of both Second Street and Timber Lake, stood behind the huge wooden counter and beckoned me over.

"Look!" He pointed down to a box that I had to stand on my tiptoes to see. "Books!"

"Books!" I repeated even though I wasn't as excited as he was about it. I thought back to the bulging shelves in my store.

"They're for you. Almost brand-new. I was going to throw them out but thought, why do that when my new neighbor has a bookstore?"

Mr. Al was of the burly, Santa-looking variety. His beard was white but scraggly, and he was completely bald. Still he had a big hearty laugh and a belly that hung over a belt he was always tugging upward. He was the kind of guy who would bark at a customer for bringing their dog in the store but would take out a bone or a container of water for your furry friend that you had tied up to the bike rack outside.

"Thank you, Mr. Al." Smile still plastered, I was trying to think where I would put the gift of books he'd just sprung on me. I could put them in storage, I thought (after I checked what shape they were in), but I'd hate for him to come to the bookstore and not see what he'd given me.

"I'm a giver," he said, placing his hand over his heart. "What can I say?"

"I'll have to send someone over to get them," I said. "Is that okay?"

"Sure. Of course. I didn't expect you to carry them yourself." He gave the box a jab with his toe. "I can bring it over if need be. I would have dropped it off this morning, but no one was there when I got here at six."

I chuckled. "We got there at eight today, but once we open, we probably won't be getting in until ten."

"Good to know," he said. "I've been thinking that Books & Biscuits, with Koby cooking up a storm, will give me a run for my money."

"I'm sure we'll all get along great."

"What can I get you today?" he asked.

"Do you have any fresh bagels?"

"You know I do. And I've got your favorite."

Mr. Al prided himself in knowing his customers, and I hoped to do the same thing when we got regular customers.

I loaded up on bagels, cream cheese, smoked salmon, breakfast quiches fresh out of the oven and sliced seasonal fruit. I headed back to the café. When I rounded the corner to go back inside, I noticed someone on the Park Street side of our building peeking in the window. Initially happy to see a would-be customer checking us out, that soon turned to shock.

Maybe horror.

It was Tessa Chaiken. From the train.

What was she doing at our window? How could she know we could be found there? I hadn't put that address on the sheet I filled out at the interrogation.

Maybe she had followed me from home . . .

Maybe that was what happened to my book.

Yeah, right, Keaton. A killer comes to your house and takes a book.

That made no sense.

The heart palpitations I was having were what made no sense. She wasn't going to kill me in broad daylight. But most important, I didn't know if she had killed anyone.

I decided to say something to her.

Just a *Hello.* And a *We won't be opening for a couple days.* Maybe even a *Don't I know you from somewhere?*

"Yeah, maybe not that last one," I muttered as I took a step toward her. But as I did, she took off in the other direction.

"Oh. Okay then. Guess I won't be doing that." I opened the door to the store, ready to go back in when a thought hit me. It made me feel kind of excited. I was thinking it must be the kind of thing that Koby experiences—a need to know.

Why was she in Timber Lake? And why had she stopped at our store? I wanted—needed—to find that out.

What exactly did I think I was going to find out by doing this? Not sure. I certainly wasn't going to try to get any information out of her. I wouldn't know what to say. Still, I was so curious.

I could only hope not so curious as to have the same fate as that pesky proverbial cat.

I tucked the packages I'd gotten from the farmers market right inside the door in a little recess so no one would trip over them, not that anyone was coming in, and turned to head back out. To follow Tessa. I thought I heard Koby calling out my name as I shut the door, but I didn't take the time to answer. He'd wonder what happened to me. Hopefully he wouldn't worry, though. After all, he was the one who had said Tessa was someone to watch.

I had decided to do just that.

As I started out, I did think it might have been a good idea to tell someone my plans.

Thank goodness the streets were still kind of busy. Not as

many cars as had been out on my way in, but enough that I felt like I'd be okay if she discovered what I was doing and confronted me.

I stayed back as far as I could.

Tessa headed toward the west side of town but didn't go any farther than a couple of blocks, stopping at the Pfeiffer Crest Pharmacy. I stood outside, tapping my foot for four or five minutes, eager to see where she was going and confident I'd be able to follow her without being seen.

It was only after I decided to go into the pharmacy that I started feeling foolish. She'd already picked up whatever it was that she came in to buy. She was at the counter, next in line to pay for her purchase.

"Hi," the clerk said. "Did you find everything you needed?"

"Yes," Tessa said. "Thank you."

She had good posture. She stood up so straight. Her voice sounded different from what I remembered from the train. Younger.

Today Tessa had on a bright red summer sweater, blue jeans and flats that were red and white striped. She would have been hard to miss.

I shook my head. That is not what I should do to get information. How did noting what she was wearing tell me anything about what she was up to? It didn't!

I needed to try to think more like my brother.

"Going out on the water?" the clerk asked, and passed something under the scanner.

What would make the clerk say that?

Dramamine? I thought.

"Oh yeah," Tessa said. She put her head down, looking into the shoulder bag she carried. "Not much else to do around here."

"No," the clerk agreed. "Not around here. But I'm used to it." She dropped the purchase in a bag. "You're not from around here?"

"No," Tessa said.

"Oh." The clerk's face lit up with an idea. "You should go into Seattle. Lots of stuff there. Plenty of people your age."

"I don't really like big cities," Tessa said, handing over some paper money. "I'm sure I won't be going into Seattle while I'm here."

Ha! She was just in Seattle. Why would she tell that clerk that?

"How long you staying in Timber Lake?"

"I'm just here a few days." She paused but then added, "To visit with my grandfather. Keep him company."

"Aww. That's sweet." With a proud smile, the clerk handed the change back to Tessa. "My grandpop just went to live with my uncle in North Carolina. Didn't realize how much I was going to miss him. But the rain around here wasn't any good for his lungs."

"Okay." Tessa took her bag from the clerk and thanked her as she turned to head out.

"Eee!" I ducked my head and ran the other way down the aisle. I couldn't let her see me. I rounded the corner into the next aisle just as she was going out the door.

I watched from the door until she got a few feet ahead of me. She didn't walk with much purpose, swinging her arms as she ambled along down the street, looking in windows as she passed stores. She waited at street corners for traffic to go by.

My borrowed Koby intuition told me that meant something.

But what?

"Well . . ." I muttered, swallowing as if that would help an idea formulate in my brain. "Maybe. Uhm . . ."

I know! She wasn't in a hurry. It wasn't like she was up to something nefarious (like coming to kill me and Koby so as not to leave any witnesses). And she seemed to know exactly where she was going.

I smiled. Happy to have come up with an observation that went beyond fashion.

But what did that mean?

Ahhh. It meant that she probably lived here.

Or had lived here.

Or knew someone who did.

Oh wait. She had just said she was visiting her grand-father.

I had to stop thinking so hard. I was trying to figure out stuff I'd already heard her say. Plus, she was getting too far ahead of me.

Tessa headed east this time and cut through the ravine just as I had that morning.

I started to get nervous again. She was going in the direction of my house.

Then I started worrying about what was in that bag other than something for seasickness.

Rat poison?

Or something less lethal. Had she'd filled a prescription for a drug that would knock me unconscious so she could take me captive to torture me to see what I knew?

Like the book *Still Missing* by Chevy Stevens that I hadn't too long ago finished. Of course, my mother would be the therapist, like the one in the book, who would help me over-come the trauma after I was finally rescued.

That gave me chills.

I was going to have to start reading romcoms . . .

But before I could have a full-on panic attack, she veered right and headed toward the docks.

The Timber Lake Marina wasn't much of anything. There were buildings—the clubhouse—I could see from the path I took to the shop. But there wasn't ever much of any activity going on when I passed by.

Once a hub for the residing boats, now it really had no purpose. Old Man Walker had run it for years, and while there were few social interactions and no restaurants or showers available for the renters anymore, it still had locked storage spaces. So he often was prone to complain when he visited the library. He had one librarian whom he seemed to like to talk to. Liz Chambers. And then she'd tell me, not that I'd asked, what he said.

Nowadays, there wasn't much for him to do—put locks on the storage spaces, take out the garbage from trash receptacles and change the lightbulbs along the dock whenever they went out.

The need for the clubhouse had faded when the slips began to be filled with fewer pleasure boats and more houseboats. All sizes and shapes, they dotted the shoreline for nearly as far as the eye could see.

The floating homes, some fully navigable, some rickety, retired steamers and some new, state-of-the-art. They were a mix of single and double story with covered patios and large windows used as permanent homes or Airbnbs. There was even one that sold cupcakes, a moored bakery of sorts. Tessa made her second stop there, picking up a half dozen, or so it seemed from the size of the box she emerged with.

I smiled at my observation.

But there was no time for a pat on the back. She was on the move again.

But not for long. She walked down the pier to a one-story pontoon houseboat docked about seven piers down. It looked homemade from its blue jay–and–white-colored aluminum siding to its tin patio roof. There was a metal rail around the bottom of the boat and a sunbathing deck on the roof.

She boarded without announcement and went inside.

Is that where her grandfather lived? I looked down the shoreline, my house not too far out of view. A random woman on the 6:44 train in Seattle was my neighbor. Go figure.

It was a coincidence that I was on the same train as someone from Timber Lake, but not so for Reef. He lived in Seattle. Well . . . I guess I shouldn't say that. He might not live in Seattle proper—there were plenty of neighborhoods around it. But he certainly didn't live in Timber Lake. I knew that for a fact.

But she did. How hadn't I ever seen her?

I hid behind one of the light posts along the dock for what seemed like forever. And then I reasoned, if she did indeed live there, she might just be in for the day. Or at least long enough that I couldn't spare the time to hang around to see her again. I checked the clock on my cell phone.

I could just leave . . .

Then Koby's voice percolated around in my brain.

She was one to watch.

I needed to see what she was doing inside.

I looked around to see if there was any way I could get close enough to see what she was up to. Boarding her boat and peeking through the window crossed my mind, but of course I knew better than to do that.

However, on the uncovered deck of a two-story canal houseboat right next to the one Tessa had disappeared into was a telescope. I'd be able to see her.

I glanced up to the top level and wondered why a telescope wasn't up there. After all, it was for gazing at the stars. Maybe the owner of that houseboat had been doing exactly what I wanted to do.

Now to hope no one was at home.

I walked with reckless abandon to the door and knocked. I had thought about calling out, but I didn't want Tessa looking out of one of her windows at me.

There was no answer to my rap on the door. Probably at work. I thought that was a good assessment and took it as a go-ahead on my plan. (I could have tried again to make sure, but why take the risk?) I made my way to the telescope.

"Shoot!"

Just as I put my eye to the rim of the scope, it started to rain. Not a downpour, just a drizzle—even the sun was still shining— but enough to collect droplets on the other end of the lens.

"Now how am I supposed to see anything?" I muttered.

I went around and swiped the lens with the tail of my shirt. Then went back. Putting my eye to it, I got a shock.

It was Jason Holiday! The nerdy guy from the train, only he didn't look so nerdy today. He was inside the boat that Tessa had just gone into. That knocked me back on my heels. Surely he wasn't her grandfather.

What the heck! Was there even a grandfather?

Probably not. Hadn't she lied when she told that clerk she wouldn't be going into Seattle? She had been in Seattle.

They had acted like they didn't even know each other on the train. At least that was what I thought. Now here they were in the same houseboat.

And how had I never seen either one of them before?

I mean, before we decided to open the bookshop café, I was working full-time at the library and wasn't usually out in the morning roaming the streets. And then again, if I had seen them, I wouldn't have known who they were and wouldn't have paid any attention to them.

And maybe they had just moved in.

But whatever the reason, here they were.

Now to figure out how that had anything to do with what happened to Reef.

I was going to have to tell Koby about what I'd seen. He had been suspicious of them from the beginning.

And I had to get out of the rain.

I'd gone back in my house that morning to get an umbrella but hadn't even thought about bringing it with me when I decided to tail Tessa.

But when I decided to leave, so did Jason and Tessa.

"Shoot!"

I couldn't let them see me. I ran around to the far side of the boat. I peeked around the corner of the house to watch until they left.

But instead of leaving, they came out and stood on the deck. Their *covered* deck. I was going to have to wait them out, but I couldn't just stand around in the rain either.

Geesh! I looked up at the sky. That sun was starting to get blocked out by grayish clouds. This might not be a quick shower. We hadn't had much rain in the last couple of weeks. I guess it was time for it. I was hating, though, that I was going to get caught in it.

In my distress, I turned and leaned my back against the outside wall of the boat. Well, I thought it was a wall. It wasn't. It was a door and it pushed right open! I ducked inside and prayed that no one was in there.

I took a look around but didn't wander too far into the interior. I let my eyes scan the area. It was a nice place, reminding me of a dorm room or college apartment. A hodge-podge of different kinds of furniture didn't match at all the modern exterior. But it was neat and clean and newer-looking.

I crossed my fingers in hope that no one rubbing their eyes would emerge from a bedroom, or still wet from the shower with only a towel wrapped around them. Or no towel at all.

Those thoughts were making me anxious. I tiptoed across the space to the window on the side closest to Tessa and Jason's boat and watched as they stood on the porch and talked.

What in the world are they doing?

Couldn't they talk inside? Or get going to whatever their destination was?

Deciding to "watch" these two hadn't turned out to be such a good idea . . .

Chapter Nine

WHEN I GOT back to the store, my mother was there, and so was Homicide Detective Daniel Chow. Both standing in the dining area with Koby. Both still in their nearly matching trench coats, so I figured they hadn't been there long.

I had come through the door and found the bookstore side like I'd left it, including the food I had set inside the door, still tucked in the corner.

I grabbed the bags and followed voices I heard to the café, and that's when I saw them.

I hadn't forgotten about my mother coming with her "feel good" cookies, but I never expected to see Chow.

"You're all wet." My mother was the first to speak. "Where have you been?"

I held up the bags. "Getting food."

Koby raised his eyebrow. "Why aren't the bags wet?"

He would notice that. I looked down at them, then put them on the table. Georgie and Pete came out from the kitchen area. "What's going on here?" I asked.

Tessa and Jason had stayed on the porch talking for just a

few minutes, but it seemed like an hour. They finally stepped back into the house and I made a dash for it. Wasn't sure if they ever came back out or if they even had gone anywhere. I didn't care. By the time I made my getaway, the rain, thankfully, hadn't gotten any heavier, but it was still coming down. I trotted all the way back to Books & Biscuits, trying to miss as many raindrops as I could. But I'd escaped one tight situation just to find myself in the middle of another one.

"I brought you cookies," my mother said. She should have known that question wasn't directed at her.

"I came to have a word with you and Koby," Detective Chow said. His presence was already the one I was questioning, but after he said that, I started to feel anxious. Dressed almost the same as he was yesterday, except today his shirt was a powder blue, he stood with his hands folded in front of him. He was looking official.

I drew in a breath. Was he there because he thought Koby and I had done something wrong?

"How did you know we were here?" My eyes asked Koby if he had told them about the bookstore café.

"I'm a detective." He patted his badge. "It's what I do."

"He has news about Koby's friend," my mother said.

"Reef?" I said and met the eyes of each of the faces of the people in the room. Koby, my mother, Pete, Georgie and Detective Chow all looked back at me.

"You asked me yesterday had your friend been murdered," Chow said.

I looked at Koby. I didn't like that the detective was letting my brother know I'd gone behind his back to affirm what he'd told me. But certainly, I wanted to know what he had to say.

"I thought I was supposed to call you," I said. "After the autopsy. In a few days, like you said."

"They finished the autopsy," Koby said.

"And?" I said.

"I was right," Koby said.

Detective Chow nodded in confirmation.

I felt a blubbering coming on.

My mother held out her arms and came over to wrap them around me.

I hadn't ever been one to show a lot of emotion. Whether I was feeling happy or sad, my nose was usually in a book, where I'd become one with the characters and slip off into another world. I wasn't too keen on letting emotions run loose with a mother who always wanted to psychoanalyze them.

But Reef being dead was bad enough without finding out that someone had intentionally made him that way.

"How?" I pulled up from my memory again Reef lying there on the floor. I didn't remember seeing anything that could have killed him. Some blood on his nose, but that might have happened when he fell over.

"He was poisoned." Koby answered the question. He wasn't letting the detective do any talking.

"Do you know who did it?" I asked, my mother dropping one arm of her hug but still holding on to me with the other. I directed my question to Koby.

"Not yet," the detective answered this time. "But I wanted to tell you two personally, seeing your relationship with the, uhm, victim." He paused, as if silently giving his condolences, before he spoke. "And I thought I'd jiggle your brains again, find out if you knew anything else that might help. Anything else you may have thought about from yesterday that you saw after you boarded the train."

My mind wandered back to Tessa and Jason on that houseboat. What kind of relationship did they have? Where was Tessa's grandfather? Was there really a grandfather?

I wasn't sure whether I should tell Detective Chow about what I'd seen because certainly nothing they'd done was criminal—pretending not to know each other and living together in Timber Lake. And even Tessa's lying to the clerk at Pfeiffer Crest Pharmacy wasn't breaking the law. It all was just fishy.

"I also wanted to find out if you knew of anyone else we should notify."

I could tell by his demeanor that the detective had determined that Koby and I weren't suspects.

"We're his next of kin," Koby said. He moved two fingers back and forth between us.

I nodded my agreement with softened eyes, happy that Koby included me in that designation.

Koby looked at me and gave me a nod. "We have some foster family that would need to know, but we can notify them."

"Okay. Good," the detective said, and gave us a tight smile. "So, did you notice anything, either on the Westlake platform or on the train, that we didn't discuss yesterday? I know you weren't there but a few minutes before your discovery."

Detective Chow, true to his word, must have checked the security camera on the station's platform. He'd found I did indeed board at Westlake and that Koby boarded only once I'd pulled the emergency cord. Now, he came seeking more information.

"Nothing," Koby answered without hesitation, and almost as soon as the words left the detective's mouth.

I took a minute and went through the things I'd seen the day before. At the time, I hadn't decided to make a determined effort to notice things (other than what people were wearing), like Koby did. Maybe that's why he could answer so quickly.

But when I did answer, it was the same one that Koby had given. "No. Nothing."

"Do either of you know anyone who would want to hurt Mr. Jeffries?"

"No, we don't," Koby said.

The detective looked at me and I shook my head. I didn't know anyone, other than my brother, who Reef knew.

The detective sucked in a noisy breath through his nostrils. He tugged on his trench coat and nodded. "Okay then. I'll go. You both have my card. Call me if you think of anything."

"And for updates," Koby said. His eyes met with the detective's. "You won't mind that, will you?"

That time we got a more relaxed smile. A warm one, even. "Not at all. Call me anytime."

"I'll walk you out," my mother said. For the first time she let go of me. She gestured an "After you" and took him out through the bookshop side.

Once they disappeared from sight, Pete's face lit up. "Wow, a real-life murder mystery." His eyes wide. "I wonder why anyone would want that guy dead. He was a such a nice guy."

"You didn't even know him," Georgie said, one hand on hip. "I'm the one sad here. I used to love when he stopped by. Never judgmental." She shot a glance my way. "Always complimentary. It's a shame." She put a hand on Koby's back and gave it a rub. "How you doing?"

"Fine," he said. "Just like before the detective came in."

"That's because he already knew everything Detective Chow told us," I said. Guess I was going to have to believe more in my brother's estimations. Every day, I was learning how many talents he actually had. "He said it was murder yesterday when no one else was sure of it."

"How did you know, Koby?" Georgie asked.

"Because I know that Reef wouldn't have ever left me on his own. Not on purpose. Not in a million years."

Chapter Ten

AFTER THE DETECTIVE left, my mom came back in and ran me through her standard set of questions—a mini examination—to make sure I was okay. The whole time sitting at the table holding my hand.

"How did finding out about Reef make you feel? Are Koby's feelings making your grief inflated? Are you feeling overwhelmed?"

I thought maybe she should have posed her questions to Koby.

Pulling my hands loose from hers, I chomped on her cookies while she talked. Assuring her I was okay and that her cookies had a part in me feeling better. That made her happy. And it kept my tears from falling. All in all, it was a good and effective therapy session for both of us.

I offered some of my mom's cookies to Koby, who declined, before I put the plastic wrap back over the plate and set them in the kitchen.

After my mom was sure I was okay, we sat and chatted about the excitement around the newly opening store. I showed her all the different areas we had—children's, self-help, genre fiction—and the area we were going to use for storytelling time and author events.

I sent Pete to get the box of books that Mr. Al from the Second Street Market had for me, and my mother and I went through it. To my surprise, many of the books were new, even some signed by the authors. I didn't know where he could have gotten them from, but they definitely weren't in the back room and not on the shelves, like I'd thought. I'd have to be sure to send him a thank-you note.

My mother suggested I give them away since I got them for free. A good marketing tactic. I thought that was a good idea. I knew just how I'd do it.

We were drinking tea—my mom's hot, mine iced—at one of the tables, without the tablecloths on, while Koby and Pete were hanging foodie prints by John Holyfield when there was a *rat-a-tat-tat* on the window.

It caught all of our attention.

"Mama Zola!" Koby said, and stepped down from the chair, handing the hammer over to Pete.

Zola Jackson, one of Koby's foster moms, was peeking through the Second Street door that led right into the café.

Koby opened the door and hugged her before she could get through it. "What are you doing here?"

"What? I can't come here? You got a ban on who you'll serve?"

"Of course not," he said, and chuckled. "You're always welcome, I just wasn't expecting you. And you know we're not open yet."

"Hi, Miss Jackson," I said. Seeing her brought a smile to my face. She was so nice and felt like the grandmother that any child would wish for.

"Well, I'd be dried up like a prune if I sat around and waited for you to come and bring me out here." She came over and gave me a hug. "Now, I've told you to call me Mama Zola. Just like all my other kids do."

"This place is nice," she said, a smile in her eyes. She let them wander around the room. She made her voice sound fancy, drawing her next words out. "I like." She smacked a hand at Koby.

Miss Jackson—or rather, Mama Zola—was fancy herself. A good-looking Black woman, her skin was dark and her hair salt and pepper. She always wore stylish clothes, and I often wondered, the times when I'd seen her, where she was dressed to go. Her hair and nails done, strutting around in heels that were higher than any I'd ever wear. Even my mother's work attire had a more sensible shoe heel as part of it.

Mama Zola was right, the café did look nice. I hadn't had time to admire what they'd done while I was out sleuthing. I came back to Detective Chow and word on what happened to Reef and had gotten all distracted.

Koby's decor was reminiscent of what he said was an old Southern kitchen. I wasn't sure how he thought one looked, but it certainly had the feel of one—cozy with smells that made your mouth water and made you want to grab a plate, pile it up high and sit down to eat.

There was an old-fashioned cash register that sat on a counter, built out like a peninsula from the wall that was made of reclaimed wood. All the tables were square and sat four. When I asked about bigger tables that sat more customers, anticipating the popularity of our new venture, Koby didn't waver in what he wanted. He said we'd just push two of them together.

Koby wanted hardwood floors (that I opted to have on the bookstore side, too), wood beams in the ceiling, gingham curtains and valances. In vases atop the white tablecloths, he found the most realistic-looking silk twinflowers. (Yep! That's a thing.) Cheery, bright, welcoming people to just come in and sit a spell. Sip tea. Gossip over a slice of sweet potato pie. Hanging from the ceiling were black metal farmhouse pendant lights and matching sconces all along the walls that were painted white and had beadboard under a chair rail.

"I know you're not open yet," Miss Jackson said after a long pause. "I came because I've got something for you."

"Something for me?" He looked down at her hands, which were empty, then looked at her with a puzzled look on his face. "Well. Come on in then," Koby said. "And I just wanted to wait to show it off to you once it was all done."

"Well, I love it," she said.

Standing behind the door, Koby went to close it, but he got some resistance.

I saw a tall guy with his hand on the knob. I moved in closer to the door, thinking it was someone who mistakenly thought we were open. We had had a couple people coming through today.

"We're not open," I said, alerting Koby there was someone there.

"He's with me," Zola said.

Koby peeked around the door. "Capt'n Hook!" He gave the big guy a hug.

So, this was the policeman Koby liked, although he had retired from the force. I had heard a lot about him but had yet to meet him.

"Thought you could get away from me by hanging out here in Timber Lake, did you?"

"I know I can't get away from you," Koby said. "But if I knew you guys were coming, I would have cooked you up something to eat."

"No worries," Koby's Captain said. "And hey, looka here. This has got to be your sister." He turned to me. "She looks just like you." His grin so wide it was easy to see under his bushy, white mustache. "Nice to meet you, Keaton."

I stuck out my hand to shake, but he grabbed me into a bear hug. "Nice. To. Meet. You. Too." I could hardly get enough air to get the words out. "Captain Hook," I said once he let me go.

"No one really calls me that anymore. Except Koby and Reef." He hung his head and looked down at his big hands, seemingly the mention of Reef's name making him remorseful. "Just call me Moran."

"Mama Zola, Moran, this is Keaton's, uh"—Koby rubbed his hands together—"m-mother. Dr. Rutledge."

My mother stood up and stuck out her hand. She stood far enough back that Moran couldn't wrap his arms around her. "Nice to meet you both."

"I've told you about them, Mom," I said.

"Yes. You did. They are Koby's family."

"*Part* of his family," I said.

"C'mon," Koby said. "Have a seat. I can bring you some sweet tea."

"Sounds good," Mama Zola said. "We'll just sit right down here with Dr. Rutledge."

"Imogene," I said. I wanted us all to be family. "You can call her Imogene. Right, Mom?"

"Of course," my mother said, giving one of her polite, clinical smiles. "Call me Imogene."

Koby took no time in getting back with two ice-cold mason jars of what we hoped would be a customer favorite.

"So, Mama Zola," Koby said, pulling up a fifth chair to the table between me and her. "Before you tell me what you've got to say, I have something to tell you."

"What?"

"It's bad news."

"Couldn't be no worse than what you dropped by to tell me last night." She looked at Moran. "I couldn't even sleep."

"That's why you were up so early calling me," Moran said.

"I guess," she said. "But I'm an early riser. I ain't no slacker. Never have been. That's what I loved about Reef, never minded giving me a helping hand."

Koby laughed. It wasn't a hearty one—it was the kind you do when you're remembering a story about someone who is no longer there. I hadn't too long ago learned all about doing that. "Well, the only thing he gave a helping hand with around here was emptying the pots and pans."

"I believe it," Mama Zola said. "He'd eat me out of house and home if I'd let him."

Everyone around the table chuckled.

"What do you have to tell me?" Mama Zola asked.

"The detective who's working on Reef's case—"

"What's his name?" Moran asked.

"Daniel Chow," Koby said.

"I don't know that I know him," Moran said.

"Younger guy," I said, adding the thing I always noticed— appearances. "Maybe midthirtyish."

"What did he say?" Mama Zola asked.

"He said that Reef was murdered. Somebody poisoned him."

"Oh no!" she said, and put her hand over her mouth, her eyes filling up with tears. Koby reached over and held her other hand.

"Who did it?" she asked.

That was everybody's question. "They don't know," I said.

Mama Zola looked at my brother. "Koby. You don't know who did it?"

"No, ma'am, I don't." He sniffed. Wasn't sure if he wasn't going to start crying. "But the police are looking into it."

Mama Zola turned to Moran. She didn't even have to say anything. "I'll look into it," he said. "See what I can find out."

"Well, this makes what I have even more important," Mama Zola said. "I didn't want to spring this on you over the phone." She wiped the tears from her cheeks. "That's why I had Moran bring me to Timber Lake. To tell you in person."

Koby placed a hand over his heart. "Mama, I can't take no more bad news either. Please," he said, and put an arm around her shoulders, "don't tell me anything's wrong with you."

"No. I'm fine," she said, and leaned into him. "It's from Reef. Maybe it'll help figure this out." She reached into her purse and pulled out a sealed envelope. "Reef gave this to me and told me if anything happened to him, for me to give it to you."

Koby didn't reach for it, he left it dangling in her outstretched hand. "What is it?"

"Only one way to find out," she said.

Koby had told me the story about how Zola Jackson was one of those foster moms who always had a house full of kids, and not just the ones who came from the group home. Even the neighborhood kids liked to hang out at her house.

He'd told me that he hadn't been there long when he found that Reef's foster family had sent him back to the group home. It was Christmastime and that, for most of the kids there, was the hardest. After Reef had looked out for him, ever since he could remember, Koby wanted to return the favor. He asked Mama Zola to get Reef from the home and give him a real home. Reef, Koby told me, didn't have the best reputation in the foster family community. But he talked her into it, and Reef got to spend Christmas with them. After that, Reef never missed spending another holiday with Mama Zola, whether Koby was there or not.

Koby took the envelope reluctantly and opened it.

He pulled out a business card and, flipping it over, looked at both sides.

"What does it say?" Mama Zola asked.

"Brian Jenkins. Attorney-at-law."

"Is that all that's in there?" my mother asked.

"No," Koby said, and took out a folded piece of paper. "It's a letter, too." He glanced over it. "From Reef."

It looked like my brother was going to cry. I knew what a private person he was and was sorry that he had opened that envelope in front of everyone. Sorry that everyone was going to see him get emotional.

But he held it together while he silently read the words contained in that letter. He finished it, refolded it and slid it back into the envelope.

"What did he say?" Moran asked.

"He said that if anything ever happened to him, for me to go and see this lawyer."

"Reef had a lawyer?" Moran asked.

"Guess so," Koby said, and laid the envelope on the table.

Chapter Eleven

"OH MY." ZOLA came out of the kitchen. Her nose turned up. Her face in a full-on frown. She was holding the plate of cookies my mother had made for me at arm's length.

Moran had left. Although he had been Mama Zola's ride back to Seattle, she didn't want to go. After Koby called Reef's lawyer and set up an appointment for Monday, she told him to show her "around the kitchen." Actually, that had translated to, "Let's cook."

"What are these?" she said. "Koby, I know I taught you better baking skills than this. These aren't even fit for your dog to eat!"

Koby had left her in the kitchen with Georgie acting as sous chef and had gone back to hanging pictures with Pete. She hadn't been back there without Koby for more than ten minutes.

I hopped up from my seat and relieved her of the cookies. "Those are mine."

"What are you going to do with them? Use them as book-ends?"

I glanced over at my mom. "I'm going to eat them," I said, words that made my mother's shoulders relax. "At home," I added.

"Why in the world would you want to do that?" Zola said. Before I could answer. "I could make you something better. I feel ashamed that Koby would want to serve anything like that to you. He claims he loves you."

"I do love her," Koby said.

"He didn't make them," I said, not offering anything else.

"Well, who did?" She didn't let up. She swung around from her hip and surveyed the room. "I know Pete didn't, he told me he worked in stock." She pointed a finger at Georgie. "Did you? Because if you did, Koby needs to rethink your position here."

Koby was right. She was a firecracker, and she didn't let up. I didn't want her starting on my mother. So I looked to Koby—maybe we could get her to move on to something else, but before we could, my mother spoke up.

"I made them." My mother stood up from the table where we'd been sitting. "Keaton was sad about her friend. I'll have you know, Zola"—she emphasized her name—"my daughter has always loved my cookies. They've always cheered her up."

"I'm surprised they didn't kill her."

The room got quiet.

I'm sure she realized what she'd just said and how it might be inappropriate. We'd just learned that had been the manner of Reef's demise. And even though I hadn't seen her shed a tear—she'd been all businesslike since she arrived—I knew she had a love for Reef.

But what she said seemed to go right over her head.

"Child," she said, and tugged the plate of cookies from my hand, "I've only got two black dresses, and I don't want to have to wear them both in the same week."

"It's fine, Miss Jackson. I like my mother's cookies." I thought better of calling her "Mama" when it felt like I should take my own mother's side.

"Then you need your head checked, or your taste buds." She smacked my hands away from the dish. "Or maybe both." She changed her focus to my mother. "Where did you get the recipe for these?"

"I don't have a recipe written down," my mother said. "It's all in my head." She tapped a finger to her temple. "I just add a little of this and a little of that. And they come out wonderful every time." My mother held up her hands like her cookies were borne from magic.

"That's why I never went to see a shrink," Mama Zola said. "They'll have you believing all kinds of crazy stuff is true."

I opened my mouth to say something. I did enjoy Koby's cooking. Just the thought of it made my mouth water, but I'd always enjoyed my mother's cookies, too.

When I was little, I wasn't allowed a lot of sweets, nor was I allowed to hang out with kids after school or on weekends. At least not much, so I really didn't know what kids were doing or eating at their houses. It hadn't bothered me. I was quite happy with the life I had at home.

But now it seems I may have been missing out on some things. Like cookies. Good cookies.

"You come with me." Mama Zola stuck out an elbow for my mother to grab.

My mother huffed. She looked from me to Koby to Mama Zola, then to her watch. "I've got . . . I need . . ."

"I. I. I. Nothing," Mama Zola said, hands on her hips. She spat out the words. "I'm going to show you how to make a proper shortbread cookie. Won't take but a minute, but you'll be thanking me for years to come."

They disappeared into the kitchen, and I slid up next to Koby. "Why didn't you take up for my mother?" I asked. "You know her cookies are good."

He raised that eyebrow of his. "Now they'll be good."

"What?"

"I just didn't have the heart to tell you before, Keaton." He put his arm around me and gave me a squeeze. "But your mother's cookies are pretty bad."

"No!"

"First time I ate one, I was kind of glad she hadn't adopted me, too."

Georgie burst out laughing, and she and Koby, trying not to laugh along with her, put a mock "I'm sorry" look on his face before the two of them headed back to the kitchen. Pete tucked his head and slid through the archway to the other side of the shop.

"I always thought they were fine." I shook my head, muttering to myself. "Who knew? Guess it's a good thing I'm not in charge of the kitchen. This entire venture might have turned out to be a flop."

MAMA ZOLA AND my mother came out of the kitchen arm in arm with big grins on their faces not an hour later. They had made fast friends, and it didn't seem that my mother felt at all bad with what Mama Zola had said earlier.

And she had sent my mother packing, in time for her next appointment, with flour streaks on her cheek, a plate full of the most delicious shortbread cookies and the flakiest, buttery homemade apple turnovers I'd ever tasted. Not that I could ever remember eating ones made at home.

She walked my mother to the door, like it was her place, and they both were laughing and planning their next visit like two old friends.

Come to think of it, I couldn't remember my mother ever having girlfriends. Mama Zola was probably fifteen or twenty years older than my mother, but she seemed to be able to relate to anyone and make them feel good, from parentless kids to analytical nerds.

After my mom left, Mama Zola headed right back into the kitchen, and there she stayed the rest of the afternoon, cooking.

I don't know what Koby had had in that kitchen for Tuesday's opening, but he was going to have to go shopping all over again.

Mama Zola made soul rolls, as she called them. Taking the leftover greens Koby had cooked the last time Reef had stopped by, she "doctored" them up with the juice from a jar of banana peppers and finely diced pimento. Then she rolled them up in a wonton wrapper with bits of cubed ham and deep-fried it. Yum! Served with a dipping sauce made from hot sauce, Worcestershire and spices. It was crunchy and spicy and scrumptious.

She made fried green tomatoes and a peach cobbler (her *famous* peach cobbler, she said) to die for. If aromas came out of the kitchen like they did when she was cooking, I'd never get anyone to stay in the bookstore long enough to buy a book.

"What day are you opening?" she asked while serving me my second helping of tomatoes. I shook hot sauce on them.

"Tuesday," I said, wiping away the crumbs from my mouth stuffed with food. "Only four more days."

"What you got planned for your grand opening?"

"We've ordered some balloons, and we're going to post all over social media. Well, I'm not. Georgie is." I looked over at my brother. "And Koby is supposed to be cooking up some free samples."

"I don't know anymore," Koby said, a sly grin on his face. "Mama Zola outcooked me today with just the items in the kitchen."

"Looks to me," Georgie said, "she could take a glass of water and two eggs and come up with a seven-course meal."

"I probably could," she said, and blushed.

"I need you to teach me how to make those soul rolls," Koby said.

"I could do that. Because, you know, they could be filled with any kind of Southern food. Peas, macaroni and cheese. I could go on."

"I'm ready to learn," Koby said. "We need to-go kind of

food, too, that doesn't take a knife and fork. Especially for opening day when people are wandering in to check us out."

"I could come out and help if you needed me."

I chuckled. The feistiness she'd shown all day had melted. It seemed she wanted to be a part of our venture, at least for the day.

"I think that'll be fun," I said, already looking forward to her being there.

"Yeah, Mama, that'll be cool," Koby said. "I can pick you up."

"Not in that raggedy car of yours," Mama Zola said. "We'll come in my car."

"You have a car?" I asked.

The traffic in Seattle was a monster. Nothing people like driving around in, and in the few times I'd met her, I would think she didn't have the patience for it.

"Of course I have a car," she said, almost making me feel bad for asking. Then she let her eyes roll up to the ceiling and shook her head. "I just hope my driver's license is still valid."

Chapter Twelve

DESPITE THE BAD news that Detective Chow had delivered, I went home Friday evening smiling. I enjoyed all the other company we'd had at the bookshop café. I imagined (and hoped) that that was how it would be when we opened and had regulars coming in.

Smiling faces. Happy customers. All day, people in and out. Gathering around the café tables sipping on sweet tea and munching on soul rolls (yes, Koby had already added them to the menu). Browsing the shelves or sitting in the back during storytelling time while I replenished inventory from shipments filled with new debut, as well as famous, seasoned authors.

My mother had driven all the way back from Seattle to pick up Mama Zola and take her home. She called after she finished her last appointment and said she was on her way, even though her office was only a couple of miles from my childhood home, where she still lived.

We closed up shop soon after they left. After Pete did such a good job on Thursday, I hadn't had much to do. And with all the company and commotion we had on the kitchen side, I didn't know that Koby had gotten much of anything done. But tomorrow we were meeting the Leaf Guy—our cousin, according to the genealogy website.

"You excited about tomorrow?" Koby asked. He was walking me home. He had insisted on it. I tried to get him to take a ride with my mother and Miss Jackson, but he wouldn't. He sent Remy back to Seattle in the car to stay with Mama Zola until he got there. He'd said he had other things he had to finish up. I didn't know anything else, other than seeing me home, that he'd done in Timber Lake after they left.

"I'm nervous about tomorrow," I said.

"Why? He's family."

"I was nervous to meet family when my parents took me to Michigan to meet my cousins for the first time." I tucked my head. "Sometimes I get nervous about new stuff."

"Don't think about it like that," he said. "Think of this more like solving a mystery. Putting a puzzle together. Wait to get nervous until we actually find Morie. Mom."

My brother hadn't ever had anyone he could call that. I knew this meant a lot to him.

"Jigsaw puzzles, I like," I said. "But I'd rather read a good mystery than be involved in one." I leaned in close to him. "I'm happy having found you."

"Actually, I found you."

"Yes. That's true. But you know what I mean."

"You don't have to go if you don't want to. I don't know how much he'll be able to help me anyway." A small smile curled up his lips. "Help *us*. But we have to follow all the leads we can get."

"I'm in," I said. "I want us to do this together."

"We're going to meet him at the Needle. Figured it would be less awkward than sitting across from him in a restaurant. Less like an interrogation."

I wanted to laugh out loud at that one. I knew an interrogation was probably more like what it would be. Koby was intent on investigating what happened to our birth mother.

"HI, MAN." KOBY gave our newfound relative some dab—a handshake and a one-armed hug. "This is my twin, Keaton." He nodded his head my way. "Keaton, this is Marcel Wade."

Koby and Remy had shown up to pick me up that morning in Zola Jackson's car.

"She wanted me to try it out," he'd said. "Said she hadn't driven it in a while."

It looked a lot nicer than Koby's car, but I think it was just as old. Evidently, Koby felt it was a lot safer. He wouldn't have ever picked me up in his heap of a car.

"Nice to meet you, cuz," Marcel said, beaming. He seemed as happy to meet us as Koby was curious. "I was hoping to find out about my *ancestors* when I did my DNA, but it's cool to find out about unknown relatives who are still alive."

"Hey, Keaton." He hugged me, too. "Yeah, so Koby was telling me that you were adopted but he wasn't."

What a way to start the conversation . . .

He didn't look anything like us. He was dark skinned, stocky with thick fingers and shoulders that sloped. He looked like he was in his late thirties or early forties. I hadn't asked Koby how distant a relation we were with Marcel. The DNA match page shows how much of a match there was. But seeing we were related, I had thought, ever since I found out about him, he would look like me and Koby. I knew that all family didn't look alike, and I'd never known any close relatives apart from my twin, but I had, I guessed, hoped to see a connection just by seeing him.

He wore his hair short and his face clean-shaven. He had on blue jeans and a T-shirt. Like he was just hanging out on a Saturday, not meeting someone new. Meeting a long-lost relative. Both Koby and I had been more thoughtful about our dress, even though we hadn't planned it beforehand.

Koby's khakis had a sharp crease, and his celery green shirt was fresh and starched. I wore black leggings and a long white top with yellow daisies and black centers. I had even flat-ironed my hair.

There I was again, basing my reaction to someone by what they were wearing. This time even comparing them to me and Koby. I knew Koby was counting on a lot to come out of this meeting.

"Even though I was adopted, my brother and I are together now," I said in response to Marcel's probing comment. "We won't be separated again."

He looked at me like he got what I was saying and could empathize. "Cool," he said, and smiled. "I hope that I can help you find your mom."

"You said you might know a Hill?" Koby asked.

"I said that I kind of remember that name." He smacked his lips. "Hey. Let's grab a couple of hot dogs. It's about time for me to take my medicine. I have to take it with food. You guys hungry?" he asked.

Koby and I looked at each other.

"Yeah," Marcel said, pointing toward the food stand. "You guys are gonna love Dog in the Park. Best place to get a hot dog." He pointed to the well-known stand. "I bet this little guy wants one." He stooped down and ruffled the fur around Remy's neck and head. Koby's dog didn't seem to be excited about him. "What happened to his ear?"

"He's a rescue," I said.

"Oh. Sort of like you guys."

Koby shot me a look and I narrowed my eyes. I wasn't sure if Marcel thought that was funny or not, but I certainly didn't. I was convinced that my twin didn't either.

We walked over to the Dog in the Park stand right below the Space Needle without talking. The amazing smells made my mouth water and made my stomach grumble. And the carnival-looking stand, with its red front and yellow-and-red-striped tentlike roof made me smile with memories of my dad. It was a place that I was used to, but sure, it was also the kind of place, if you were visiting Seattle, you wouldn't want to miss. But we weren't visiting. Seattle was our home.

I could see meeting someone for the first time who is supposed to be family can be awkward. And maybe since we met at the Space Needle, Marcel used it as a conversation starter—like if we were tourists. Just saying what one would normally say to someone who came in from out of town.

Although I had never felt that way with Koby. Never awkward. Never like he was a stranger.

I ordered my hot dog with mustard only, which both of the men scoffed at. Koby got a Seattle Dog—topped with cream cheese and sautéed onions—and so did Cousin Marcel. But Koby wouldn't let him pay for our lunch, even though Marcel tried to insist, saying that he had invited us.

We took our hot dogs back to the bench, and as soon as we sat down, Koby started in with his questions.

"So, did you find out if anyone you're in contact with knew our mom?"

Marcel took a big bite of his hot dog and held a crumpled napkin over his mouth. "I wasn't able to get in touch with my great-aunt." He pushed food into his cheek. "The one who would know. But I did ask my mother, and she says she can't remember anyone named Hill." He swallowed, then took another bite.

"So you didn't find out anything?" Koby asked.

"Maybe if you knew whether Hill was her married or maiden name, that might help."

"We don't know anything," Koby said. He wrapped his sandwich back up, tossed it into the trash and stood up. "That's why we're out here looking."

"AT LEAST THE hot dog was good," I said as Koby drove me back home. "Because we didn't find out anything worthwhile."

"Maybe we did," Koby said, putting on a blinker to go around the car in front of him.

"You're kidding, right?"

"No."

"Cousin Marcel said nothing to help us find our biological mother."

"No. You're right about that, but maybe he said something that might help us with Reef."

"What?" I said, raising both eyebrows. We hadn't even mentioned Reef's name.

"I was trying to figure out how Reef was poisoned on the train. Everyone on the train said they didn't see anything."

"That's true. Unless they're lying."

"Which is a possibility."

"But?"

"Remember when Marcel said it was time to take his medicine?"

"Ohhh," I said, nodding. I knew just what he was getting to.

"You know what I'm talking about?"

"Yeah. I do. Reef was taking medicine."

"Vitamins."

"And he set an alarm so not to forget." I didn't remind Koby that Reef had initially said *pills*. "The poison could have been in the vitamins."

"Exactly," Koby said. "Detective Chow was vague on the poisoning."

"Maybe not vague, but cautious."

"Either way, it would be a good way to kill him remotely."

"Put the drug in the vitamins," I said. "Just lie in wait until he took them."

"Exactly."

And that was the last thing we said on the rest of the drive home. And the last time we mentioned Cousin Marcel.

When we got back to my place, Koby let Remy play in my backyard, with Roo giving him a run for his money by swip-

ing her claws at him and taking off up the Pacific yew tree
when he gave chase. After Roo grew tired of him, she came
and curled up in my lap as Koby and I sat on my paprika-
colored twin lounge chairs and talked.

"It's weird," Koby said. "All the times I looked through
the obituaries looking for our biological mom, I never
thought what that meant."

"You mean other than she's dead?"

"Yeah. Like somebody had to compose the words about
her life to even have an obituary."

"You're thinking about who knew our mom?"

"Yeah." He looked over at me. "And about Reef."

"He'll need an obituary," I said.

"And a funeral."

I pursed my lips. "There's a lot to that," I said, remembering my father's.

"I thought the funeral home did everything. You just had
to pick out what you wanted."

"I don't mean going through the motions—selecting music, a casket and a flower spray." I groaned. "I mean preparing to not ever see a person you love again."

"Who do you think did it for our mother?" Koby asked.

I hunched my shoulders.

Until Koby came into my life, I hadn't ever thought much
about her. Now I sometimes wondered if she ever married.
Had more kids. Was she somewhere thinking about us—
looking for us—like we were thinking and looking for her?

"How much is this going to cost?" he asked.

"A lot," I said.

"Like how much? Twenty thousand?"

"No, not that much."

"Good. Because I don't have that much."

I didn't know that my brother had any extra money at all.
He'd put in all he could to start Books & Biscuits. At least
that was the way it seemed. He'd sold a motorcycle he had,
and he tried to sell his car, but no one would buy it. That was

what Zola had told me—in confidence. I hadn't ever asked Koby about it, but there was no reason not to believe it, especially after I saw that heap he claimed was an automobile.

After Koby left, I sat down at my kitchen table with my laptop. We'd called the funeral home we'd used for my father, and Koby made an appointment.

But I could tell, even though I was learning that he wasn't one to wear his emotions on his sleeve, that what happened to Reef had mixed in with his feelings he'd been having for Morie Hill.

It was like he hadn't ever associated looking for obituaries with the fact one would mean she was dead. It was just a way to find out what happened to her. A possible answer to why she'd given us up.

Marcel Wade hadn't helped us. And Reef, the only person Koby knew who had given him a link to his past, was now gone.

I opened up my laptop, typed in my password and pulled up a browser.

Koby had never wanted to ask my mother if she knew anything about our birth mother. I'd never asked him why, but I think it was because he didn't want to somehow veer into a conversation that would lead to the question of why my mother and father hadn't adopted him, too.

I hadn't asked my mother either. I would have asked my dad, but by the time Koby found me, he was gone. But without asking, there was something I could do.

Adoption records usually are sealed—forever—after the adoption is finalized. I had looked up information about adoptions when I first found out I had been, but it was nothing I wanted to act on. I was happy with the parents who had chosen me. But I had discovered, without going through the legal system, that some states, including the state of Washington, allowed adopted children access to nonidentifying information. The state, however, didn't allow the adoptee's siblings to gain that information. That meant Koby, who hadn't ever been adopted, didn't have access to it.

But I did.

I could get the nonidentifying information without cost, registering with the state or asking my mother. It would save face for everybody. And it might be that giant leap my brother needed toward finding what was most important in life to him. Finding his mother.

Our mother.

I typed in "KingCounty.gov" and found the link for the Adoptions Department of Family Court Services. I printed off the information request form.

As the term *nonidentifying* implied, I could only get information that wouldn't identify Morie. Things like her education, occupation, how old she was when I was adopted, other children she may have had, the reason the child was given up for adoption, and photographs.

Probably a long shot, but wouldn't it be something if they had a picture of her?

I filled out the form, found an envelope and tucked them into my bag and gave it a pat. It needed to be notarized. I wouldn't be able to do that until Monday, but just knowing it was going to be done made me feel like a weight had been lifted. Not from me, but from my brother.

Chapter Thirteen

IT RAINED MOST all of Sunday morning.

I sat, curled up, in my reading nook built under a window. My fur baby napping at my feet, lulled away by the drops gently drumming against the panes of the window. A wide-rimmed, steaming cup of peppermint tea, in remembrance of my friend Reef, and a book with a brooding tone, *Wuthering Heights*, like the weather outside, helped me pass the dreary morning.

By noon, the rain had receded, and the grayish skies were swapped with a bright blue one with white fluffy clouds.

"I'm going out for a walk," I told Roo as I washed out my cup. Standing at the sink, drying my hands on a tea towel, she came and rubbed against my legs.

"You want some love?" I said, stooping. I picked her up, cradling her in my arms like a newborn, and sprinkled kisses over the soft black fur of her head. "I would take you with me," I told her, "but it may start raining again, and I know you wouldn't like that."

She followed me into my room, where I stepped into a

pair of jeans and slipped my favorite T-shirt over my head. Black, it had a white cat napping atop a stack of books that read, **Once Upon a Time, There Was a Girl Who Really Loved Cats and Books**.

"How do I look?" I asked her. "You like the T-shirt?"

"Meoww."

"You should," I said. "You got top billing."

She followed me into the living room and climbed up on top of one of the bookshelves. It was naptime.

"Guess you're not going out with me anyway, huh?"

From the time I moved to Timber Lake after I graduated from school, I'd often put her in the basket on my bike and we'd tour the city. Although our community was small, there were too many residents to ever think I'd come to know them all, but everyone I'd encountered had been friendly. Everyone was neighborly and I'd felt at home right away.

I grabbed an umbrella and a rain slicker but returned the jacket back to the peg by the door when Mr. Jones caught my attention.

"It's going to be hot today," he said, waving his trowel. "Probably won't see any more rain."

I looked up. The sun beaming down on me made me close my eyes. It was beautiful out.

"Your flowers are looking good, Mr. Jones," I said, opening my eyes up and training them on him.

"Yes, but I've got a lot of work to do." He pointed to the garden hose that was stretched across his lawn and a wheelbarrow of dirt.

He and Mrs. Grayson, my neighbor on the other side, were big on gardens. My grass was nice and green, and I kept it cut, but a yew tree in my backyard and a Douglas fir in the front were the extent of my garden. I didn't have one flower. I had been planning to invite the two of them over and get schooled on what to plant and how to take care of it. But after switching from working for the Seattle library system to being an entrepreneur, I wasn't sure if I was going to have the time.

I walked down by the marina. It was a normal route for me to take to head into town, and although I had left home with no set destination in mind, it seemed like a perfect day to be near the water. And maybe I'd come that way because I was being nosy.

I didn't get too close to it, but I got near enough that I could see the houseboat that Tessa and Jason occupied. I had forgotten to tell Koby about seeing the two of them. I'd gotten back to Books & Biscuits and Detective Chow was there, which discombobulated me. Then Mama Zola took up all of Koby's attention.

And then, after Saturday hadn't turned out the way Koby had hoped, it just didn't seem important enough to bring up.

My brother wasn't one to show how he was feeling. Putting his range of emotions out for people to see just wasn't him. He always seemed to take things in stride. I hadn't even seen him mourn Reef—not with tears or slowing down to take it all in—and I knew how much that guy had meant to him.

I saw Old Man Walker, the handyman at the marina, out emptying trash on the pier. He was on a golf cart and made a stop at the waste containers that were placed every couple dozen feet apart. He stopped when a woman in high heels, frosted hair, and a navy, double-breasted raincoat come storming down the pier after him, wagging a finger.

His body language didn't change, but she showed a lot of emotion with hers. It was easy to see she wasn't very happy with him or with something he had something to do with.

I didn't know much about the old man, not even how he'd gotten the moniker. When I worked at the library, he'd come in every now and then with a box of books. He told Liz, his and my librarian friend, that he'd find books in the storage closets when people's memberships to the clubhouse ended and they failed to clean their spaces out. It seemed to me that Liz also had mentioned to me that the clubhouse had once had its own library. I vaguely remembered that. I never knew if some of those books had come from there.

Other than Old Man Walker getting chewed out by that woman in the navy coat, nothing else was going on. No motion was detected from Tessa and Jason's place, and I wondered what they were up to.

What do you do after you've killed someone?

Do you just go back to life as usual?

"Stop, Keaton," I said to myself as I started to move on. "You don't know who killed Reef."

I shook my head, not wanting those kinds of thoughts to fill my mind. I knew I wouldn't want anyone blaming me for it just because I was there. And that was all I knew about the two of them. They were there. And that's it.

I cut through the park and across the ravine. There was no hustle and bustle in the downtown area today. Sundays were slow. It was like Timber Lake was a sixties kind of town. Sundays were a leisurely, lazy kind of day. Stores closed. People staying home with family, attending church, having a big Sunday meal and whiling around the rest of the day.

But just a few miles away in Seattle, Sunday was like any other day. Streets and roadways crowded with people and cars. Businesses open and in full swing. It was noisy with smells of exhaust and food filling the air.

I like the slowed-down pace of Timber Lake. I had strongly advocated for Books & Biscuits to be there when Koby and I decided to start our own business.

I walked along Eighth Street and naturally gravitated toward Books & Biscuits. Our corner store was visible from two blocks away. The name of it in big white letters, in the Awesome Birds font, and the ampersand large and curvy, connected the two words.

Even though it was dark inside, the large picture windows showed all the imagery and excitement within the store. Well, at least for me. Stacks of books and upholstered sofas and chairs. And through the large archway, which I could just make out from where I stood, was the charming café.

Just the sight of it made me happy. Which, I guess, was a

good thing. Being the owner of a brand-new business, I was going to spend much of my life there from opening day on out.

Which was fine with me. And I loved having my brother as my business partner. I hadn't ever met anyone else—living—I would have done it with.

When I was little, I hung out with both my parents, not with other kids. Nowadays when I think back on it, like my mother, I didn't have any friends. As I got older, I spent all my time with my dad. He was the complete opposite of my diagnostic mother. Creative and funny, he doted on me. And after he left, I realized what a singular life I had. Then Koby came along.

Chapter Fourteen

"WHATCHA DOING, KEATON?"

Koby had called me. His voice was low on the other end of the phone and his words monotone.

"Uhm. Nothing. Why?"

"Can you meet me somewhere?"

I glanced at my watch. We were supposed to meet later in the afternoon to go and decorate Books & Biscuits. We'd ordered a tank of helium, colorful balloons and a big step-and-repeat sign to take selfies in front of, in lieu of a hiring a photographer, which we couldn't afford.

I had expected him to call me to tell me how his day had gone. It was Monday. The day before opening day, but also the day he was going to see Reef's lawyer as the letter had instructed him to do.

"Sure," I said. "Are you okay?" He didn't sound like he was.

"I found something out."

"At the lawyer's office?" I glanced at the clock on my phone. It had been a couple hours since his appointment time. "Are you still there?"

"No. I'm in Timber Lake. Right down from your place."

"Oh. Well, come over here."

"No. I need you to come to me."

"O. Kaaay." He was sounding weird. "Just tell me where you are."

"Down at the marina."

"The marina?" I swallowed a knot that had suddenly balled up in my throat. I had forgotten to tell him about Tessa and Jason. How could I have forgotten to tell him that? Now did something happen with them? Had they kidnapped him? Oh my! Maybe they told him to call me and lure me down there, too.

Only Koby wouldn't ever do that. I knew that for sure. No matter how much they tortured him.

"Keaton? You still there?"

"Yes. I'm here." I shook the thought out of my head. "Is there someone there with you?" I asked. "Just say my name again if there is. I can call the police."

"Keaton!"

"Oh! There is someone there! I knew it! Are they holding you hostage?"

"What are you talking about?"

"I'm calling 911."

"No! Don't."

"Oh my goodness. Did they hear me say that? Oh, please don't hurt my brother!" I yelled into my phone.

"You need to calm down," he said. "Check your twin radar. Does it feel like I'm in danger? Or does it feel like you're just flipping out?"

I stilled myself. I let my eyes drift up and to the left. Radar. Did we have that? I knew sometimes it felt like I knew what Koby was thinking or how he felt.

I stood up straight and exhaled. Okay. If I did have a "radar," there weren't any discernable blips on it. Not that I could feel.

"I just wanna show you something," he said, maybe sensing my concern. "Can you calm down and meet me?"

"Okay." I nodded, not that he could see it. "I can do that."

"Just start walking toward the marina. I'll walk up and meet you."

"Okay."

I grabbed an umbrella—a big one with a metal tip in case Tessa really was up to something—and a yellow windbreaker before rushing out of the door. Might have to protect myself from Jason and her grandfather (if he really existed), too.

I had been thinking that we might have twin telepathy. And there were times, it was becoming more frequent, that we said the same thing at the same time, but I hadn't ever thought about radar. Twin radar. I liked possibly having that superpower.

I hadn't gotten far when I saw my twin. His windbreaker was flapping in the wind. It was yellow, too.

"Hey," I yelled, and gave an exaggerated wave.

He waved back.

"Am I not going to be able to call you with news anymore?" he said as I got closer to him.

"No." I shook my head then nodded. "Yes. I mean just don't call like something bad is going on. Especially when it's about something I had just learned."

"What are you talking about?" He tugged my arm and we started. "C'mon. I want to show you something."

"I didn't tell you that I followed Tessa down here." I didn't move. I figured since we were so close to where she was, I should tell him what I'd learned.

"Who?"

"Tessa Chaiken."

"The girl on the train," we both said at the same time.

"Where did you see her?"

"Here. At the marina. Well, not at first. I followed her here."

"What? You followed her? When was this and why didn't you tell me?"

"It was Friday. After I got food from Second Street Market. I saw her, put the bags inside the door and followed her."

"Followed her where?"

"First she went to the pharmacy. While she was in there, I overheard her—"

"Overheard?"

"Okay. I eavesdropped. She went in the pharmacy, I followed her in, hid in one of the aisles and listened as she and the salesclerk talked."

"What did she say?"

"That she lived with her grandfather and that she'd never go to Seattle. She wasn't a big-city girl."

"Then what was she doing on the train?"

"My question, too," I said. "Then she left and I followed her here. To the marina."

"And you're just now telling me all of this?"

"I meant to tell you when it happened, but when I got back to Books & Biscuits, Detective Chow was there. Then Mama Zola and Capt'n Hook showed up."

"That was two days ago."

"I know. But then we met Marcel and you went to the funeral home."

"Never mind." He held up a hand. "Where did she go when she came to the marina?"

"Right here," I said, and pointed. We were walking down the pier as we talked, but when I pointed to the boat, Koby stopped. "She went in there. And Jason Holiday was there, too. I saw them both. I never did see anyone who could be her grandfather, though." I tried pulling on his arm as I talked to keep him moving. Didn't want Tessa or Jason to see us. I wasn't worried about the grandfather, if he even existed. He wouldn't know what we looked like. But Koby wasn't budging.

"What?" He held his head and spun around to take a good look at their boat. "You have got to be kidding me."

"No. Not kidding." I gave him another tug. "And if we keep standing here, they'll see us."

"What were they doing?"

"I don't know. I couldn't tell." I glanced at the boat. "Now can we go?"

"They're going to be seeing me anyway."

"Why? We are not going to talk to them. I'm not getting on that boat."

"Because that boat"—he pointed to the one next to it, the one that I had stowed away on to get out of the rain—"now belongs to me."

"You bought a houseboat?"

"No. Reef left it to me."

"Wait. I don't understand. That's Reef's boat?" I shook my head. "Right next to Tessa and Jason?"

"I guess so. You said you saw them there."

"I did." I stuck one foot in front of the other and anchored myself. "So they were neighbors? They knew each other?" I looked between the two boats. "I thought Reef lived in Seattle. Or somewhere."

"Evidently not," he said, jabbing his finger to the boat again, this time with an exclamation. "Because that was his."

"He sure had me fooled."

"Me, too." Koby blew out a breath. "And it's a really nice houseboat."

"It is. Nice on the outside, at least."

"What do you mean?"

"I've been inside that boat. It didn't look anything like you'd expect after seeing the outside. Scarcely decorated. Little furniture."

"You've been in the boat? When?" He turned and looked at it, then turned his eyes on me. "Reef took you in the boat?"

"No. Of course not. I just said I didn't know he lived in Timber Lake."

"So how did you go in it?"

"When I followed Tessa here. She went into her boat. I

couldn't see what she was doing, but I saw that telescope"—
I pointed to the deck of Reef's boat—"and thought I could
look through it and see what she was up to."

"I can't believe you did that." I could see the amusement
in his eyes.

"Yeah. Well, I can't either. But I did. She was in there with
Jason, and while I was trying to make out what they were
doing, the two of them decided to come outside. I couldn't let
them see me, so I hid."

He was chuckling and shaking his head.

"Not funny." I gave him a smirk.

"How did you get inside?" He held up a set of keys and
gave them a jingle. "I just got these from the lawyer's office.
You climb into a window or something?"

"The side door was open."

"Really?"

"Really. Well, unlocked. I went around the side of the boat
to duck out of sight and leaned up against it. It came right open."

"I can't imagine Reef leaving a door open. He's always
been one for locking up stuff."

"Maybe the lock on that door is broken."

"Maybe." He glanced back at the houseboat. "This is such
a coincidence. And," he said, "I was thinking I'd wait until
you were here to see it for the first time. We could see it together."

"And I've already been in it," I said, exactly as Koby was
saying, "And you've already been in it."

"Whatever possessed you to follow those two?"

"I only followed Tessa. And I did it because *you* said she
was someone to watch."

"Oh wow." I could tell by his face that he didn't think I'd
take that literally. "I didn't mean *you*. You weren't supposed
to go and watch her."

"Too late now," I said.

"So, what happened? What did they say? What were they
doing?"

I hunched my shoulders. "I got nothing. I didn't hear anything, and the only thing I saw was the two of them."

He outright laughed that time. "You are like the worst sleuth."

I shrugged.

"C'mon. Let's go take a look inside." We boarded the boat. I stood behind Koby at the front door as he tried one of the keys on the ring. It didn't work, so he tried another one, and the door gave way.

We stepped inside. Koby blew out a breath and gave a nod before turning to lock the door behind us and take a gander around the room.

"Wow. You would have thought it looked a lot . . . uhm . . . nicer in here." He scanned the boat he'd just inherited. "You know, with the way it looks on the outside."

"I just told you that."

We both stood in place and let our eyes wander around. It looked the same as it had on Friday, when I'd hidden inside.

But then, why would it look different? It was Reef who had lived there, and he had been killed Thursday evening.

"And why didn't I know about this place?" Koby said.

"Or that Reef was right here in Timber Lake."

"Right," Koby agreed. "Probably why he was popping up so often at the restaurant." He narrowed his eyes. "I don't know why I didn't notice that before. He'd come and stay for a minute. Why didn't I realize he hadn't come all the way from Seattle?"

"I don't know." I hunched my shoulders. "I never thought about it."

"You were just happy to see him."

I didn't give an answer to that comment, but it was true.

Koby walked over to the kitchen area and looked in a couple of cabinets and pulled open a few drawers and then the fridge.

"What else did he leave?" I asked.

"Not much food," Koby said.

"I mean to you. Did he leave anything else?"

"He had a life insurance policy."

"He did?"

"But it was just for five thousand dollars."

For the little while I worked at the library, an insurance policy had been included in my benefits package. After leaving there, I'd gotten back on my mother's health insurance since I wasn't quite twenty-six, but I hadn't ever thought about getting some on my own.

But then again, I'd never thought about dying young. Evidently Reef had.

"I bet you're thinking, why would Reef have a life insurance policy?"

I smiled. "You're right. That was just what I was thinking," I said. "Why did he have one?"

I saw Koby's jaw tighten. He slowly shook his head back and forth. "I don't have a clue."

"And why did he leave a will with a lawyer?"

"It really wasn't a will." Koby went and looked out the window that faced Tessa and Jason's boat. "It was a letter, but it was still weird. Him having a lawyer. Instructions on what to do if he died." Koby turned around. "Or this secret houseboat."

"A houseboat moored right next door to where two people who were on the train when he died live."

"I wonder, does this thing actually float?"

"Don't change the subject."

"I'm not." He frowned. "We're talking about the houseboat."

"No. We were talking about the neighbors."

"Tessa and Jason," he said, and chuckled. "You were talking about them."

"How could you not talk about them?" I put a hand on a hip. "Can't you see?"

"See what?"

"How weird it is that you thought something was up with

them the first time we saw them. And how suspicious it is that with the way they acted on the train, you wouldn't know that they knew each other."

"And they live next door to Reef."

"Right!"

"Right." He nodded in agreement.

"And for some reason, Reef left instructions on what to do when he died. Like he knew."

Koby looked at me out the side of his eye. "Like he knew he was going to die."

"Yes."

I waited for Koby to say something else. He didn't.

"Do you think they told the detective?"

"What? That they knew him or that they were neighbors?"

"Either one." I flapped my arms. "Both."

"I don't know," he said, but he seemed distracted. Maybe he was just digesting all of this.

"Koby. They are probably the ones who killed Reef."

"Yeah, I wouldn't jump to that conclusion."

"How could you say that? They knew him. They were on the train."

"I read that book," he said.

How was that an answer to my question? "What are you talking about? What book?" I asked, confusion written across my face. I needed him to stay on topic.

"You never told me there was an alternate theory to how the murder was committed."

"What! Book?"

"The one where they all killed the guy. They each stabbed him."

"*Murder on the Orient Express*?" I squinted my eyes and shook my head. "I've been looking for that book." My tone became more thoughtful. "But I don't know what you mean. There is no alternate ending."

"Oh. I took it from your house. That night. The night I rode back home with you."

"You did? No wonder it was missing."

"Yup. You kept talking about it. I wanted to read it."

"What ending are you talking about? They all killed the guy."

"The other theory that that detective had."

"Hercule Poirot?"

"Yeah. Him. He said that someone boarded the train, killed the man, then got back off the train."

"But it had snowed. Remember? Did you read the whole book? They determined it couldn't have happened. That's how they figured out what really happened."

"I know, but the other theory gave me an idea. What if someone killed Reef who wasn't in that train car with him once it was stopped?"

"Like someone other than Tessa and Jason?"

"Right. Or the Pussetts or that Aubriol girl."

"Why would you think that?" I didn't understand his thinking. "No one else was around."

"Because," he said, "I picked up Reef's personal property, and there was only one phone in it."

"I don't understand."

"Reef had two phones. One was an iPhone. One was an Android."

"Yeah." I nodded slowly. I did remember that. "And you're saying they only had one of them?"

"Right. Exactly."

"And?"

"And the one they gave me"—he pulled a phone out of his back pocket—"is not the one he texted me from when he said he was on his way."

I frowned. "How is that possible?"

"I don't know." He drifted off in thought, turning the phone around in his hand. "Unless his killer has it."

"So . . . what? The killer took his phone after he texted us?" I didn't give him time to answer. My mind was putting the story behind his theory together. "Then that would mean whoever killed him had to have gotten off the train at West-lake. Westlake, where *we* were." I shouldn't have had to remind him of that. But I did. "And no one got off the train when we got on."

"Or maybe they got off before that. Maybe they got off at the Capitol station."

"Nooo. Because if they had, he wouldn't have been able to text us to tell us he was passing that station."

"Not unless *they* texted it instead of him."

"Why would someone do that?"

"Really, Keaton?" He wrinkled his eyebrows and shook his head. "They did it so they wouldn't get caught. It would seem that he was still alive, at least until after he had passed that station."

Chapter Fifteen

OKAY, SO MAYBE my brother wasn't the next Hercule Poirot, because that theory sounded crazy.

How would the killer know to text us?

But I didn't have time to ask that question before someone knocked on the door.

"Don't answer that!" I said, jolted from my thoughts.

"Why?" Koby said, and walked to the door. He was already making himself at home. And he didn't even wait for me to give him an answer. Which would have had to do with a killer being on the loose. "Hi," he said, pulling the door open.

"Hi," the guy at the door said. "Uhm, is Reef home?"

"No," Koby said.

I stood there with my mouth open. Not sure if the guy at the door was friend or foe of Reef's, because evidently there was at least one person who didn't like him.

"Oh. Okay." The guy acted as if he didn't know what to say next.

"I'm Koby. A friend of Reef's. Who are you?"

"I'm Darius. I'm a friend of his, too. Well, my brother is."
He peeked around Koby to see inside and caught sight of me.
"My brother told me to come and see about doing some work."

Darius was what my father called a redbone. Black man
with fair skin, reddish hair and a sprinkle of freckles across
his nose and cheeks.

He was lanky, and he didn't look like he'd been long out of
his teens. His jeans were baggy, and he kept pulling them up.

"Some work?" Koby asked.

"Yeah, you know, for his business."

"Who is your brother?" Koby asked.

"Sam." He seemed to start to fidget. "Sam Anderson," he
added. "You know him?"

"Nope. I don't." Koby pulled the door open wider. "Why
don't you come in."

Now why was he inviting this guy in?

"Uhm, I can wait until Reef gets back." He fidgeted some
more. "Can you tell him I stopped by?"

"Reef won't be back," Koby said. "He died."

"Died?" Darius looked from Koby to me and back. "How?
When?"

"Thursday." Koby paused before he finished. "Someone
killed him."

I saw Darius' knees go slack. His mouth dropped open and
his face turned pale. "Oh wow. I didn't know." He cleared his
throat. "I guess that's why he hadn't been answering my texts."

"You okay?" Koby asked. He'd seen, too, how that news
affected Darius. "You wanna sit down? A drink of water or
something?"

"No." Darius shook his head. "What . . . What are you two
doing here?" His tone accusatory.

"Reef was my foster brother," Koby said. "And this is my
twin, Keaton."

"Oh. Koby. Yeah." Darius mustered up a smile. "I know
who you two are. You're opening that new store on Second
Street."

"Yep," I said. "That's us." The table had turned. Now I was trying to assure him that we weren't the bad guys.

Darius stepped into the living space, I guess feeling more comfortable now. Koby shut the door behind him, and Darius looked back at it, seemingly weighing whether it was okay not to have an easy egress. He probably would have felt more comfortable with it open. I knew because I would have, too.

"So, do you know how it happened?" Darius asked.

"Nope," Koby said, shaking his head. "We were meeting him on the train, at the Westlake Station. But by the time we got on, he was dead."

"Oh wow." He scratched his eyebrow and took a look around the room. "You guys planning a funeral?"

"Yeah, we are," Koby said. "We're his only family, you know. We gotta put something together."

"I heard about his foster family," Darius said. "My brother told me." Then he frowned. "But what about his girlfriend? She probably would want to have something to do with everything."

"His girlfriend?" I said. Oh, that made my stomach clench. Hadn't he been flirting with me? Inviting me to come and hear him play his sax? "What girlfriend?" I looked at Koby, trying to gauge whether he knew about this.

"Yeah," Darius said, looking at the two of us. "You don't know her? She lives right around here."

"Tessa?" I blurted out. How was he dating Tessa and she was with Jason?

"I'm not sure of her name." He stopped and narrowed his eyes at us. "Why don't you know this stuff about Reef if you were his friends? His family, or whatever?"

"I'm wondering the same thing, bro," Koby said. "I'm wondering that same thing, too."

DARIUS GAVE US his number before he left, although he seemed to have a renewed skepticism about us. I was skeptical about us, too. I had been so proud to be included whenever Koby introduced Reef and himself as family. But family should know about each other.

But more than that, I was kind of steaming over the fact that Reef had had a girlfriend. Was he just inviting me as a friend? Or worse, as family, like as in his "sister"? What the heck!

"Let's take a look around," Koby said, interrupting my inner rant. "I didn't know that Reef was so secretive."

"Neither did I." I didn't like the way my words came out. It sounded like I was sulking.

"And now it seems like he wants me to find out what's going on instead of him just telling me in the first place."

I frowned. "Why do you think he wanted you to find out?"

"The letter Mama Zola had. Him leaving me his boat. Clues all around."

"And you thinking you're a detective."

"He was the one to say that. Only because I've always been observant."

"And because out of the seven million people in this state you found me."

He gave me a lopsided grin. "Yeah. And that."

"I really don't see this trail of breadcrumbs, though." The story of Hansel and Gretel popped into my head. They got lost in the woods and into a lot of trouble because of breadcrumbs. *Maybe I should have used another metaphor . . .*

"Reef was turning thirty. He had stopped drinking, although he never had a problem with it."

"Just trying to get healthier." I repeated what Reef had told us.

"Right. He stopped getting into trouble, bought real estate." He wagged a finger around. "And he got a lawyer."

"You think he knew someone was trying to kill him?"

"I don't know. But I need to find that out."

"What about Detective Chow?"

"What about him?"

"Well, that's kind of his job."

"And I'll let him do his job." He held up both hands, as if

showing they were clean. "No one is trying to stop him. I'm just going to follow the breadcrumbs, as you call them, that Reef left for me."

"Okay," I said. "Where do we start?"

"You with me?"

"Of course." I was hoping we'd fare better than the story-book siblings.

"Probably the best place to start would be here," Koby said. "He did leave me the keys."

The boat wasn't that big, and with the open floor plan that I had admired before, it didn't seem like it had many places to hide things.

"Maybe there's a safe somewhere?" I asked.

He pulled the keys out of his pocket and flipped one over, then the second one, then the third one. "Nope. These two look like they go in a door. I don't know what this third one is for." He looked down at his feet. "What about a secret hatch?" He started stomping across the floor, listening for a hollow sound underneath the area rug.

I watched him march across the room, and I started gig-gling. "Do you even know what we are looking for?"

"No." He stopped and did an about-face toward me. "But we do know whatever it is, it isn't underneath the floorboards."

"What about a bedroom?" I looked around. "Gotta be one."

Koby looked over past the last cabinet in the kitchen. "Two doors. One I'm thinking is a bathroom, the other might just be—"

"The bedroom," I answered.

He agreed with a nod. "Let's see."

We each went and stood in front of a door. "You go first," I said.

Koby opened his door. "Bathroom," he said, and looked at me.

"Bedroom."

"Good," he said, and came over to stand by me. "See any-thing?"

"Not really," I said. "Nothing much in here."

Koby stepped inside the room. "No, there isn't."

There was a bed. A chair with a couple pair of pants laid across it. A dresser with a book and some papers on it, a few drawers hanging open with clothes coming out of them. An ironing board with the iron sitting on top of it. And, sitting in a corner all by itself, Reef's saxophone.

"He must not have been living here long," I offered.

"Well, maybe not, but he wasn't living in the apartment he had in Seattle either. I went there and checked. The apartment manager said he'd moved out a little less than a month ago. And according to the title I got from the lawyer, that's when he bought this boat."

"And you didn't know?"

"No. And now I could kick myself. I was paying so much attention to getting Books & Biscuits up and running."

"That was important."

"I know. But man, I feel bad for not knowing."

"It's not like you hadn't seen him," I said.

I didn't want him feeling bad. I hoped he wasn't thinking he'd chosen being with me over his friend. Did brothers ever feel like that? "You talked to him on the phone. And he was there all the time."

"Yeah. That's true."

Koby wandered around the room. "I just feel like there is something I'm supposed to find." He scratched his head. "Something that he thought might cause him harm, and he was taking precautions against whoever was threatening him by leaving me stuff to figure out so they wouldn't get away with it."

That seemed like a tall order, I thought. I wondered, even with Koby's deductive skills, were we going to find something that elusive?

"They?" I said, nodding. "Like his neighbors?" I said, not wanting him to forget about Tessa and Jason. "I think we should tell Detective Chow about them."

Chapter Sixteen

BEFORE I COULD whip out my phone to tell the good detective my suspicions, we heard a noise out in the living part of the boat.

"What was that?" I asked.

"Shh! I don't know. Maybe Darius circling back for some reason." He looked at me. "You stay here."

"No," I whispered. "You stay here. We'll wait until they leave." I was too afraid to stay by myself, and I didn't want him to go either.

Hansel and Gretel leaving breadcrumbs had gotten themselves captured by a wicked witch.

Someone had killed Reef. Someone, according to Koby, Reef thought might be after him. With so many people coming to his house, odds were getting better that we might just run into that someone.

"We need to know who it is," he said. "We're following breadcrumbs, remember."

He'd gotten the gist of what I was thinking, but he didn't get it all. He must have missed the part about what we might find maybe not being a good thing. I needed him to think "evil witch."

"Hello." Koby had not attempted to grab anything to protect us with, nor had he taken any caution in announcing us. He stepped out of the bedroom.

I grabbed the big book that had been on the dresser and followed out behind him. Didn't know what I thought I'd do with it. I didn't even have good aim.

"Oh!" The intruder was startled by Koby's greeting.

Our witch was a young woman. Probably about our age. Long, dark, curly hair, a light brown tan covered her, which I wasn't sure how she'd get in our rainy part of the world. The little clothing she had on was tight—her blouse stopping way above her navel, her shorts the Daisy Duke variety, and she was barefoot. She was a pretty girl. No. I had to correct that. I was sure anyone who saw her would say she was beautiful.

As soon as she saw us, she hurriedly put her hand behind her back. (So not only should she be classified as beautiful, I thought I should add "sneaky" to her list of attributes.)

"I didn't think anyone would be here." She kept her hand hidden but tilted her head and stared at us. "Who are you?"

"Who are you?" Koby asked, turning her question around on her. He folded his arms across his chest.

That seemed to be the question of the day.

"And how did you get in?" I added, trying to get more out of her. I kept the book in her eyesight in case she tried anything with whatever she was hiding behind her back.

I must have looked less menacing, even with my make-shift weapon, because she answered my question first. "The side door." She pointed with her one free hand. "The lock is broken."

"I told you it might be," I said to Koby. We'd come in and hadn't ever checked it. Now someone had come through it.

"I'll have to take a look at it," Koby said, "but that still doesn't answer my question."

"Isabella Ramirez," she answered. "But everybody calls

me Izzy. I live a few boats down." She pointed down the pier, opposite from where Tessa and Jason lived.

"Are you in the habit of letting yourself into other people's places?" Koby asked.

"I didn't think . . . I thought . . ." She opened her mouth and didn't say anything, like she was thinking. Getting her story straight. "Reef and I are dating. Sort of." She looked up, her eyes shifting to the right like she was making this up as she went along. "I always let myself in if I need something." She pulled a screwdriver from behind her back. "I just got back in town and found I had a leak. I needed to fix it." She waved the tool back and forth like a metronome.

"A leak?" I could tell Koby didn't believe that.

"In my sink."

I didn't believe it either.

What under a sink required a screwdriver?

Nothing.

Koby looked at me and I let him know, with my facial expression that agreed with him, she didn't seem to be truthful.

I really hoped the girlfriend part, in particular, wasn't true.

"I'm Reef's brother," Koby said. "Foster brother. How about if I help you with the sink?"

"Uhm. Sure," she said. "If your girlfriend doesn't mind."

"No." He seemed to blush. "Keaton?" Koby swung around my way. "She's my sister."

"Okay, then." She tucked her head and looked up at him.

"Koby," I said.

I wanted to say that I didn't think that was a good idea. Going somewhere with someone we didn't know. Someone he had just seemed to soften to and was seemingly taken with and who might just be the wicked witch of the story. But I didn't get a chance to.

"I'll be right back," he said, not even to me, just in the air, and was out the door.

I only hoped she wasn't planning on fattening him up with her lies just so she could stick him in her oven.

I SAT ON the couch, my tennis shoe–clad feet propped up on the coffee table.

Koby had been gone ten minutes, fifteen tops, and I had worried about him every minute he'd been away. He was acting just like those people in scary movies—going toward the danger instead of running away from it. Reef's murderer was somewhere out there, and while we weren't aware of anything we'd done to draw attention to ourselves, the killer might not like us being around. Koby already thought there was something in the houseboat that would lead him to Reef's killer.

Maybe Izzy and her screwdriver had come to find it.

"Time you got back." I looked at my watch then up at my brother as he came through the broken side door.

"I gotta get that door fixed."

I gave him a smirk.

"You ready to go?" he asked.

"Where to now?"

"Books & Biscuits," he said, like where else would he be talking about? "We have balloons to blow up."

"Are we finished with the search here?"

"Uh," he groaned. Looking around, he let out another one. "Well . . . we did look." He hunched his shoulders. "Yes." He bobbed his head from side to side. "No." He shook his head. "We are not done here, but we do have to leave."

"Okay," I said, and stood up. "Let's go."

"Whatcha think of Izzy?" he asked as he locked the door behind us. "She seems good, huh?"

"Yep," I said. "A good suspect."

That made Koby chuckle. "What are you talking about? What has she done?"

Other than her coming around when we were talking

breadcrumbs and how it reminded me of how perilous such an innocuous act could be, there was nothing much to make me suspect her. But there was that one thing that made me think she might have wanted something more than she'd indicated.

"Who fixes a sink with a screwdriver?" I asked.

He laughed again. Something about talking about Izzy sure did tickle him. "Yeah. It was really a pressure issue. The flow of water coming from the sink was low."

"I thought it was a leak?"

"Oh yeah." He smiled. "She did say that, didn't she?"

"Did you fix it?" I ignored his question.

"I did the best I could."

"Hmmmmm."

"What?" He laughed. Again.

"Nothing," I said, shaking my head.

When we got to the shop, Koby still had a stupid grin on his face. And I wanted to remind him that she had said she'd been Reef's girlfriend, but I didn't.

I knew that would have wiped that crazy grin off his face, though, just like it had done mine.

Chapter Seventeen

BOOKS & BISCUITS looked so cute!

We did one heck of a good job putting everything out, and it hadn't taken any more than a couple of hours to do with Georgie and Pete to help. But I could barely stand back and admire it before Koby was pulling me out of the door again.

"We gotta go," he'd whispered in my ear.

"Go where?" I lowered my voice, too. Didn't know why we were changing the volume of our voices. Georgie had disappeared into the kitchen and Pete was resweeping an already swept floor.

"Izzy told me what the other key is for."

"What other key?"

"Remember there were three keys on the ring I got from Reef's lawyer?" He was still in my ear.

"Oh yeah. Front-door key. Side-door key—"

"And storage key," Koby finished the list.

"Oh," I said thoughtfully. "That's what it's for." He nodded. "I knew there was a storage area at the marina, should have thought about that."

"You knew?" He frowned. "Why didn't you tell me?"

"Uhm. I don't know." I hunched my shoulders. "I didn't think it was relevant."

"Relevant?" I felt him lean back from me. I turned to look at him. "We were searching his house for trap doors, hidden safes and secret files."

I rolled my eyes. He made it sound so Dan Brown–ish.

"Maybe I would have thought of it," I said, "if you hadn't stopped the search to fix that girl's sink."

"Oh." He smiled. Entire face lit up. "Izzy." The name came out breathily.

I shook my head. I had to refrain from rolling my eyes again.

"But if it wasn't for her," he said, "we wouldn't have known what the key was for."

"We would've figured it out eventually," I said.

This time it was Koby who shook his head. "Keaton, to work as a team, you have to remember to tell me things when you find them out." Koby glared at me, like this hunt for clues was real and a serious thing. "Not tell me at some random time because of some tangential reference that jars your memory."

"Tangential reference," I mumbled. I bit on my bottom lip and nodded. "Got it," I said. A little sarcasm seeping out.

He bumped into me. I stumbled and we both laughed.

"Okay guys, time to lock up," Koby announced. He hit his fist into the palm of his other hand. "We'll meet back here tomorrow morning at nine thirty."

We all got out of the door and I locked it.

"C'mon," Koby said, and tugged me in the direction of the marina.

It was still nice out. Koby had left his yellow slicker at the bookstore. I carried mine over my arm. I glanced up at the sky. With it being springtime in the Pacific Northwest, you have to be prepared for rain at any time.

"Are we looking for anything in the storage space?" I asked as we headed into the wooded park area.

"Clues."

"The ones that Reef left you because he felt someone was after him?"

"Yes."

Again, he didn't seem to notice my sarcasm.

"Do you have any idea what those clues might be?" I asked.

"No." He looked at me, a grin on his face. "But I think we'll know when we see them."

As we crossed the ravine and came out on the other side, I was thinking that I was glad he had that much faith in me. That I'd know a clue when I saw it, seeing as I didn't even know what the clue was leading to. I was a bad Captain Arthur Hastings to Koby's Hercule. I couldn't even remember to tell him stuff I knew—stuff he felt was critical to Operation Decode Reef's Secret Life. What kind of power of deduction did I possess that would help determine the value of something I saw in a storage closet?

"You know where the storage is?" Koby asked as we neared the clubhouse area.

"No. I just know there's one because I've heard Old Man Walker talking about it."

"Who is Old Man Walker?"

"The guy who maintains all the property at the marina. We should see if we can find him. He can tell us where it is."

The marina was an eyesore. On the side we entered was an asphalt parking lot filled with holes and uneven ground. The only good thing about it was the lunar blue Mercedes that sat in it.

There were a few buildings that made up the marina, collectively called the clubhouse. I hadn't been past any of the buildings recently because they were on the other end of the long property. But the last time I saw the clubhouse, it looked like it was on its last legs.

We walked across the parking lot and down alongside the back of the buildings. On the other side of them was another long wooden structure nestled between a black wrought iron fence and a wooded area behind it. We cut between two of the buildings and came out on the other side near the water and onto the boardwalk. At the far end were gas pumps and a waterway for boats to pull up and fill up.

"Those are in bad shape," Koby noticed.

"Yeah," I said, and scrunched up my nose. "And can you smell the gasoline?"

"No."

"You don't smell that?"

He breathed in. "No," he said again.

The entire time we had made our way down the marina, there hadn't been anyone around. The only activity was from the gulls overhead—squawking and wings flapping among them.

"What's the purpose of all these buildings?" Koby asked as we neared them.

"It used to be nicer," I said. "My father used to bring me up here when I was little." I pointed back to the buildings we had passed. "There used to be a restaurant and bar." I pointed ahead of us. "A little park area with picnic tables, then the boardwalk continues to the beach and . . . Oh! A store." I looked down the walkway in front of me. "Let's try there."

"Where?"

"Right down here. It sells food and drink, like beer and distilled water and fishing stuff, like licenses, tackle and bait."

"Is it still open?"

I shrugged. "I don't know. But people around here still fish, I'm guessing. And it might be worthwhile to have since people are living on houseboats down here instead of just coming down to sail around for the day."

"Okay. Lead the way." He pointed in front of him. "You remember where it is?"

"I think just down here."

There was a smell that hit us in the face as soon as we

opened the door to the clubhouse store. It was fishy, like sea-water, the store musty and dark. Old, worn posters on the walls, an outdated calendar, and cookware and fishing gear hanging on walls.

The little light that drifted in when we entered showed an abundance of dust motes seemingly suspended in the air. It was easy to see that whenever they landed, they covered the items stacked in disarray on the shelves. And it seemed no one bothered to displace them.

The place was a mess.

"Gotta love shopping local," Koby said, lowering his voice.

"I said, give me a minute!" a man called out, his voice rough and scratchy. The announcement made both of us look behind us. We weren't sure if he was talking to us. Out of sight, his voice seemed to be coming from behind the counter.

"Okay," I said hesitantly.

To my surprise, Old Man Walker stood up and looked at us. "Who are you?" he asked.

"We needed to talk to someone about getting into the storage area."

"I'm the somebody you need to talk to, but I don't know you, and that means you don't have any storage here."

Old Man Walker, whom I remembered from my child-hood but had only seen at a distance since, looked just the same. Old. Scraggly. He had sprouts of washed-out white hair along his jawline, atop his mouth and sticking from under the skullcap he was wearing.

"My friend Reef Jeffries has a boat here," Koby said.

"Him I know."

"Did you know he died?"

Old Man Walker eyed us. "I might have heard something like that."

"Well, what you heard is true," Koby said.

"And who are you?" Old Man Walker asked again. But this time he meant as it was relative to Reef.

"Reef was my foster brother," Koby said. "He left the boat to me."

"And who's this?" He nodded toward me.

"Oh, sorry," Koby said. "This is my twin sister, Keaton."

"Is she going to live on the boat, too?"

"No," I said. "I have a house." I swung around from my hips and pointed toward where my house was located.

He leaned across the counter and squinted at me. "Don't I know you?"

"I used to come here when I was little, but you might remember me from the library. I used to work there."

"Oh. Yeah. You left to open some shop."

"With my brother." I nodded. "We're opening up a bookstore café called Books & Biscuits."

"So." His eyes left mine and shifted over to Koby. "You wanna get inside of the storage?"

"We just need to take an inventory of his things. Find if he had anything we could bury him in, and there are a couple things in there that he wanted me to have."

I looked at Koby. I didn't know where he'd gotten those tall tales from or what made him spew them, but I kept quiet. I'd have to talk to him about that later.

"You got the code?" Old Man Walker asked.

"To the gate?" Koby asked.

I tried not to let surprise show on my face. We hadn't known where the storage area was, but after his saying it, it made sense the storage was behind that gate we saw coming in. It was a security gate.

"Yep," Old Man Walker said. "You can't get in without the code."

"I lost it," Koby said. "Things have been kind of stressful lately." He blew out a breath like he had a weight sitting on his shoulders. "But I need to go through his clothes and get them to the funeral home."

I couldn't keep a straight face, so I wandered around the store. I landed by a shelf that carried dog food and motor oil.

Standing close to it, I tried not to sneeze and concentrated on a can of tuna whose expiration date had long ago passed.

I watched the two of them out the corner of my eye, not letting the other eye stray from the green and gold Neptune label on the tuna until I smelled something. Something familiar.

Peppermint.

I scanned the aisle, sniffing until I spotted it. It was a bag of peppermint candy. I ran my finger on the cellophane and smiled, then I leaned over and took a good whiff.

Reef.

My mind went right to memories of him. And this time the smell did make me sad. Maybe being close to where he lived. Or thinking maybe this is where he bought the ones he was always sucking on.

Old Man Walker took in Koby's words, then paused, but only for a minute. Koby's sob story did the trick. "He left that boat to you, huh?"

"He did," Koby said.

"What are you going to do with it?"

"Not sure," Koby said. "It's a nice vessel, though."

"It is," Old Man Walker said, and nodded. "Well, c'mon then." The storekeeper hit a key on the cash register, it *cha-ching*ed as the drawer came open. He came from behind the counter and headed toward the door. He held it open for us. After we were out, he flipped one of the signs to say, BE BACK IN 5 MINUTES and then locked the door.

I was glad to leave that smelly store, but when we stepped outside, I smelled the gas again. I hadn't ever smelled it on the other end of the marina, but now it was giving me a headache.

"What is that gas smell?" I asked. "Is it coming from when boats fill up at the tanks?" I did a head nod toward them.

"No. Those pumps are under repair. They're not working." Koby looked at me as if to say, "I told you so."

"You don't need to worry about that, though," Old Man Walker said, still walking, keeping his face forward. "Reef's boat isn't seaworthy. You can't go anywhere on it."

"Good to know," Koby said.

"I'm real sorry about Reef," Old Man Walker said as he led us around the back of the store. "He was a good egg. Always stopped by to check in on me. Say hello. Real stand-up kind of guy."

"That was Reef," Koby said.

Old Man Walker put in the code, and the black wrought iron gate creaked open and stayed put. The door was only a few steps from the gate's entrance. It didn't have a lock on the door, probably because the gate was secure, but there did seem to be a lock on the outside. Wasn't sure it was even operable, though.

The front of the building was made out of cinder block, the rest was wood. It looked like mortar was coming loose between the bricks, and it was crumbling in some places. It didn't seem to me that it would be able to support the rest of the structure for long. It was in as bad shape as the other buildings on the property.

Old Man Walker grunted as he pulled open a heavy metal door. As he did, a turpentine stench wafted past us. I wiggled my nose. There were too many smells around here. It was making my head swirl.

He walked ahead of us. "Not many people use the storage area," he said.

I could see why.

"Somebody's storing paint stuff," I said. I wiggled my nose, trying not to sneeze, but it didn't work. "Achoo!"

"That's the owner's stuff. She uses that first space there."

"It smells," I said, and scrunched up my nose.

The building on the inside was one long corridor and appeared to have only one way in and out. It looked longer on the inside than it had on the outside. But maybe I hadn't been paying enough attention as we had walked by to make an accurate assessment. (I was going to have to become more aware of my surroundings, like Koby.) And, I thought, maybe some of the building was hidden behind the trees on the other side of it.

But at least the strong smells diminished as we moved down the long hallway. It turned from paint and varnishes to must. My nose handled that a little better.

"Any lights in here?" Koby asked.

"Yep. Motion-activated. You walk, they flick on."

"Energy-efficient," Koby said.

"Cheap," Old Man Walker said.

We followed him about halfway down the corridor, five- or six-feet-wide metal gates every few feet, some with locks, most without. As the lights popped on, I saw what looked like boxes of papers and trash. There were mattresses and wood standing up on the walls. Someone needed to take a broom to the place.

I looked up and saw security cameras. I wondered if they were motion-activated, too. And I wondered, why spend money on surveillance cameras for such a trashy, run-down building?

Old Man Walker stopped halfway down the structure and stood in front of a door. He scratched the stubble on his cheek and kicked crumpled paper in front of the door away. "Well, this ain't right."

"What?" I asked.

"This one's got a double lock on it." He looked up at the number over the door, then back down at the lock. He tugged down on his hat.

"What does that mean?" Koby asked.

"We do that when the renter hasn't paid their slip fees for the month."

"I can pay it now," Koby said.

"That's the thing," Old Man Walker said, scratching his head. "I could have sworn that he paid." He lifted the second lock and let it drop. It clanged against the metal of the door and other lock. "And I didn't put this one on."

Koby and I looked at each other.

Maybe this was one of the clues I was supposed to keep my eye out for.

"Who would have done it then?" Koby asked.

"Only one person I know," he answered. "Historia Krol."

"Who is that?" I asked.

"She's the owner." He shook his head. "And she doesn't play when it comes to money."

Chapter Eighteen

OLD MAN WALKER gave us a card for Ms. Krol, which he had in his pocket, and an unceremonious nod good-bye.

We headed back out toward my house. I wasn't sure how Koby had gotten to Timber Lake, but I knew he was going to have to get back to Seattle soon to see about Remy.

"I should have gone back with him." He stopped walking and glanced back toward the clubhouse store. "I can have him check his records to see if I need to pay Reef's slip fees."

"He said Reef paid it."

"Then why is it double-locked?" Koby asked.

I didn't have an answer for that.

"This place doesn't look so well run," I said, "so it might just be a mix-up."

"Right." I could see in Koby's face him weighing what to do.

"How about we call the woman who owns the place?" I held up the business card. "Maybe she can tell us. Or talk to Old Man Walker to see where the mix-up is. We might get it done quicker going straight to the top."

"Okay," he said, giving in. "Call her."

I dug out my phone and called her number. I heard it ringing in my ear, but a ring was coming from somewhere behind me as well.

"You hear that?" I asked Koby.

"Yeah. It's her." Koby pointed behind me.

I turned around and smelled her before I saw her, but when I did, I knew she was the same high-heeled, frosted-haired, navy blue, double-breasted-coat-wearing woman I'd seen the other day. Digging in her pocket, she was trying to get her ringing phone out. She was the same one—I was almost sure—I'd seen pointing a finger at Old Man Walker when he was trying to empty the trash.

"I've seen her before," I said to Koby.

"Oh. Not again." Koby shook his head at me and headed over toward the woman.

I didn't know what he was huffy about. I didn't know who the woman was at the time, and I had no idea she'd be part of our clue-finding expedition.

"Ms. Krol!" Koby held up his hand to get her attention. She was headed toward her car. The lunar blue Mercedes I had noted earlier. The only nice thing in the crumbling parking lot.

I hung up the phone. Didn't need to call her now. I followed behind Koby. Her perfume was so strong, it made me sneeze.

"Achooo!"

Historia Krol took a step back from me.

"Hi," I said, self-consciously wiping my nose.

"Can we talk to you for a minute?" Koby asked.

"Who are you?"

There's that question again.

Historia Krol looked from my face to Koby's and back again.

"I'm Koby Hill. This is my sister, Keaton."

"If you're interested in renting a slip, you need to talk to

Mr. Walker. You'll find him down at the store. And, just so you know, there's a nonrefundable application fee."

"We already have a slip lease."

That made her look at us again.

"Which number?"

I decided to take over the answering of the questions. I didn't know what Koby was going to say, if he was going to come up with more of his tall tales. "It's Reef Jeffries' houseboat."

"Okaaay," she said. She seemed to try to think of who that was.

"We needed to get into his storage closet."

"I'm sure he can help you get in it. It's his space." She narrowed an eye at us. "If you have permission."

"We do," I said.

"Are you saying he can't help you get in it?"

"That's what I'm saying," I said.

"Well, you're gonna need a key for his lock. We require locks on every door. And a code to get into the gate."

"We have a key," Koby said.

"The problem is, there's another lock on his door," I said. "Mr. Walker said he didn't put it on there."

"Why are you bothering me with this?" she said. She pulled out her fob and unlocked the car door. "I didn't put it there either," she huffed out the words. "If there is an additional lock, Walker put it on. I swear, he'd forget his way home if he didn't live here." She started walking. Pretty fast in those heels over that broken-up asphalt. "We added a lock, then that means we didn't get a payment. Thirty days late, we put our own lock until we receive payment." She grabbed her car door, signaling she was finished with our conversation. "Mr. Walker takes care of late payments. Tell Mr. Jeffries to pay, then if you really do have his permission to go into his storage, Mr. Walker will take the second lock off."

"Reef is dead," Koby said.

I looked at him with big eyes. I was trying to avoid that. I remembered my mother had a hard time getting into an account my father had only in his name after he died. We had to go through probate court.

That stopped her. "Oh. Reef Jeffries." Her voice got low and sympathetic. "I can't let you in there then."

"Why?" we asked in unison, although I was sure I knew the answer.

"Because he's dead, and I can't let people take his stuff. Next of kin has to come to get it."

"We're his next of kin," Koby said.

She looked skeptical.

"The only family he has. We grew up in a group home together."

Her eyes drifted off toward the water. "That explains a lot," she mumbled. Then she focused on us again. "Look. I just can't give his things away to any Sam Hill who comes by and says they want it. That puts me and my marina at risk of liability. I don't need anybody suing me." I opened my mouth to say something, and she put up that same finger I'd seen her wag at Old Man Walker. "Bring me something that says you're the executor of his estate, or something to that effect, and it's all yours." She nodded, indicating she had spoken, opened her car door, threw her bag inside and followed in after it.

She pulled away while Koby and I were still standing in the parking lot, her unfriendly coldness lingering in the air.

Chapter Nineteen

IT WAS LIKE opening up a fairy-tale book.

Tuesday morning was bright and sunny. And through my bedroom window, birds were singing, and Mrs. Grayson's lilac tree, yellow roses and colorful alstroemerias were dancing in the gentle breeze.

It was opening day.

Koby had walked me home the night before and told me he had to catch the train back home. He was going to be up late.

But for me, even with the anticipation humming around inside me exciting every nerve ending in my body, I went to bed early. I wanted to be fully rested for our first day.

I swung my feet over the side of the bed and stretched. I noticed Roo still curled up snoozing.

"How can you sleep in?" I asked, stroking her fur. I glanced at the alarm clock. It was seven thirty. "Okay, baby"—I stood up and bent over to kiss her head—"maybe it is a bit early for you. I'll shower and see if you're ready to celebrate with me then."

I showered and dressed. I'd gotten a new sweater set for the first day, pink and pretty, with some black-and-white-checkered pants and pink shoes with a wedge heel to complete it. I turned and twisted in my cheval mirror. I liked the way I looked. Cute! My hair was curly today. I decided not to take the time to flat-iron it. I figured I was going to be in a mad rush all day with the gazillion customers streaming in, and I'd sweat out any hairdo I tried to have. I pulled it up in a top ponytail and let it flop where it would.

I made toast for breakfast and drank a glass of orange juice. I was happy and excited, but nervous, too. It was the first day of Books & Biscuits. We were going to find out if people liked what we'd come up with—not only a soul food restaurant in Washington State cooked by a twentysomething, but one attached to a bookstore. Soul food recipes are usually handed down by grandmas, not perfected by younger generations. And for us librarians, books aren't kept anywhere near food. This was going to be a whole new experience for me.

But we had done it, and I couldn't wait for the day to start. Fingers crossed that it was a hit.

"Breakfast!" I called out to Roo. She sauntered in, walked past her bowl of food and, brushing up against me, made a figure eight around my legs. "Oh, now you want to congratulate me, huh?" I picked her up and we rubbed noses. "Is that what this is about? Or is it you just want attention?"

I had to leave a little earlier than I normally would. We had decided on store hours of ten a.m. to seven p.m. But this morning, I had a stop to make.

I washed up the glass I used and swiped the crumbs from the toast off the counter. I grabbed my bag and gave a quick look inside it to make sure I had the envelope.

"I'm leaving," I yelled out to Roo. Nothing. "She probably went back to sleep," I muttered. "How could she sleep today? Too many butterflies."

At least in my stomach.

I stepped outside on the porch and pulled in a breath. I

looked up at the sky and smiled. No umbrella today. I pulled the door shut and headed toward town.

I needed to go to the bank and get my application for nonidentifying information related to the adoption notarized. Just thinking about it set off another flutter of those buggers in my belly. I was almost as excited about helping Koby solve his mystery of our biological mother as I was about opening Books & Biscuits to the public for the first time.

Lake Community Bank opened at nine, a good hour before we were set to, giving me plenty of time. I wanted to get to the bookstore café early, so my plan was to be at the bank before they opened and be the first through the door.

We'd already done the decorating. Georgie and Pete had met us at Books & Biscuits the afternoon before, after we'd left the houseboat. We blew up balloons and sprinkled confetti around book stands. Koby had put the final touches on his menu.

The Books side was finished, so there was nothing for me to do this morning. Koby, of course, needed to cook. We were giving away free food. That meant we were going to have a lot of people coming through. He didn't need my help for that, Mama Zola was coming in. And he never let me in the kitchen anyway. I guess now I knew why—he probably thought I cooked like my mother.

The bank was on the outskirts of the town center, just another two- or three-minute walk past our store. And right outside of it was a mailbox. I hoped to get my morning mission done and get back to Books & Biscuits no later than a quarter after nine.

But I hadn't thought about the library opening at the same time. Walking past it headed to the bank, I ran into one of the librarians I used to work with and got distracted.

"Keaton!" It was Liz Chambers. She waved me over. "Hi! Today's the big day, right?" She rubbed my arm.

"Yes, it is." I blushed. "Opening day."

"Congratulations! I'm so proud of you, and I know your dad would be, too."

Liz was a reference librarian who had worked with my dad at UW. She'd left the college after she'd gotten pregnant, wanting to stay closer to home. She'd been the reason I applied in Timber Lake—she had suggested it to my father right before he passed away.

Liz was friendly, not just to me, but to everyone. Like Old Man Walker. She was the reason I knew anything about him and what I knew about the marina.

Even with her amiable personality and past relationship with my father, she was never more than an acquaintance to me. Someone to chat with between the stacks. We didn't talk on the phone or visit each other at our homes, but I had a warm affection for her and appreciation because I knew my father had.

"Thank you," I said. "I'm really excited. But I've got to get moving. I have to stop at the bank and then get to the store."

"Of course. Of course," she said, a smile beaming on her face. "And I'm going to stop by on my lunch break. Show my support."

"Thank you," I said again, then leaned into her. "I have something special for you."

She squealed. "I love surprises! Especially when it's book-related."

"It's book-related." I smiled my confirmation. I didn't know why I said it. I really hadn't thought before to give her anything. But the books Mr. Al had given me popped into my head, and I wanted her to have one.

I glanced at my watch to give my cue it was time to leave, but when I looked back up, something out the side of my eye caught my attention.

"Oh."

"What is it?" Liz followed my gaze. She saw what had stopped me. "Jason Holiday. I see he made it back." She turned back to me. "You know him?"

"Uhm, not really," I said, still watching him. He'd gotten

out of a blue shiny car that seemed familiar and gone into the employee entrance on the side of the building. He hadn't been driving because the car pulled off after he'd gotten out. Who needs a ride to work when they live within walking distance? "He works here?" I asked.

"He's one of the new pages. Just started." She tried to get my attention by coming to stand in front of my view. "Why did he catch your eye?"

"He's a . . . uhm . . ." I turned my face toward hers. "A new neighbor."

"Oh." She frowned, confused. "I thought he lives on the marina?"

"He does," I said, digging myself into a hole. I didn't want her asking how I knew this stuff about him. "A down-the-street kind of neighbor. I pass by there when I'm on my way downtown."

"Oh yes, right."

"Is he married?" I asked.

"Not sure," she said, her forehead crinkled in thought. "Can't say that I remember him wearing a ring." She glanced toward the door where he'd just gone through and back at me. "You want me to find out?" She gave me a crooked smile.

"Oh! No. Nothing like that," I said, and waved a hand. "I just wondered about him, that's all. You know, what kind of person he is."

"Oh," she said, nodding like she thought I was hiding my true reason for wanting to know.

I actually was doing that, but it was far from the reason she thought I wanted to know.

"Well, he's kind of quiet. And I know that he likes music. He's always humming."

"Happy guy, huh?"

"Yeah. He did miss a couple of days last week, which with him being on probation, probably wasn't good. But if you're sick, you're sick."

"Which days?"

"Which days what?"

"Was he out sick?"

"Ohhh." She turned her head, thinking. "He left early on Thursday, I think, then missed Friday and Saturday." She tightened her lips and gave a curt nod. "I remember because we had to scramble to get someone to work the weekend."

Weekend, like for the rest of town, only included Saturday. Even the library was closed on Sundays.

"Oh. That wasn't good," I said.

"No. But he's a good worker and people do get sick."

And some of them commit murder, I wanted to say.

"I have to go, Liz," I said instead. I pointed to my watch. I wasn't going to get to the bank before they opened and be the first in line, but I'd be there, if I hurried, just as they were opening the door.

"WE WON'T BE open for another thirty minutes," I called through the door.

The man standing on the other side was too early. Maybe he was as excited as I was about opening day. But it was making me more nervous that he was standing there wanting to get in when it wasn't quite time to open the doors.

I had just made it in myself. I'd had to wait a couple of minutes before the bank representative called me over to her desk, and a couple more while she located her seal. But I got it done, licked the envelope and dropped it in the mail. I noted the pickup time was noon. Then it would be on its way and hopefully give us some answers.

As I had walked toward the store, I heard, before I saw, Koby's car making its way down the road. I couldn't believe he'd driven it in. Mama Zola hadn't been with him, which was what I expected. She had said she wasn't ever riding in that piece of junk (her words, not mine). I wondered how she'd plan on getting here. I would have bet that Koby would've wanted the two of them to come in together.

Pete had been standing outside the door, waiting for me. He was the most punctual guy. I had looked around to see if Georgie was anywhere in sight. She hadn't come in until nearly nine thirty.

"I'm here to see Koby." The guy wouldn't go away.

I frowned. I didn't want to be rude. I knew Koby was busy. I could smell the biscuits, the aroma of the flour and butter wafting into Books. But this guy didn't understand what the sign on the door read. Opening hours posted meant he wouldn't be able to see anyone in here, face-to-face, for another thirty minutes.

I held up my arm and pointed to my watch. "We open at ten."

"I'm a friend of Reef's, and I need to talk to your twin."

I guess he thought showing he knew who I was and knew someone we thought of as family would work to get me moving.

It did.

I held up a finger. "Hold on. I'll get him."

How could I tell him to go away and he came about Reef?

I grabbed Koby and practically had to do a tug-of-war with Georgie, who claimed she needed him, to get him to come back to the door with me.

"Who is it?" Koby asked when I wrenched him away. He swiped his hands down the front of his moss green apron before pulling it over his head and taking it off. He had on a Books & Biscuits T-shirt and blue jeans.

"I don't know," I said. "But now that I think about it, he does look familiar."

"Familiar, like how?"

But even before he opened the door, he knew what I meant. I could see the recognition on his face.

Koby unlocked the door and pulled it open. "Sam. Right?"

"Yeah. Have we met?" The man at the door seemed as surprised as me with Koby's guess. He stepped inside the door.

"You look just like Darius."

Sam chuckled. "Darius looks like me. I'm the oldest."

That was why he looked familiar . . .

"What can I do for you?" Koby asked.

Sam Anderson had more weight on him than his younger brother. More muscular. He was light skinned, but not a ginger, his hair was dark and he had no freckles. He was taller. At least six feet. He had more facial hair and definitely didn't have a baby face. He looked about thirty, but still they resembled each other enough that it was easy to see the relationship.

"Reef has some stuff that belongs to me, and I wanted to get it."

"It isn't here," I said, making a face. Why would he come to the bookstore café with his demands?

"Yeah, I know that." He gave me the same face.

"Look, I don't know anything about what you're talking about," Koby said. "But we're getting ready to open our store today for the first time, and I just can't help you out right now."

"I know, man. I didn't think you could give it to me now. And I'm sorry for dropping by when you guys are busy." He took a look around the store. It was easy to see we weren't busy. In our defense of poor sales, though, we hadn't opened yet for the day. "But I didn't know where else to find you. And I didn't want you selling off that houseboat, and I lose my tools and stuff."

"We're not selling the houseboat," Koby said.

"No?" He shrugged. "Okay. Like I said, I didn't know what was up. But I need my stuff."

"So you keep saying," Koby said. "But there wasn't anything in that houseboat like what you're talking about."

"No?" he said, and scratched his eyebrow. He looked just like his brother when he did that. "Maybe it's in the storage?"

"Storage?" Koby asked, and shot a glance my way.

"At the clubhouse," I said, and nodded. I knew just what my brother was thinking. What was behind those two locks on Reef's storage space?

"Yeah. You didn't know?" Sam asked Koby. "There is a storage closet." He nodded like he was schooling us.

"Okay," Koby said, not acknowledging he did know.

"That's probably where it is. You know, my stuff. I can just get the key from you and get it. No bother to you at all."

"What kind of stuff is it?" I asked.

"Like I told you, tools . . . equipment and stuff I need for work."

Koby glanced at the clock over the register area. "Tell you what, I'll get your stuff together for you and give you a call. How about that?"

"Uhm . . . you know . . . I—"

"That's the best I can do," Koby said, interrupting his stammering. "I haven't gone through Reef's stuff yet, and I'm really cutting it close with my opening by standing here talking to you."

"Okay. I just don't want to lose my stuff, man."

"Understandable," Koby said.

"Sorry we're late!" My mother and Mama Zola came rushing through the door. "Traffic was the worst!"

My mother grabbed me and kissed me on the cheek. "Today's the day!"

I smiled.

"Who is this?" Mama Zola asked, pointing to Sam.

"He's a friend of Reef's," Koby said.

"Uh, we used to work together." He seemed to correct Koby's interpretation of his and Reef's relationship.

"But he was just leaving," I said. "So we can finish everything and do opening day." I went toward the door.

"That's cool," he said. "But I need to leave my number so I can get my stuff that Reef had. You know, when you can get to it, which I hope won't be too long."

"Sure," Koby said. He grabbed a pad and pen off the counter and handed them over to Sam, who scribbled his info across it.

"Be sure to call me," Sam said, handing it back.

"Bet," Koby said. "And if not, you know where to find us, Sam."

Sam left and Koby locked the door behind him.

"Why are you letting people in here and we're not open?" Mama Zola smacked Koby on the arm.

"Keaton let him in," Koby said.

"Wait! What!" I smacked him on his arm, too. "You are such a tattletale," I said. "I did not know that about you."

"You don't want to be in trouble with Mama Zola," he said. "It ain't no fun."

"We've got to get cooking," Mama Zola said.

"I'm working Books," my mother said.

"Thank you both for coming in this morning," Koby said. "And you taking off from work, Mrs. Rutledge."

"You are quite welcome," she said. "I wouldn't have missed this for the world. It's so good to watch my little girl do this."

"What I need to see is what the biscuits look like that I smell," Mama Zola said. "Can't go around serving flat biscuits."

"They're gonna be perfect," Koby said, putting his arm around her shoulder. "I had a good teacher."

Mama Zola smiled, then pointed a finger at the two of us. "And you both need to watch people coming around saying they're Reef's friends."

"You're talking about that guy who just left?" I asked.

"I am. Because if that Sam was Sam Anderson, Reef wasn't so keen on him."

"He wasn't?" I asked.

"Nope," she said. "Called him a knucklehead."

Koby and I looked at each other.

My twin radar was telling me Koby was thinking the same thing I was.

We might have just located ourselves a murderer . . .

Chapter Twenty

FIVE! FOUR! THREE! Two! . . .

Koby and I were standing at the front door on the Books side. Everyone else—my mom, Mama Zola, Pete and Georgie—gathered around as we counted down.

"One! Open the door!" we all said in unison.

And with a hand each on the doorknob, my twin brother and I officially opened Books & Biscuits for business.

We had at the last minute wiped the crumbs of Koby's first batch of biscuits and soul rolls from our faces and the countertops. Both items were going to be a big hit.

There wasn't a long line at the door when we opened. I guess that was what we got for opening on a Tuesday, when a lot of people were at work. But new books always came out on Tuesdays, and I wanted to give a nod to that tradition.

Liz the librarian stopped by, just like she said she would, right after noon. She browsed the shelves and chatted with my mother before I gave her the "surprise" I had for her. A signed copy of Alyssa Cole's *An Extraordinary Union*.

Liz loved historical romances, and this one had been in the

box of books that Mr. Al had given me. When I saw the Civil War love story, I had immediately thought of Liz.

And since I was giving out surprises, I'd also spotted a book about fruit trees I had set aside. I thought I'd give it to Mrs. Grayson when she stopped in. There was one titled *Growing Your Garden* that I thought I'd give to Memphis Jones, although he never said he was going to visit. Mrs. Grayson would probably say I needed to keep that one for myself.

Liz stayed most of the hour she had for break and grabbed a soul roll and sweet tea for food. She said both were "sublime." I laughed. I knew Mama Zola would eat that compliment right up.

And Liz bought a book, too. Sales on my side were kind of slow, so that made me happy when she paid for one.

"I came to support," she said.

People trickled in during the morning and early afternoon. But foot traffic picked up around three.

At first everyone who came in the door (we'd decided to use only the door that straddled both streets and left the Second Street door that came directly into Biscuits closed) made a beeline right to the café for the free food. But Koby's food must have mesmerized them, making them fans, because a lot of them wandered back over to the Books side—to the shelves, shopping for books, a few even buying—dropping crumbs along the way.

I giggled to myself, remembering the association I'd made with breadcrumbs and Izzy Ramirez. I hoped me thinking of it wouldn't conjure her up and she'd come waltzing through the door.

THERE WERE FOUR or five people in the line when I first spotted her. A girl who seemed lost. Not quite sure what she was looking for. She stood in the middle of the floor, a stack of papers in her hand, and was looking lost. I knew I had to help her. It was what librarians did.

I glanced around and found Pete helping or watching, not sure which, a couple by the sci-fi/fantasy bookshelf.

Mom had been bagging up the purchases as I rang them up.

"Mom, can you take over? I want to help that customer."

"Oh!" she said, and looked at the cash register like it might not be safe to touch. "You think I can?"

"I do," I said. I had trained her on it in the thirty or so minutes we had before the store opened after she'd gotten in, and she'd been watching me all morning. "The scanner does most of the work, remember?"

"I can try," she said. "I'd probably do better here than helping someone out in the stacks. Your father always teased I'd get lost trying to find a book."

"I won't be long," I said as I made my way around the counter.

"Hi," I said. I gave the girl a "May I help you?" smile.

"Hi," she said. "I was looking for the owner."

"I'm the owner."

She frowned. "I thought it was a guy."

"My brother and I own it together."

She nodded. "I'm Maya. I work at the Hemlock."

The jazz café where Reef had invited me to come hear him play.

I offered a warm smile. "I'm Keaton Rutledge."

"We're having a memorial for Reef Jeffries Thursday night." She handed me one of the sheets of paper in her hand.

I glanced down at it, reading what it was advertising.

"Come with me," I said.

I found Koby just bringing out a rack of biscuits, and it sent a whiff of buttery goodness up my nose. My stomach started to grumble.

"Koby," I said. "This is Maya."

"Hi, Maya," he said, and smiled.

"She gave me this." I handed Koby the flyer.

He set the biscuits down and wiped his hands on his apron and swiped them together before taking the paper from me.

He read it. For a long time. Longer, it seemed, than it took to read the few words on there.

The flyer's background was swirls of different shades of purple and a picture of Reef playing a saxophone. He was on a platform with the blur of other people behind him. It said words like "our friend" and "soulful homegoing" and gave the time and place. Hemlock's logo was in one corner and below it was written "Food Donations Needed."

Koby finally looked back up, still holding on to the flyer, first at me then to Maya. "Can we keep this?"

"Sure," Maya said. "I can leave a few for the counter, if you'd like," she said. "I was on my way to take them to Mac's, the place where Reef used to play in Seattle."

"I know Mac's," Koby said. "I'm sure some of those guys would want to know about this."

"He talked about you a lot," Maya said, looking at Koby. "His brother, he called you."

"We *were* brothers."

She smiled. "That's why I wanted to be sure to let you know."

"And how about I bring the food?" he said.

"That would be great if you could bring something." Her smile grew wide. "It smells heavenly in here." Looking around, she said, "And it seems like everyone is enjoying it." She fished a phone out of her shoulder bag. "What can I put you down for?"

"Everything," he said.

"Everything?" she repeated.

"Yeah. Keaton and I will take care of the food and all the accessories. You guys can supply the drinks, right?"

She looked from Koby to me and back, her dark hair flopping back and forth with her head. "We're planning for maybe thirty people."

"Thirty? No problem. We got you covered."

"You don't . . . We can get . . ." She closed her eyes momentarily and shook her head. "Okay." The word came out with an exhale. "Okay." She smiled. "Thank you." She put her phone back in her purse. "That's very generous of you."

Maya followed behind me back to the Books side, and I got a few flyers from her. I watched as she walked out the door and headed in the direction to get to the Sounder station.

I was happy to help with the memorial for Reef, but we had just opened and hadn't made any money. I mean, really, all the food we'd passed out today was free (although, just like Koby predicted, getting people in the store had gotten us some book sales.)

My brother was planning a funeral, an expensive endeavor, and now feeding at least thirty more people than we had fed today for free. I wasn't sure where he was going to get all that money he was spending. He'd told me the insurance policy was for only five thousand. Nor did I know where he was going to find the time to do all the things he said he would.

I was beginning to worry about him. My mother would probably say that Koby's grief was causing him to suffer a strong emotional reaction, manifesting itself through guilt—thinking that he could have done something to keep Reef safe and away from what, or rather who, had killed him. And, she'd say, those feeling were causing him to overextend himself physically and financially to make up for the missteps he felt he made. That, she'd warn, wasn't good.

I was beginning to think that that was true about him, myself. And that made me sad.

Not only sad about my brother, but sad that I was starting to think like my mother.

Chapter Twenty-One

I HAD SO much fun on opening day!

After it started off with Liz stopping me from getting to the bank before they opened, me seeing Jason Holiday and Sam Anderson stopping in demanding we give him tools—whatever those were—the day hadn't started out too stellar-like. I worried that the rest of the day might be like that, but nope. It was good. All good.

We gave away balloons to kids, soul rolls to everyone, and books to not as many, but I was happy. For those who did buy books, I passed out come-back cards that gave a surprise discount. It was a scratch-off that offered different incentives to get people to come back to the store. Underneath the silvery circle was anything from *20 percent off* to *Buy one, get one free* to a free book, courtesy of Mr. Al, to a gift of one Books & Biscuits' merchandise, their choice.

The merchandise choices right now, though, consisted only of a T-shirt like the one Koby and Pete were wearing. I hoped to add more.

Everyone who came in was all smiles. Most of them

strangers, but all seemed happy for us and our new venture all the same.

Pete worked with me and, for the day, so did my mother. Georgie and Mama Zola worked with Koby, and the day just sailed along.

The day passed so fast, and I didn't want it to end. I hoped every day in the bookstore café was going to be like today had been. Although, I must admit I was feeling a little exhausted when I looked up at the clock. It was 6:40, and I wondered if my feet were going to hold out for another twenty minutes. I made a mental note to only wear flats from here on out.

I glanced at my mother. She'd been such a big help. I wondered how Pete and I were going to handle it by ourselves from here on out.

I had worried about Pete, even down to how he was going to look coming to work. I gave him a Books & Biscuits T-shirt, and unexpectedly, he had on a new pair of jeans. But he surprised me.

Pete was good out on the floor. Really good, although he didn't smile much. I was going to have to talk to him about that.

And when he saw the line was long, he'd step up, without me asking, and help bagging up books or looking for a book a customer wanted who'd come up to the counter to inquire about it.

But then the day ended the way it had started out. Messy.

"Hi, Moran," I said. Koby's Capt'n Hook walked in the door. I suspected he'd come to pick up Mama Zola but made getting there before we closed only by a hair. I knew Koby would want him to see it in full swing.

"Hi, Keaton," he said, and pretended to tip a hat. "Looks good in here." He gave a proud smile.

"It's quieted down some now," I said. There were only three or four people still browsing the shelves. And maybe a few more in the café. Mama Zola's soul rolls had been a hit for sure. "Let's go find Koby." I came from around the counter and headed toward the other side. My mother could handle ringing up the few customers left if they decided to buy anything. And Pete was keeping an eagle eye on them. "Maybe some of the free food will be left."

"I ate an early supper before I came," he said, and patted his stomach.

"Why in the world would you do that?" I asked, my voice going up an octave. "You couldn't have forgotten that we were serving food."

"No. I didn't forget." He appeared to want to say something else but was hesitant. I could see lines in his forehead and the tautness in his jaw.

"Is something wrong?" I asked. I stopped and turned to face him. I sure didn't want any bad news on such a momentous day.

"We should wait so I can talk to you and Koby together." He nodded for me to continue walking.

My stomach started doing somersaults.

What could have happened now?

My breathing came in short spurts, and I was ready for everyone to go. Push them out the door and find out what Moran had to say.

Like I thought, Biscuits had more customers than we did on the Books side. All smiles, stuffing their faces, which any other time would have pleased me. I wanted to hide away in a corner, away from all the noise, and see what it was that had Moran's face filled with concern.

"Koby," I said, trying to get his attention. He was being the consummate host. Walking around, smiling and chatting with the customers. "Koby!" My voice a little louder. More urgent.

He turned to look at me, his smile still plastered on his face. "Hi, Keaton," he said as if he couldn't see the anxiousness written all over my face.

"Come here," I said, and waved him over to me.

I watched him excuse and extricate himself.

"What's up?" He glanced at Moran. "You made it!" His attention averted from me just that quickly.

"I don't think he's here to just pick up Mama Zola," I said, leaning in to him.

Koby's eyes went from me to him. "What's going on, Moran?"

"I think we should talk after you guys close up."

Now he says that. Why even mention it when he came in the door if he wasn't ready to tell us what was going on?

Koby wasn't as irritated as me. "Okay," he said. "How about I get you a soul roll? What kind you like? Greens? Black-eyed peas?" He gave Moran a pat on the back and led him to a table to wait to be served.

I stood there for a moment. Flabbergasted. I wasn't sure if I was going to make it through—I checked my watch—the next ten minutes.

I spun around and headed back to the bookstore, my head spinning.

At least, I thought, *no one else is dead*. At least no one close to me. I knew that for sure because they were all here at Books & Biscuits with me.

Those last minutes ticked down at a snail's pace, that second hand moving slow as molasses in January.

I was happy to see Pete hustling people along, herding them over to the counter like a collie on a cattle ranch once it turned seven p.m. He got them in line and then stationed himself at the door, unlocking and locking it back as each one left. I hadn't been sure if it was a good choice when we hired him, but now I knew it was, and tonight I was especially happy to have him.

"SO," MORAN SAID, and clapped his hands together.

Koby and I were sitting at a table in Biscuits with Moran. Mama Zola, over squawks and protest, had gone back to

Seattle with my mother. She wanted to stay, clean the kitchen and prep for tomorrow.

Pete came over and helped Georgie in the kitchen after dusting and sweeping on the Books side.

"I talked to your Detective Chow," he said.

"He's not *our* Detective Chow," Koby said, landing on that distinction first before asking what he wanted to know. "Did he find out anything?"

"Not yet." Moran drew in a breath. "He's got a couple of leads. A couple of suspects."

"Good," I said, my head nods quick and slight. "That's really good."

"Don't know how good." He used his nail to scratch something off the tabletop. "Those couple of suspects he's got his eye on are the two of you."

"Us?" We said the word at the same time.

"We didn't do anything." My face screwed up. "I'm the one who found him."

"I know," Moran said.

"He saw us on surveillance, didn't he?" I said.

"He did," Moran said, and gave a nod.

"So how . . . How in the heck . . ." I looked at Koby, who was had leaned back in his chair, his arms folded across his chest, not saying a word. "Why would he think we would do something like that?"

Koby might not have been upset, but I definitely was.

"He said he thought it pretty coincidental that you two showed up at the exact time it happened."

"Reef called us," I said, getting exasperated. "We met him because he called us."

"He had a copy of Reef's phone records, and it doesn't show any calls to you," he said to me, then turned to Koby. "Or to you. At least not in the hour or so before he died."

"He didn't call us from that phone."

"What do you mean?" Moran asked.

Koby unfolded his arms and sat forward. "Reef had two

phones." Ahh, my brother talks! "The one he called us from wasn't the one that was in his property."

"Didn't you show him the call?" I asked Koby. I remembered Detective Chow had asked me to see where Reef had called us. I told him then that it was on Koby's phone.

"That doesn't matter," Koby said.

"Did you show him?" I asked again.

"Yes, Keaton. I showed him the call, but as you can see"—he waved a hand Moran's way—"that doesn't seem to matter."

I let my head roll back. "Ugh!" This was craziness. "Now what?" I felt tears coming on. "He's going to arrest us?"

"I don't think he has enough evidence to arrest anyone," Moran said. "I just wanted to give you guys a heads-up. To let you know to watch out for him."

"Because he's gunning for us," Koby said.

"Exactly," was Moran's response.

Chapter Twenty-Two

WE SAT WITH our backs against the wall in the downstairs hallway in my house. We had come there after work. My legs stretched out straight, Koby's long legs bent at the knee. Our animals scampering back and forth, getting between us or on top of us, paws in face, crowding us in. That would have made anyone dizzy. But it was Avery Moran's message that put a hole in the close of our first day with Homicide Detective Daniel Chow's suspicions, that had my head spinning.

"At least we know," I said.

"I told you I didn't trust that guy."

"You don't trust any police officer."

"Except—"

"I know—Capt'n Hook."

"Right. You saw how he came and told us what was going on."

I nodded.

"He's a genuine guy," Koby said.

Remy came and laid his head on Koby's knee, like he

knew Koby needed a little sympathy. Koby absently rubbed Remy's head.

"He didn't tell us what to do about it," I said.

"I know what we have to do about it."

"What?" His answer worried me.

"Find out who really did it."

Oh. So now *he* was thinking he was Hercule Poirot.

Roo came over and swiped a paw at Koby and Remy, causing Remy to lift his head and give Roo a stink eye.

I picked up Roo with one hand and with the other gave a swipe of my own. "How are we supposed to do that?"

"What do we know?" Koby asked.

Roo jumped out of my arms, and since they were empty, I held them up. "I don't know. I got nothing." I blew out a breath. "Oh. Wait. We *know* that Detective Chow thinks we did it."

"No." He sucked his tongue. "I mean about the murder. What do we know about the murder?"

"That one of Reef's phones is missing," I said.

"Why would someone take Reef's phone?" We were talking in unison again.

"And how," I said, "was someone able to get his phone in the time it took from when he texted you to when I found him on the train?"

"Maybe the killer is the one who texted us."

I held up a hand to stop him. Roo must've seen me do it because she popped up out of nowhere and lifted her paw in protest, too. She understood me well. That theory was giving me a headache. "How?" I asked.

"I don't know, that's what we have to figure out."

"Or we can think about the people on the train." My voice went up, signaling I was trying to noodle him into going into a different direction.

If we were going to solve this, we had to follow viable leads.

He shook his head. "I just don't like that idea."

"What idea?"

"That people on the train killed him."

I remembered how he had ruled out everyone on there as murderers even before me, and the detective was sure it had been murder.

"Okay," I said, scooting myself into a different position. "You think that no one on the train did it, right?"

"Right."

"And you think there wasn't time for a big cover-up, right?"

"I don't think anyone on the train did it, so why would I think they covered it up?"

"I mean if someone else did it. Like in *Murder on the Orient Express*."

"The other theory."

"Right."

"Someone got on the train, did the deed and got back off."

"Did the deed?" I chuckled at his turn of phrase. "But yes. If there was someone else, in addition to the five people we know were on the train. Someone who got on, killed Reef and then got off."

"Okay, so you're asking me if that person had time for a cover-up?"

"Yes," I said.

"Between the time that he called me and the time you found him?" Koby asked, and then answered before I said anything. "No."

"Because, according to you, no one wants to be on a train with a murderer. And, I guess, if the killer got off the train, no one would know about who the murderer was."

"Right."

"So then I got nothing," I said. "You've knocked down both of my theories. And I am definitely knocking down your theory of the killer texting you." I hit my head on the wall behind me. "Where does that leave us?"

"Why are you knocking my theory down?" He spoke with conviction. "The killer texting me would alter the timeline. It would be a good alibi, and now it seems"—he looked at me—"it would cast suspicion on us."

Mmmm . . .

He'd added to his theory. And I couldn't deny the addition did seem to make it more probable. Especially since that part of it had already worked.

"Unless you have another idea?" Koby looked at me.

I thought for a minute. I didn't.

"But," I said, "I just can't see them taking the phone just to text us. They, like the people on the train, only had a short time, like two or three minutes, to kill him and think to take the phone to cover it up."

"Maybe they killed him for the phone," Koby offered.

"They poisoned him," I said. "You don't just carry poison around and use it because you see a phone you'd like to have."

"True," he said. "And that's something else we know."

"What?"

"That he could have been killed remotely." I knew what he meant. We had just talked about that after meeting with Marcel. "Someone could have put something in his vitamins and just waited for him to take them."

"On the timer he'd set," I said.

"Right," Koby said. "And that brings us back to the phone." He cleared his throat. "So maybe the murderer thought something was on that phone that would hurt him."

"Or incriminate him in some way."

"Exactly."

Then Koby snapped his fingers and gave me a sly smile. "What if . . ." He pulled a phone out of his pocket, looked at it, then put it back. "What if we could find the other phone?" He lifted up his other hip and pulled out another phone from his back jeans pocket and held it up.

"Oh."

"Oh is right," he said, a pleased look on his face. "This is Reef's phone. Maybe there might be an app like Find My Phone on here."

"Ohhh. We could locate Reef's other phone." My eyebrows went up, a smile curled up my face. Then it faded. "If there is an app like that on the phone, we should give it to Detective Chow."

"No," Koby said, frowning. "Why?"

"For one, it would clear our name. And two, the person who has it is probably the murderer. We don't want to tangle with him."

Then I had another thought, and before Koby could respond, I posed it as a question. "That's the phone that was in his property, right?"

"Yep," he said. "Didn't we just establish that?" He was busy trying to get into it.

"Why didn't they keep it in the first place? They could have used the Find My Phone app."

"If there's one on here." He was looking at the phone, biting his lower lip. "And, for the same reason I'm not in it yet. No password."

"So?"

"So, it's an iPhone. Apple won't open up their phones."

"That's for lawsuits, I thought."

"Maybe," he said, punching numbers in on the keyboard of the phone. "But I guess they just figured it was easier to find out what they wanted to know from the phone carrier. List of calls, texts, all that stuff they can subpoena for."

"How do you know that?"

"I listen to the news. And"—he finally looked up from the phone—"because Moran told us they checked the phone records, remember?"

"Oh yeah." I looked at Reef's phone, the screen still black. I gave a nod toward it. "Doesn't look like we're going to be able to get into that phone either."

"I'm still thinking," he said.

"You think you might know how to get into it? You know the password?"

"I thought I did." He held up the phone again and stared at it. "I tried the things I thought he'd pick. His birthdate. My birthdate. Mama Zola's."

"They didn't work?"

"No." He showed me the phone. "And now I gotta wait five minutes to try again."

That meant the phone was punishing him for getting the password wrong too many times.

"Remember when you said if you were running the investigation into Reef's death, you'd keep your eyes on Tessa Chaiken and Jason Holiday?"

"Are we through with the phone?" Koby asked, still looking at the phone like that would make the time go faster.

"Just trying to use the five minutes we have to wait wisely."

"Good thinking," he said. "Tessa and Jason, huh?"

"They live next door to Reef."

"They do."

"And you thought they were fishy even before we were sure they knew each other or found out they lived next door to Reef."

"I always knew they knew each other," Koby corrected.

"You didn't know they lived together."

"No, I didn't. You found that out." He looked up at me and smiled. "Although, I have yet to see them."

"I saw Jason today."

"You did? Where?" Koby asked. "Did you go down to the marina?"

"No. I saw him at the library's parking lot. I stopped to speak to my old coworker Liz, and he was going into the building."

"This morning before we opened?"

"Mm-hmm."

"Why were you at the library?"

"Because . . ."

Shoot. I didn't know what to say. I couldn't tell him what I was doing by the library, but I didn't want to lie to my brother either. "Shouldn't you save your questions for Tessa and Jason?"

"I guess I should," he said, letting out a grunt as he stood up. "But I have to save those until tomorrow. I've got a date."

"Date?" I said. "We have more suspects to talk about, like that Sam Anderson who Mama Zola doesn't like and who came barging into our store demanding stuff and—"

"Yep." He cut me off, not letting me finish my list of suspects. "Can you watch Remy for me?"

"For your date?"

"Yep."

"Who is this date with?" I didn't have to answer the question about babysitting. He knew Remy was always welcome.

"Izzy," he said with a grin.

She was the next person I had planned on naming as a suspect before he cut me off. Now he was going on a date with her? *Geesh!*

"Isabella Ramirez is someone else we need to question," I said. I tried to make it sound like a warning for him to be careful.

"I'll see what I can get out of her tonight." He winked. "Wish me luck."

Chapter Twenty-Three

"HEY. WAKE UP."

Koby was at my house at six o'clock the next morning. I opened my eyes, one at a time, to him sitting at the bottom of my bed, shaking my leg through the covers.

"I've been dreaming about this all night," he said, looking at me to make sure my eyes stayed open. "I could barely get in my five and a half hours of sleep."

He could barely sleep. I hadn't slept at all. Even when I opened my eyes and saw him, it wasn't him waking me. I think my eyelids were just too weary to hold themselves open.

"We don't have to open for four more hours." He shook my leg again. "Get up. Let's get this investigation started and see what we can find out."

Hadn't we already started the investigation? I had followed Tessa. He had stomped around the boat looking for hollow areas where something could be hidden. What else were we supposed to do?

I didn't say any of that, though. I didn't say anything. I couldn't. I put the sheet over my head and didn't move.

"I went and got Mama Zola already," he said. He was talking fast, trying to get everything out, it seemed, in one breath. "Drove her car in and dropped her off at Books & Biscuits to start cooking." I heard him sigh. "I don't know what I'm going to do about getting her here every day. I'm moving into Reef's houseboat, and that would really be a feat for me. Every day catching a train to go and get her, driving her here in her car, driving her back home and then taking the train back." He clucked. "I'm going to have to figure something out. And you might have to put Izzy at the top of your list."

In one swift move, I folded the covers down off my face and sat straight up. "Whoa!" I squeaked out. I stared at my brother. "Do I need to make an appointment with my mother for you? Because you are doing too much."

"What?" he said, like he couldn't understand what I was talking about. He stood up and grabbed my arm. "C'mon! We have to investigate this."

"You just said a lot. What am I supposed to do with all of that?" I pushed him out of the way and swung my legs out of the bed. "First. Do you know how much food we'll have with Mama Zola cooking for four hours?" I remembered what she'd whipped up in the little time she'd spent in Biscuits' kitchen a few days before we opened. "We can't sell all that food."

"Second," I said. "There is no way you can drive Mama Zola back and forth from Seattle to Timber Lake six days a week!" I was standing in front of my closet trying to find something to put on. "Although, I must say I am super stoked you are moving here, but I am going to hold back my excitement. For now. Because it seems you need someone to tell you that you can't go catching trains before we open and after we close." I turned and looked at him. "That sounds crazy!" I threw the outfit I'd picked out onto the bed.

"Third," I said, making my way down the hallway to the bathroom, Koby following at my heels. "What is there to investigate? There is nothing we can do." I stood in front of

the sink and squirted toothpaste on my toothbrush. "And"—
he was listening to me fuss with a grin on his face—"I didn't
sleep at all. Wasn't asleep when you came in my room. And
although I didn't hear you"—I pointed my toothbrush at him—
"don't ever do that again." I laid my toothbrush on the counter. "I was up all night thinking about the predicament we're
in with Detective Chow and what we could do. But I came up
with nothing." I made a circle with my fingers and thumb.
"Zero. There was nothing I could think of that we could do."

"Fourth." I put a plastic cap over my head and turned on
the water in the shower so I could hop in once the water was
warmed. "What did Izzy do?" My voice had started squeak-
ing. "Nope!" I held up a hand. "I don't wanna know. I knew
nothing good would come out of you seeing Reef's girlfriend. I don't know how you could do that." I clucked my
tongue. "If this is what it's like having a brother, him driving
you nuts, then I'm going to have to start making weekly appointments with my mother in her professional capacity!" I
pushed him from where he was perched, leaning on the
frame of the door with his arms crossed, and closed the door.

"And," I yelled through the door, toothbrush still in hand,
"don't think I'm going to be getting up at six a.m. with you
to traipse around playing your Sherlock Holmes games when
we need to worry about staying out of jail!"

After scrubbing the heck out of my teeth, which helped me
to calm down, I stepped into the shower. With the hot water
beating down on me, I felt all the stress my brother had just
caused me dissipate. I probably stayed in there longer than I
should have, seeing that I had someone else in the house. Roo
would keep him company, I knew, but with me not having a
television, he'd probably get bored pretty quickly.

I got out of the shower and, on the way to my bedroom,
could smell the bacon wafting upstairs from my kitchen.

"Mmmm. Smells so good," I muttered, and smiled as I
put lotion on and got dressed. I still hadn't done anything
fancy to my hair. I pulled it up into a floppy high ponytail

like the day before. I went downstairs and stood in the door-
way and watched as my brother moved deftly around my
kitchen. He was pulling plates out of the cabinet when he
caught sight of me.

"I fed your cat, too," he said, setting the plates on the table, where he'd already filled two glasses with orange juice.

I turned and, for the first time this morning, noticed Roo.
She was eating. I'd never seen her come to her bowl without
coaching, and she usually ate after I had left the area.

"Thank you," I said.

"Now sit so I can feed you, too." He brought the food to
the table, serving it family style.

Koby had made a batch of his yummy biscuits, a pile of
bacon, cheese eggs and grits.

"Who told you you could cook in my kitchen?" I scooped
up a heaping amount of everything and piled it on my plate.

"Roo," Koby said as I ate a forkful of the grits. They were
so good. I closed my eyes and enjoyed the moment. "She
gave me permission. You know, contingent on her getting
food first."

I glanced at my cat. She was enjoying her meal, too. I'd
have to thank her later for giving Koby the go-ahead.

"And one." Koby hopped up from his seat and grabbed
the grape jelly out of the fridge. "Or should I say *first*?" He
emphasized the word, amusement in his eyes. "Mama Zola
is cooking food for the memorial. We went to the grocery
store before we came here. Five o'clock this morning she had
me pushing a grocery cart. She picked up three whole chick-
ens, a ham, all the ingredients for her cold shrimp pasta salad
and all kinds of sides. Nothing we'd have to sell. No inventory sitting around our kitchen going to waste because we
couldn't sell it."

"The memorial isn't until tomorrow."

"She'll probably cook until then."

"And for the funeral, too?"

"I thought we'd just make the memorial do. Still have a

viewing, though, for people who want to see him one last time or can't come to the memorial. But no formal funeral, you know?" I nodded. "Me, you and Mama Zola can pick out a nice urn for him and sprinkle his ashes on the water by his boat. I already told everyone about the memorial."

"That sounds like a good idea." Less cost, but still I worried about his spending. "Where are you getting money from for all of that?" I asked, finally voicing my concerns. "And how are you paying for the viewing and stuff?"

"GoFundMe."

"You started a page to collect funds?" I stopped midair with the eggs I was ready to stuff into my mouth. "Why would you start something like that"—I let the fork clang on my plate—"and not tell me?"

Hadn't he just fussed at me about not sharing information? I'd been worried that he was overextending himself when all along he'd been gathering resources. Gathering but not sharing.

"I didn't—"

"You didn't what? Do the same thing you told me not to do? You didn't share information with your team member. Your sister. Your *twin* sister."

"Well, if you'd let me talk, Twin Sister, I'd tell you that *I* didn't start it. Our group home community network started it. Us foster kids. We have a Facebook page."

"You're on Facebook?"

"No, but when they heard about Reef, they created the account and made it so the donations came to me."

"How much did you raise?" I asked. In awe of how they'd come together. Sometimes I wondered why Koby was so interested in finding family. He had one that was close and there for one another without one of them being a blood relative.

"Twenty-five thousand dollars."

"What!" My mouth hung open. "Wait. In . . ." I counted on my fingers. "Six days? You raised more than twenty thousand dollars? Wow."

"Right, so I'm not spending money we don't have." He drank some of his orange juice. "Two," he continued. "It is crazy for me to go back and forth to get Mama Zola here. Of course, I need to talk to you about it, but I was thinking we could hire her, and she could live in Timber Lake."

I raised my eyebrows.

"Hear me out," he said, reaching across the table. He held on to my wrist as if he thought I might leave. "She wants to do this, and if I'm moving here, I'd want her to be close so I can look out for her anyways."

"You're moving here," I said. That made me smile. He'd said that earlier, but it was sinking in. It would be great to have my brother right down the road from me.

"I don't know that we have it in the budget to pay her," I said.

"It sounds bad to say, but we don't really have to pay her, pay her." He squinched up his face. "You know what I mean?"

"No," I said.

"She doesn't have a job now. Right? She lives on a fixed income and that pays all her bills. So it's not like she'd need anything more to live here. We'd just need to find her a place to rent that is the same or less than where she lives now."

"Everything in Timber Lake is cheaper than in Seattle." I crunched on a piece of bacon. "I'm sure we could find something inexpensive but nice, and we can work to find a way to give her something money-wise."

"See." He smiled at me. "I knew you'd know how to help so we could do this."

"After we start making money, we can start paying her for all of her time."

"We'll see," he said. "She has so much energy. I don't know if we'll ever be able to pay her for all she wants to offer."

I laughed. From what I'd seen of her in the kitchen, he was probably right.

"I'm going to skip over your third point for a second, we'll circle back to it."

I looked up at him. Was he going through the points I'd enumerated to him before I got into the shower? I didn't even remember everything I'd said, let alone the order I said them in.

"Okay," Koby said, pouring more juice in his glass. "Where are we? Fourth. That one was about Izzy. Right?"

I took his word for it.

"Izzy was not Reef's girlfriend."

"How do you know?" I asked. "She said she was."

"Trust me," he said. "She wasn't."

"How do you know?"

He hesitated. Dropping his head, he acted like he wanted to pick his words carefully. He lifted his eyes to look at me. "Reef liked you. He wouldn't have tried to date you if he had another girl he was messing with. He wasn't like that. Plus, he knew if he hurt my sister, I'd kill him."

"Don't say that out loud!" I said, a blush coming on my face. Although, I knew the fear I was feeling from him saying he would kill someone who hurt me showed in my eyes.

"Don't get all upset. I'm just saying."

"Reef liked me?"

He let his eyes roll up and pursed his lips.

"Anyway," he said, letting me know we were moving past that. "She lied. Izzy. She wasn't telling the truth about her relationship with Reef and about her sink."

"Oh, I thought you believed her about her sink."

"Who fixes a sink with a screwdriver?" Koby said, reiterating the same thing I'd asked him.

"So if you knew she's been lying from the beginning, why are you dating her?"

"It's not dating . . . Or that I like her, like her." He weighed the thought, his head going from side to side. "She's interesting."

I held up my hand. I didn't want to know. "Moving on," I said. "Let's get back to my third point."

"No, you had a fifth point we need to get to first."

I frowned. I didn't remember saying the word "fifth."

"You didn't actually list it that way," he said, reading my mind. "You just yelled through the door that you weren't going to be getting up at six to play detective games with me."

"Oh yeah," I said. I scraped up the last of my grits and slid them off the fork into my mouth. "I do remember that." I wiped my mouth with a paper towel. "But if I get breakfast like this, I might agree to participating in the games you have afoot."

"Good segue to get us back to your third point."

"Which was?" I said.

"That we can't investigate." He held up one hand. "We don't know where to start." He held up his other hand. "We don't know what to look for." He was trying to sound like me. He put both hands up to his head, shaking them like he was going crazy.

He thought he was being funny.

"Okay. Okay," I said. "You must have an idea."

"Not so much an idea, but a revelation." He got up and dragged a chair next to mine. "One that might help us get started on figuring out what happened."

"And what is your revelation?" I asked. I reached across the table and stacked up the plates.

"I got into Reef's phone." A pleased look on his face. "And it's got a bunch of stuff in it that'll help us."

"You did?" I got the same pleased look on my face as Koby had.

"I did," he confirmed.

"Ah," I said. "So the game really is afoot?"

"Yep." He smiled. "And we're diving in with all four of ours."

Chapter Twenty-Four

I PUSHED THE stacked dishes out of the way. I had no interest at the moment in cleaning up anything.

"How did you figure out how to get into the phone?"

Looks like we did have something to investigate after all.

"When I went to see Reef's lawyer, he had me show him ID, you know, to prove it was me. I gave him my driver's license, and then he asked me, *Is this your real birthdate?*"

I turned up my face. Feeling disgusted that the lawyer would think Koby was showing a fake document. "That was rude."

"It was a joke between me and Reef. Reef must've told him about it."

"What was the joke?" I asked.

"I used to tell people I was older than I was when I was younger so I could hang out with Reef. Go where he went. Plus, I didn't want him thinking of me like that, you know. Just a little boy."

I nodded, enjoying hearing a story about the two of them.

"One time," Koby said, "it was for a birthday. He gave me

a prank gift, this fake ID, putting my age up. It had my picture and everything. He told me, *Now you legit*."

I laughed. Koby was enjoying the memory, too.

"But it didn't have the correct birthdate on it, and I was like, *My birthday is wrong*. He took it, looked at it and, handing it back to me, he said, *Well, that's your birthday now*.

"And over the years, every now and then, he'd call me on that day, or we'd hang out that day, and he'd tell me it was for my birthday."

"And that was the passcode on his phone?"

"Yep. 1121." He nodded. "One of the many things I thought about last night when I couldn't sleep. Came to me when I was thinking I needed to call the lawyer to get the proof we need to get into the storage at the marina."

"That's not even close to our birthday."

"Yeah. I don't know how he got it so wrong." Koby shrugged. "Maybe at the time, he didn't know my real birthday. When you get moved around a lot like we were, those kinds of details fall by the wayside."

That was a sad commentary.

"Okay," I said, and slapped my hands together and rubbed them back and forth. Didn't want to dwell on anything sad. "What did you find?"

Koby whipped out the phone. "All kinds of stuff. Like Reef had an Instagram page, which really surprised me." He put the passcode in.

"Lots of people have Instagram."

"Do you have one?"

"No," I said.

"Neither do I, but Reef had one for his business."

"Reef had a business?"

"Yep. And after looking at his, I think we need to get one, too."

"What was his business?"

"He was sort of a handyman. At least that was what his

posts were about. Call him if you've got a leaky sink. Need your gutters cleaned. Stuff like that."

"And how is that a clue?" I asked.

"It's the link he had with Sam and Darius."

"Right," I said. "Darius wanted to get a job. Sam said he had his equipment, tools or whatever."

"Exactly," Koby said. "But why, if it was Reef's business, did he need to have things that belonged to Sam, and why would Darius need to come to Reef for a job? He could have worked for his brother."

"One of them is lying," I said.

"Sam is the one that wanted to get into that storage place."

"Even saying you can give him the key and he'd go in and get his stuff."

"We need to get into that storage."

"You have to show Owner Krol that you're in charge of Reef's estate."

"I know. Didn't I tell you I had thought about that last night? I called Reef's lawyer this morning."

"Already?" I glanced at the clock. It wasn't quite seven thirty.

"I left a message. Told him I needed the proof." I saw Koby click on the Instagram icon as he talked. "But look what else I found." He scrolled through the pictures on Reef's account.

He found the picture he was looking for and, using his thumb and forefinger, stretched it out. "What do you see?" He handed me the phone.

It was a picture with Reef in it. He was the first thing that caught my eye. I felt myself choke up. I really liked him, and according to my brother, he'd liked me. I blinked away tears. "Is this in a bar?" I asked, trying to stay on track of what we were doing.

"Yeah. That's the Hemlock."

"You've been there?" I asked.

"Yes," he said, sounding exasperated. It wasn't what he wanted me to take note of. "Look at the picture."

"Reef," I said. "Oh, that's Maya and Sam in that picture, too."

"And who else do you see? In the background?"

I stretched the picture out a little bit more. "Oh! That's Tessa!" I turned and looked at Koby. "They were friends."

"Maybe. They hung out at the same place." He took the phone. "And look at this one." He found another picture.

"Maya," I said. Koby started to reach for the phone. I pushed his hand back. "Wait. I'm still looking. Oh!" I could see Koby's smile out the side of my eye, happy I'd seen what he wanted me to. "It's Sam and Tessa. They've got their heads together."

Sam Anderson was sitting in a chair, and Tessa was leaning over him, talking in his ear, it seemed. Maybe, I thought, because the music was loud.

But it reminded me of something . . .

"Yeah. They look pretty cozy, huh?" Koby said. "How well do they know each other? That's the question."

"Yes. That's a question . . ." My words were hesitant and low.

"What is it, Keaton?"

"See how she's leaning over him . . ." My voice trailed off. "Her hair in her face . . ."

"What?"

A fuzziness in my brain seemed to be coalescing into something . . . Someone.

"This is the same T-shirt she had on that day we were all on the train," I muttered, mostly to myself.

"What?"

"This T-shirt." I pointed.

Koby took the phone from me, stretching the picture out a little more. He nodded. "I remember her wearing that shirt that day." He handed the phone back to me. "So?"

"Someone . . . Well . . . A female." I stopped talking. It was like I could almost see it. I squinted my eyes.

"A female what?" I could tell Koby was trying to be patient.

"A female stooped down next to me. After Reef fell onto the floor."

"Is this something else you knew and didn't tell me?" Koby didn't sound happy about my coming realization.

"You were there, too," I said. "Did you notice who it was? Or that anyone else was even there?"

He tilted his head and made a face.

"Okay. So, let me try to remember," I told him.

"If I was there, I can't believe I didn't see it." He rubbed a hand over his forehead.

Then my eyes went wide. I remembered. I could see it now. I looked at Reef. "I think Tessa took Reef's other phone."

"What?" His eyes got as large as mine. "The one he texted us on and was missing from his stuff when I picked it up?"

I nodded. "Yes. I think it was Tessa. She's the one who leaned down next to me. She took it." I blinked my eyes to focus. "A phone fell to the floor when he fell over onto the seat. I reached down to pick it up, the train jerked and he fell over." I looked at Koby. "I never picked that phone up, and if he had the other one on him—"

"Then the one he texted me from was the one that fell to the floor."

"Unless that's the one they had because the police or paramedics picked it up."

"They didn't," Koby said. "I watched every move they made."

I could attest to that.

"Wow," he said. "We didn't even need the Find a Phone app"—he smiled—"not when we got you."

That made me blush.

"Sooo. Why would Tessa take his phone?" I asked, liking this detective stuff.

I knew I thought differently from Koby. I would think she did it because she was the murderer. Since the day I followed her down to the pier, I felt like she had something to do with

Reef's death. Koby, on the other hand, would say, *Don't jump to conclusions*. He'd want to simmer over the information and think it through.

Even if she didn't do it, though, I was thinking we should tell Detective Chow what we'd learned. Help him focus on who was really important in solving this. Like he needed, right now, to strike us from his suspects list.

Chapter Twenty-Five

"SO WHERE DO we start?" I asked, then answered my own question. "First, I think we need to tell the detective about this." I glanced down at my watch. It was already eight o'clock. "I don't think we should do it over the phone, though." I looked at my brother questioningly, eager for his input on how to do it. "And we don't have time to go into Seattle now, even with Mama Zola's car. The traffic would be a monster this time of day. We'd be late getting back to open the store."

"Slow down," Koby said. "Don't start numbering stuff again." I thought I saw him making a face. "We aren't telling Detective Chow anything. Why is that always the first thing you say?"

Was it? I tilted my head and thought about it. Then I thought, why wouldn't I tell Detective Chow? This was his job, and it was the right thing to do.

"Because," I said, "he needs to know stuff we find out."

"No." Koby shook his head the entire time we discussed whether to tell the detective. "Not until we know something concrete," he said.

"What! Why?"

I was standing at the sink washing the breakfast dishes. Koby was standing next to me, back leaning against the sink, his arms folded across his chest.

"Because. He'll think we're just trying to deflect guilt away from us."

"We are," I said. "What are you talking about?"

"We are not trying to 'deflect'—that's what people do when they are guilty of something. It'll make him think we are trying to hide something and blaming what we've done on someone else."

"Ugh!" I moaned. I flung the excess water off my hands and grabbed a paper towel to get them dry. "So, what do we do?"

"Think."

"Think?"

"Maybe rethink," he said. "Initially, I thought that Reef was trying to leave me a message to who killed him. And maybe he did. He knew how I was always the detective. But first we need to find out what Reef had been up to. What he could have done to make someone so upset with him."

"You think we can do that?" I asked.

"Maybe so. But it'll be harder to go around and find out what we need when we've got to keep off the radar. Now we have to worry about not getting pegged for a crime we didn't commit."

"I agree."

"I think that we need to talk to Darius and Sam."

"Okay," I said, thinking that being in Timber Lake, when the murder happened in Seattle, might help us keep below the police's radar. "About what?"

"They probably know better than me what Reef had been up to as of late." I could feel the hurt in Koby's voice. "He was kind of part of Timber Lake. Living on the lake. Playing at the jazz club. And evidently working around here. Maybe even partners with Sam."

"Okay." I nodded. "What else?"

"We ask Tessa why she took Reef's phone."

"Oh no we don't," I said. I wasn't agreeing to that one as readily. "She might be a killer!" I shook my head.

"Sam or Darius Anderson might be the killer, too," Koby said. "You're willing to talk to them."

"Sam and Darius Anderson were not on the train when Reef died. They didn't steal Reef's phone. And as far as we know, they haven't lied to us or the police."

"You think Tessa lied to the police?"

I stopped and thought about that. It was possible she hadn't. She could have told the detective that she knew Reef. Him having that knowledge wouldn't have meant that he thought, or had enough evidence, to hold her for the murder. And at the time, to be fair to Tessa, Detective Chow wasn't even sure that a murder had been committed.

It seemed only Koby had known that for sure.

"Okay," I admitted. "I don't know that she lied to the police. But she definitely lied to that clerk in the store. Because Jason Holiday is not her grandfather, and she has gone into Seattle before.

"I don't even have a television, and I've seen shows where people go toward the danger. It doesn't ever work out well."

"You've already followed her. She didn't do anything to you."

"Doesn't mean she won't try if we tell her we know she's the one who did it."

"We don't know that she is," Koby said, which is just how I suspected him to think. "But we'll have the element of surprise, she won't be prepared to do anything. Plus, she can't take us both down."

"I don't know."

"Keaton, think. If she is the killer, she didn't do it face-to-face. She doesn't want to get caught."

"You think, Koby. Because if she is the killer, like I've been saying all along, then she was right there when he died."

"That's why I'm not sure she is. Why poison so she'd have an alibi and then end up being right there?"

"Because she's a psychopath," I said. "Isn't that why people kill people in the first place?"

Koby thought that was funny.

"I was thinking we could go over to the houseboat and talk to her," Koby said.

Was I really going to go along with him on this? It didn't seem too smart. I was beginning to change my mind about liking the detective stuff.

"Now?" I asked.

"No. Not now," he said. "Didn't you say that Jason worked at the library?"

"Yeah," I said.

"And they live together?"

I nodded. I know Koby claimed he'd never seen the two of them, although I didn't know how much time he had actually spent in his new residence.

"Well, we don't want him to be there when we talk to her. Our two-to-one advantage would be shot, and she might not talk in front of him, just in case he had something to do with anything that happened."

"The library doesn't open until nine."

"Exactly," he said. "So, we go and talk to her then. That'll give us plenty of time to talk to her and get Books & Biscuits open at ten."

"Don't you have to cook for the day?" I asked.

"Mama Zola's there," Koby said. "I think we're good."

I had forgotten she was there, and he was definitely right about that.

As we talked, I had dried the dishes and put them all away. Koby didn't help, but that was okay. He had prepared breakfast and washed most of the things he used as he cooked.

"So what are we going to do until then?" I asked.

"I was thinking that we could finish going through his phone."

"Did you find anything else before you showed it to me?"

"I found that Instagram is very distracting," he said. "I started following links to people that Reef tagged and then following links from there to who knows where." He chuckled. "That's why I waited to finish looking until I got here."

"Yep. I hear it's addicting."

"People put their lives on there. Taking a picture of everything from what they ate to the bandage covering where they cut themselves trying to cook."

"I couldn't do that," I said.

"I don't think I could either," Koby said.

"Yeah, social media only for our business," I said. "I think it would be a good idea for us to get on social media. Look how people connected through Facebook to get Reef's GoFundMe page going and what we found out from his Instagram account."

"I hope that works," Koby said. "People coming all the way from Seattle, or anywhere, to come to our bookstore and café."

"Yep, I think it will work," I said. "As soon as they get a whiff of your cooking."

Koby blushed. "Okay. C'mon. Back to the task at hand. You know what I didn't find on Reef's page?"

"What?"

"Anything about taking vitamins or trying to get healthy."

"So?"

"Well, he put stuff on there like him playing at jazz clubs, about his business, some personal stuff. He reposted other people's personal info."

"He did say he was changing. That would be something to post about."

"Exactly," Koby said. "So why not that?"

I hunched my shoulders. "Don't know. But what I do

know"—I put up a finger to signal the lightbulb that had just gone on in my head—"is we didn't find any vitamins on the houseboat either."

"Oh wow," Koby said. "That's true. I was looking for clues to who did it, never crossed my mind to look for *how* they did it."

I stretched my eyes, saying that was true.

"Did we look everywhere?"

"We didn't really look, but I've been in there twice, and I don't ever remember seeing any powder or pills that could have been tainted."

"We need to look again," Koby said. "Look specifically for it. That might be the murder weapon."

I nodded my agreement.

"C'mon. Let's take a look at what else we can find on the phone, then we'll go."

We checked phone messages next. It seemed that Reef didn't keep his text messages, if he ever had any, because there weren't any in his phone.

"He probably deleted them after he finished the conversation," Koby offered.

I didn't know why he did that. No one called me but Koby and my mother. I rarely even had my cell phone on, but I kept all my messages.

"Let's move on," was Koby's response.

So we did.

Reef had a Twitter account, but there was nothing of note. He liked to retweet people mostly, and occasionally he would make his own comment on something someone had posted.

There were no emails. The only reference to one was the address he used to sign on to his provider account.

And by the time we'd gone through all of that, it was time to go search the houseboat for the murder weapon and to confront Tessa.

I slouched into a rain slicker and thought how I, for one, was not looking forward to the Tessa part of our mission.

I hung out at the front door longer than I should have.

"You can always tell spring is on its way when you smell the almonds on Mrs. Grayson's tree," I said, and stared at it like I was pondering the wonders of the world.

"I don't smell anything. Let alone almonds," he said, and pulled me down the sidewalk.

But I moved much slower. I walked four or five paces behind Koby all the way down to the marina, stopping every now and then to adjust my raincoat or shoulder bag.

"C'mon," he said a few times.

When we were still about twenty or so yards from the property, Koby's cell phone rang, making me jump.

"Nervous?" he said. Looking back at me, he chuckled. He didn't even attempt to answer it. He just let the phone keep ringing.

"Will you get your phone, please?" I said.

"It's the lawyer," he said, looking at the caller ID. Answering, he put it on speaker and held it in front of us so I could listen in.

"Hi, Attorney Jenkins," Koby said. "Thanks for getting back to me so quickly."

"Yeah, I got your message," he said. "Reef didn't leave a formal will, just instructions, so we don't need to go to probate and name you as executor or anything. But I can give you something official if you need it."

"That would be great," Koby said.

"And . . ." He drew the word out. "I did get his death certificate, if you want a copy of that."

Koby looked up at me. I nodded, thinking it would be a good thing to have.

"Okay. That'll be good," Koby answered. "When can I come and pick it up?"

"How about if I bring it to you?" the attorney said. "I have to come out that way for court today, and I know you've started a new business that you have to tend to."

"That'll be good," Koby said. "We'd really appreciate that."

"And I wanted to talk to you about the boat, especially since that was the problem you were having when you left me the message."

Koby frowned. "Not so much with the boat," he corrected, "just getting into storage."

"I get that," he said, "but when Reef bought that boat, he'd planned all along to give it to you. It was why he bought it in the first place." Attorney Jenkins paused, like he was expecting an answer from Koby. But that bit of information, I think, blew us both away. Our eyes caught each other's.

"Excuse me?" Koby finally spoke.

"I'd rather not talk about it on the phone," Attorney Jenkins said. "It's okay to come to the restaurant, right?"

"Sure. Sure."

"About twelve thirty or so? I have court at two."

"That'll be fine," Koby said. "And don't eat, I want you to try some of what's going to make us famous."

Reef's attorney laughed. "I heard about how good a cook you are. Sounds good," he said. "Looking forward to it."

Koby hung up, and we still didn't know quite what to say. He hadn't just inherited a boat from Reef. Reef had bought it with the intention of giving it to Koby.

"No wonder there wasn't any furniture in there," I said.

"Yeah, well. That answers that question." He shook his head. "But it makes me think even more that I knew less about Reef than I would have ever guessed. And that the only way to solve this is to find out what in the world he was up to."

Chapter Twenty-Six

DETECTIVE CHOW WAS standing on the deck of Reef's—well, I guess now I'd have to say, Koby's—boat.

Had I accidentally summoned him? *Geesh.* I had just been warned by Koby not to tell Chow the stuff we knew, and there he stood.

And there also went our safe harbor. Although I wasn't keen on talking to Tessa, I'd thought we were free to investigate in Timber Lake because he'd be looking in Seattle. But I guess I thought wrong. Especially with Koby and me being on his list of suspects, it made sense that he'd be coming to check up on us.

He'd been bent forward looking through the telescope but stood up as we approached. Like he was waiting for us.

"Come aboard," he said, and smiled.

I didn't feel the least bit hospitable about his presence or comfortable with him telling us to come onto the boat.

What was he doing there? How did he know about the boat?

"You have a key?" the detective asked. "I didn't want to

break the door in since I don't have a warrant to search your property." His smile seemed to turn wicked. "This is yours, isn't it?"

"It is now," Koby said. He didn't seem fazed by the detective's presence.

It gave me the jitters.

Koby and I climbed up on the boat, and he unlocked the door.

The first thing that went to my mind was, *Where was that murder weapon?*

Koby and I had just talked about the fact that we hadn't found the vitamins that Reef had claimed he was taking anywhere in the house. At least so far. And we had decided long ago, after hearing Cousin Marcel talk about taking his pill, that someone might have killed Reef from afar by spiking his pills and waiting for him to take one. What if we'd overlooked the vitamins, or the poison used, the last time we were there? What about if the detective found it while we were all inside? Or maybe he'd already discovered it and now was back to arrest us. Because for sure, he wouldn't have had to break a door down with the side door lock broken. He could have walked in just like I had. Like Izzy had.

"What can we do for you?" Koby asked.

"I'd like to know why you didn't tell me about this boat when I talked to you on the train."

"We didn't know about it," I said, jumping in. Koby looked at me. I knew my anxiousness came through in my voice.

"How did you find out about it?" Koby asked.

"Let me ask the questions," Chow said. The same thing he'd told me the first time he questioned me. Signaling to me that he was there on official business, unlike when he stopped at the bookstore café.

"So now that Reef is gone, you get this boat?" Detective Chow looked around, as if he was admiring it. Like Koby and I had noted when we both came on for the first time, there wasn't much to see.

"He left me the boat," Koby said. "Like I said, we didn't even know he owned it. I didn't even know he lived in Timber Lake."

"I find that hard to believe."

"He'd only lived here a few weeks, it seems, if you even want to call it that. He really didn't have anything here," Koby said. "And we were opening up Books & Biscuits. That kept us busy."

"Or was it because the two of you had been feuding?" He walked over to the kitchen and ran a finger over the countertop. "You were angry with him."

"We didn't feud."

"What poison was used to kill Reef?" I said. It just came out. Him swiping a finger made me worried that there was some trace of what killed him around. Inside the boat, in the same room we were in.

If the gleam in his eye was any indication, Detective Chow seemed amused with my blurting out. "Cyanide," he said.

Dame Agatha had used that a lot in her books, so I was quite familiar with it, something I probably shouldn't mention out loud.

He leaned back on the sink, folded his arms across his chest and one leg over the other. Getting comfortable, it seemed.

"So that's what they put in his vitamins?" Koby asked.

"Vitamins?" Chow tilted his head. "Where'd you get that from?"

"Reef was taking vitamins," Koby said. "He had a timer set as a reminder. That's how they would have done it on the train without being there."

"He was working on getting healthier," I added.

Chow pressed his lips together and shook his head. "Don't remember seeing anything like that on the autopsy report."

"Then what?" Koby asked.

Detective Chow gave us a smirk, saying he'd play our

game. "It was brushed onto a piece of candy. As a matter of fact, most of the candy was still in his mouth."

"Peppermint," I said under my breath. I remembered smelling it when he fell over.

"How do you know that, Keaton?" The detective didn't seem to be surprised. I guess he wouldn't be if he thought I was the killer. He seemed to mentally add that to his list of reasons to suspect the two of us.

"Reef always had a piece of peppermint candy in his mouth," Koby said. Seemed like he was taking up for me. "Some people chew gum, he sucked on peppermints."

"So. Whoever did this," Detective Chow said, "knew he liked that candy."

"Anyone who came around Reef knew he liked that candy," Koby said. "Easy to smell on him."

"Did you find any peppermint in here?" Chow asked, his eyes scanning the room.

"No," Koby said.

"None that you left?" he asked.

"No. None we left or at all. There was hardly any food here," Koby said. His eyes met the detective's. "We haven't touched anything, take a look." He gestured around the room, giving the detective the go-ahead.

"I believe you," Chow said. "That wouldn't be smart to leave it lying around. And I take you for a smart guy, Koby."

Did that mean he thought Koby would kill Reef and just clean up after himself? How terrible.

"When was the last time you saw Reef?" The detective looked my way. I guess that question was for me.

"Alive?" I asked. I was too nervous to think. I realized as soon as the words came out that that was what he meant. "Wednesday. The day before . . . the day before . . . you know."

"Where did you see him?"

"He was at Books & Biscuits."

"Do you sell peppermints at Books & Biscuits?"

"We sell books and food," I said.

"You've been there," Koby added. "Did you see any peppermints?"

"I'm asking the questions, remember?"

"Well, you're asking questions to the wrong people if you're really trying to solve Reef's murder. Because we didn't do it."

"So you say," Detective Chow said, standing up straight and walking toward the door.

Koby didn't say anything. I was sure he could match the detective's sarcasm, but he didn't.

With hand on doorknob, like he was ready to leave, not expecting us to have an answer, Detective Chow asked the question that Koby and I had just agreed to find out the answer to. "What in the world had your friend done to someone to make them want to kill him?"

Chapter Twenty-Seven

"WHAT IF THE peppermints had've been here, Koby?" I said, shaking my head. I went over to the window to watch where Chow went. "You telling him he could look." I clucked my tongue. "We would have been in a world of trouble. Murder weapon right where we were." I took in a breath. Just thinking of what would have happened made my heart race. "We'd just said we were going to look for it when we got here."

"What else was I supposed to do?" Koby asked, his hands up in the air. "*Not* let him look?"

"You're right, you had to let him look." I shook my head. "I still can't believe someone would do that to Reef. He was such a good guy."

"He'd done something to someone."

"And evidently the homicide detective thinks it was us. Why isn't he looking at anyone else on the train?"

"Maybe he is," Koby said.

"He walked right past Tessa and Jason's boat," I said, pointing out the window. And then, "Why aren't we looking at other people on the train?"

"We are," he said, a sly look on his face.

"Tessa." I pointed back toward the window as I walked over to the kitchen and started opening up cabinets.

"Right."

"I mean the Pussetts or Aubriol Meijer."

"With a 'j,'" we said in unison.

"Exactly." I shut one cabinet and opened the next. Nothing. "What about the other people that were there that day?"

"We already talked about that," Koby said. "We start with the places and people where Reef interacted, and that seemed like Timber Lake."

"The other riders may have some connections here, too," I said. "Tessa and Jason did."

"And if we see them, we'll investigate them just like we're doing Tessa and Jason. But I don't think so. They didn't know Reef. No reason to kill him."

"You don't know that," I said. I put my hands on my hips. "It ended up that two people on the train lived right next door to him."

"See. That's just what I'm talking about." Koby patted me on my back as he walked by. I pulled away just in case he was trying to patronize me. "By concentrating on his life here," he said, "we found out about them." He disappeared into the bathroom. "Going to check this room out again."

"No, I don't see," I said. "And didn't you use that bathroom this morning?"

"Doesn't hurt to check again," he yelled out. "I only used this bathroom once, and I was concentrating on washing my face and brushing my teeth."

I let out a grunt.

"And maybe that's what Chow is doing, too." Koby stuck his head out of the bathroom. "Maybe he talked to them before we came."

"Who?"

"Tessa and Jason. Maybe that's how Chow knew about this boat."

"Oh. So they're the nosy neighbor types? Telling people what goes on in the house next door?"

"In this case, houseboat next door," Koby corrected. "I guess I have to be careful what I do if they're going to be watching and telling people my goings and comings."

"Especially if it's the police they're telling," I said.

Koby disappeared back into the bathroom for a few minutes before coming out. "Nothing in there. No vitamins. No pills."

"Maybe he wasn't taking vitamins," I said. "Seeing there's nothing here." I cocked my head. "Why would he tell us that?"

"I don't know. Hiding something?"

"I agree. And whatever he was hiding, you think that got him killed?"

"Maybe," Koby said. "But that goes to my theory about talking to people on the train." He stuck out his neck and wagged a finger. "They didn't know him, they wouldn't have known his love of peppermint."

"Did he just grab peppermints from anywhere?" I asked. "As much as he crunched on them, you'd think he'd have an apartment full of them."

"Wherever he saw some, he'd take a handful." Koby came back out and looked around the room. "I slept in the other bedroom last night. Didn't want to sleep around Reef's stuff. But there was nothing in there."

"And where do you get cyanide from?" I asked.

"I don't know." He eyes looked off like he was thinking. "Rat poison?"

"That's arsenic." I pulled my phone out of my bag and asked Siri. "'Cyanide is found naturally in peach, apricot and nectarine pits.'" Standing in the kitchen area, I read the search results, skimming over the information on the first page that came up. "It says that it smells like almonds, but not everyone can smell it."

"Interesting," Koby said.

Then I clicked on a few other links. "It's used to develop film." That search result caught my eye.

"No one does that anymore," Koby said. "It's all digital."

"Cyanide gas is used to exterminate pests and vermin in ships and buildings." I kept reading.

Koby raised his eyebrows. "Tessa and Jason have a ship of sorts."

"So does Izzy," I said. "We didn't finish talking about her." I gave him a face that said I didn't approve.

"She's on the list."

"Which list? *Girls Koby Wants to Date* or the one for *Who Killed Reef?*"

"Sometimes, Keaton, I think you think you're funny."

"Here's another one worth looking into," I said, ignoring him. "'If accidentally swallowed, chemicals found in acetonitrile-based products that are used to remove artificial nails can produce cyanide when metabolized by the body.'"

"Sam Anderson said that he had tools and or equipment. Maybe he had chemicals, too," Koby said.

"Not used for construction." I pointed at my phone. "So, unless his tools are for mining gold, he might not have had it. But it is used to fumigate. That means we probably have something in our utility closet with it to keep vermin out of the kitchen."

"Let's hope the detective doesn't want to come back to Books & Biscuits snooping around for that."

"Speaking of which, we need to get to work," I said.

"You're right. Although I'm not worried about food being ready for today."

I chuckled. "I guess not with Mama Zola there."

"C'mon, let's go," he said.

After our unannounced visit from Detective Chow and our second time checking out Reef's place (did we really believe the killer used the things from Reef's houseboat to kill him with?), we didn't have time to go and interrogate

Tessa. Which I can't say upset me. Although I was sure Koby wasn't going to give up on that.

We cut through the wooded area, and after coming out the other side, Koby noted a FOR RENT sign in the front yard of a duplex.

"That might be a good place for Mama Zola," he said, and pointed.

I couldn't say I had noticed the sign before he pointed it out, and I had walked that way every day twice a day since we rented the shop. But then again, as I pointed out to my brother, I noticed things only when they were relevant.

"Are you serious about this?"

"About what?"

"Moving you and Mama Zola here to Timber Lake."

"Yeah. I'm serious. Why would you think I'm not?"

"You never said anything about it before."

He shrugged. "I did. Maybe not to you. But I can remember saying something to Reef about it. How I wanted to find a way to help Mama Zola." He looked at me with a grin. "Not that she needs help."

"I understand."

"Didn't know then I'd have the opportunity like I do now." He stopped on the sidewalk by the sign and stared up at the house. "You don't think it's a good idea?"

"I think it's an excellent idea. I just didn't know you'd thought about it."

"We just have to get your mother to move here, and we'll all be together."

I laughed at that. "My mother will never move from Wallingford. She loves that place. Plus, all the memories of my father are there."

"You carry memories with you wherever you go." He gave me a soft smile. "You haven't forgotten about him, have you?"

I looked down at my feet and shook my head. "Nope."

"And neither will she."

Both of us were lost in thought as we made our way down the couple of blocks through downtown Timber Lake to our store.

I'm sure he was thinking about renting that house and getting everyone to Timber Lake.

For me, I was grateful. It was nice that Koby included my mother in his plan to have us all together. I didn't try to get them to like each other or get along, but that was a hope I'd carried in my heart since I found out I had a biological brother.

Chapter Twenty-Eight

WHEN WE WALKED into the store, the aromas coming from our kitchen could have lifted us and carried us, feet dangling, right to it. It smelled so good.

A waft of sweet onions and green peppers sautéing, bacon and cinnamon. I didn't know if they were going all into one dish, but they had my mouth watering.

I followed the scent into the restaurant and found Mama Zola sitting at the table gulping up a cold glass of iced tea.

"It's hot in that little kitchen," she said. "Thought I was going to fall over into my sweet potatoes."

"There's a fan back there," Koby said. "It's pretty powerful."

"Good Lord," she said, and stood up. "Now you tell me. Come show me how to work that thing, otherwise I'll spend half the day trying to cool off with tea and the other half of it in the bathroom. We won't get nothing done."

I chuckled and headed back over to my side of the business to get ready for the day.

Our second day of opening and the first day where everything was officially for sale went slowly.

I had thought of our bookstore café serving just the three thousand or so souls in our little town. But why not get people to come across that bridge just for us? Maybe even perhaps for the few people who still moored their boats here but didn't live here. I'd have to look into that.

I thought about opening all the windows and doors. I was sure if people walking by could smell what was coming out of our kitchen, they wouldn't be able to help but to come in.

I spent the morning reflexively dusting and straightening books, Pete following behind me, redoing whatever I'd done. I sent him to lunch early. Koby gave him food, and now he was sitting out back with Remy, my brother's dog.

When I peeked over to the Biscuits side, Georgie was sitting behind the counter, elbows propped up and chin cradled in hands. There was one person at the counter nursing a glass of sweet tea, and when I leaned around the corner, I could see one person sitting at the table.

I was expecting a shipment of books. I had ordered it in anticipation of the bookstore selling out on opening day and just knew I'd need more inventory soon afterward.

Of course, that didn't happen.

But hey, there was no such thing as having too many books. Was there?

I kept my eye on the front entrance for the UPS man, and one time I looked up and saw Sam Anderson. Not coming in, just lurking around without trying to look like he was lurking around.

What the heck was in the things he had left behind with Reef? Maybe I should get Pete to come back indoors.

I hoped Sam wasn't going to come in and ask again about his tools. The attorney was supposed to come around today and give us what we needed to prove we were legit and able to take care of Reef's affairs. Well, that Koby was. I was go-

ing to tag along now, though, for sure. I definitely wanted to
see what was in that storage room.

Sam didn't hang around long, and it was a good thing, too,
because we started to get customers. A set of twin girls, who
couldn't have been more than fifteen, came in and giggled
through buying matching copies of *Waiting for Tom Hanks*
by Kerry Winfrey. An older couple wanted travel books so
they could do it from their armchairs, and I had the perfect
one for them, filled with bright, color-filled pictures and
wonderful descriptions. And then there was Charlie, the cutest
four-year-old.

"Do you have *The Story of Ferdinand* by Munro Leaf?"
he asked, tugging on my arm. I was impressed with just that.
What kid knows the author's name? "I'm thinking about going to Spain and I want to learn about it."

"You're going to Spain?" I asked, then looked up at his
mother. She shook her head in the negative.

"I said I was thinking about it." He corrected me. "I'd like
to read about it first."

"You are in luck," I said. "I do have a copy of it." I went over
to the children's section and pulled the only copy of it I had
from the shelf. "You know"—I handed him the book—"that
book is more about bulls than about Spain. I have a book about
that if you want it."

"No thank you," he said. "I think I can find out all I need
to know from the bulls." And with that, he walked over to the
counter, cradling the book in his arms, and waited for me
and his mother. I rang it up, she paid for it and then he told
me if he changed his mind about Spain, he'd be back to pick
out another book.

"Come back anytime," I told him, a wide smile on my face.

It was time to take a break from my busy morning by the
time Reef's lawyer arrived. And I was ready to eat.

"What smells so good in here?" he said when he walked
in. "Didn't expect this from a bookstore."

"We have a soul food café attached," I said, putting on my customer service smile.

"Looks like I might have to turn this appointment into a business lunch," he said.

"Sorry?" I asked. I didn't know what he meant.

"I'm Brian Jenkins," he said. He put his dark tanned leather briefcase up on the counter. "Attorney-at-law. I'm here to see Koby Hill."

Attorney Jenkins was dressed in a brown and white plaid jacket and a brown-and-wine-colored paisley tie. His shirt was white, and I couldn't see his pants without leaning forward over the counter and giving away my superpower—noticing what people are wearing. (But I think they were brown, that was my best guess.)

"Oh! Hi, Attorney Jenkins," I said, and stuck out a hand. "I'm Keaton Rutledge. Koby's twin sister."

"I see the resemblance." He shook my hand. "Nice to meet you. And please call me Brian." He had a pleasant smile and really white teeth. "I've heard a lot about you—from Koby and Reef."

Reef . . . That made me blush.

"Let me just grab someone to man the front, and I'll take you over to Koby."

"I tried to get in the door on the restaurant side," he said.

"Forced marketing," I said. "Whoever comes in the door is forced to see, or smell, all we have."

"Good idea," he said. He turned to look at the display books as I came from behind the counter.

"I've got legal thrillers," I said, and pointed to the stack to direct his attention. "I'll be right back."

I stuck my head outside and told Pete I was leaving the front of the store under his watch.

He was happy about that.

"Wait here," I told Brian. "Have a seat. I'll get Koby and see if we can't get you some food."

"Excellent," he said.

I walked into the kitchen and got dizzy. There was so much food that it was scary. I knew Koby had said that the money didn't come out of the company's budget to buy all that food, but I was concerned that it would all go to waste. And even if there were enough people at the memorial tomorrow night to eat it all, I wasn't sure where we'd be able to store it so it wouldn't be spoiled by then.

"Hi," I said.

"Don't worry," Koby said.

Had he heard the tremor in my voice?

"Not worried," I said, and tried to put on a smile. "I just came to tell you that Reef's lawyer is here."

"Oh good," Mama Zola said.

"You want to go out and talk to him, too, Mama Zola?" Koby asked.

"No. No." She stirred the pot on the stove. "I've got too much cooking to do." She opened the stove and peeked inside. "Didn't you say he came to see you?"

"About Reef," he said.

She shut the oven door and wiped her hands on a tea towel. "Just tell me later if it's something that needs sharing."

"Okay, I will," Koby said, and pulled his apron over his head. "But I also told him we'd feed him lunch."

"Good idea," Mama Zola said, and snapped her fingers. "I'll bring something out." She looked at me. "Keaton, how is your day going?"

"Slow," I said. "Happy it's lunchtime, because I'm starving."

"We've got plenty of food," she said. "No reason for you to be hungry." She got a plate off the shelf. "Go sit down with your brother and talk to that lawyer. I'll bring out something to eat for everyone."

I said, "Okay." But I was thinking she wouldn't know what I liked or what the lawyer wanted to eat either. I didn't want to have a plate of food set down in front of me and not eat it in front of someone coming to our restaurant. What would he think if I didn't like what we served?

"You need me to help you bring the plates out?" Koby asked Mama Zola.

"No, baby," she said. "I'll get Georgie to help me. Just go on."

"Hi, Koby." Attorney Jenkins stood up when we came out of the kitchen.

"Hi, Brian."

"Nice place you got here." Brian beamed a smile.

"Thank you," Koby said, and shook the lawyer's hand. "Have a seat." He pointed to the chair Attorney Jenkins had just vacated. "Make yourself comfortable."

"Thank you," he said. "But it won't be easy getting comfortable and taking care of business with all that good-smelling food wafting under my nose." He rubbed his stomach. "My belly will probably be grumbling."

"No worries," Koby said. "We can get you food."

"I don't want to be any trouble."

"No trouble." Koby shook his head. "We're hungry, too. Right, Keaton?"

I nodded.

"We'll eat with you," Koby said, and started to get up.

"Let's take care of this first," Attorney Jenkins said. He put his briefcase on the table and popped the lock on the flap. "That way I can enjoy my meal and not mix it with business." He reached in and pulled out a mustard-colored folder.

"Sure," Koby said. He rubbed the palms of his hands together. "What do we have?"

"Like I alluded to, Reef died intestate."

"Which means?" Koby asked.

I knew what it meant. I had learned it when my father died, but I let the lawyer answer.

"It meant when he died, he didn't have a will." He opened the folder. I noticed a key taped to the inside of it. "And usually, it's the will that designates who is the executor or executrix."

"But we can still do that, right?" Koby asked.

"We can show his intentions, which is something that would hold up in court if anyone was to contest it."

"There's no one to contest."

The attorney smiled knowingly, he was used to people jumping in and assuming the law. "That's right," he said. "I have a survivorship deed on the boat, recorded with King County." He took the top sheet of paper out of the folder and slid it across the table.

Koby pulled the sheet of paper in front of him and studied it. "And this is all I'll need?"

"It shows you own the boat and everything that goes along with it. Also, I have this." He pulled a few sheets of paper paper-clipped together out of the folder.

He flipped them around so they faced Koby and pointed to some numbers. "This shows all the slip rental payments through this month."

Koby looked up at Attorney Jenkins and then at me. I could see the amusement in his eyes. "How did you get this?"

"I made—well, my office—made the monthly payments. I can keep doing that if you like." I saw a grin rise on his face. "Of course, there'll be a fee to retain my ongoing services."

Koby laughed. "I think I can handle it myself."

"Good deal," Brian said. He picked up both of the pieces of paper. "Now I suggest you don't give this woman the originals. I don't have any other copies, and you'd lose the only copy you have. Not to say this woman who owns the marina—what's her name?"

"Historia Krol," I said.

He cocked his head to the side. "Why does that name sound familiar?" He stared off for a moment, then shook off the thought.

"Anyway, it's not as if Miss Krol wouldn't give it back to

you if requested, but it's always good to keep a copy of everything for your records."

"We can make a copy." Koby looked at me for confirmation of that. I nodded.

We couldn't actually make a copy at Books & Biscuits.
We didn't have a copier in the office. We'd bought one, but it
had yet to be delivered. But I knew that I could go over to the
library and have copies made, no problem.

"And in here"—Brian patted the folder in front of him—"I
have Reef's death certificate, if you need it." He looked at
Koby, but Koby didn't move. "But no need to look at it if you
don't want. I also have the title search we had to do." He
shook his head, seemingly in disgust. "That's what I referred
to this morning when we spoke."

"A title search?"

"Yes. It was a mess. The things that people do to get
around the law."

"What is it exactly?"

"You have to have a title that's free and clear"—he used
his attorney voice—"in order to pass the title from one owner
to the next."

"And this one didn't?"

"No. I actually had to go to court and do a quiet title in
order for it to be legally Reef's. Once we got into it, Reef said
he knew who the owner was."

"Reef knew everybody," Koby said.

Brian laughed. "He was a popular guy. Always sending
referrals my way." He coughed into his hand. "Anyway, Reef
said he spoke with them but couldn't get anywhere. So we
went to court."

"What happened when you went to court?" I asked, thinking maybe, if Reef had confronted them and made them
mad, they may be responsible for what happened to him.

"Never saw the inside of courtroom," Brian said. "We
won on a default judgment."

He must have noticed the confusion on our faces.

"It means the other party never answered our Complaint, and so we won by default."

"Oh," Koby said. "Like the other team not showing up for the basketball game."

"Exactly," Brian said.

So, I guess there was no reason for the previous owner, at least, to kill Reef. They didn't care enough about the boat to come to court.

"We had to wait for that," Brian said. "That was why it hadn't been transferred to your name yet."

"Yeah, I remember you saying that." Koby gave a bittersweet kind of smile. "Reef had bought it for me."

"He was so proud of you. You know, owning a business and everything, especially since you'd never been, you know, adopted."

I saw the attorney look out the side of his eye at me.

"I was a foster kid, too," Brian said. "Reef had been in a foster home with me. He stayed in touch."

"That was Reef," Koby said.

"But I was lucky. I was adopted when I was six. Got good parents. Was able to get a good education."

"So back to the title search." Koby didn't seem to want to talk about that. I hadn't ever known him to voice any grief about not being adopted. "Do I need to show that to anyone?"

"No, but it might be good to have. Reef was just starting to get his foot in the business world. Said he was going to follow your lead."

Koby let his eyes drift down to his hands, which were folded in front of him on the table. I know all this talk of Reef was making him sad. Me, too, but I was more worried about my brother's feelings than mine.

"So he came to me for advice. On what to do and what not. He got wind of this boat and thought that'd be perfect for you. He said you thought it was a killer commute from Seattle out here every day."

"I did say that," Koby agreed. "But never with the intention of him buying me a boat."

"He wanted to show his appreciation for all that you've done for him."

I saw the tears well up in Koby's eyes, and he couldn't stop them from falling. He looked at me and wiped them away. "It was Reef who gets all the appreciation. If it wasn't for him, I might not have ever known I had a sister." He leaned back in his chair. "I couldn't ever thank him enough."

Chapter Twenty-Nine

MAMA ZOLA BROUGHT our food out.

"Here you go," she said as she and Georgie put plates in front of us.

"Oh, this looks good. I love biscuits," Attorney Brian said, turning his plate around to get a view from every side. "What's between it?"

"Georgie, go and get them some iced tea," she said before answering Brian's question. "Buttermilk-fried chicken breast coated in a spicy hot sauce."

"Like Nashville style?" he asked, seemingly getting excited.

"No," she said. "Like Mama Zola style."

He chuckled. "Okay."

"Now let me finish telling you."

"Yes, ma'am," he said.

"On top is thinly sliced glazed ham, and it's all topped with my special slaw."

"Vinegar based?" Brian asked, like he was the judge on a cooking show. He hadn't learned.

She leaned over him, lowering her voice. "Just eat it," she said.

"Okay." He picked up a fork.

"With your hands."

He put the fork down.

"And the slaw is made with mayo."

Mama Zola let him eat without her scrutiny but came back out when we were just finishing up. I don't know if she'd seen he was getting ready to leave or just had some sixth sense.

"Was it good?" she asked.

She didn't have anything to do but look at his plate. It looked as if he had licked it clean.

"Very tasty," he said.

That made her laugh. She knew how much he loved it. "Listen," she said, "I want to thank you for everything you've done for my boys." She swiped crumbs from the table with one hand and let them fall into her cupped hand under the side of the table. "Helping Reef get things turned around for himself and making sure Koby got what he was supposed to, even coming all the way out here."

"It's my job," he said.

"Just say thank you," she said. "Because I know you went beyond for them."

"Thank you," he said.

"Now, after you see him to the door, Koby," Mama Zola went on, "I need you to go to the store for me. I need a couple slabs of ribs."

"Oh my," I muttered. As if we didn't have enough food.

"Okay," is what Koby said.

"I saw that grill out back, by the picnic tables earlier when Pete was out there. Does it work?"

I chuckled and so did Reef's lawyer. I guess we were thinking the same thing, to check whether it worked before deciding to use it.

"It works," Koby said.

Koby walked Brian to the door, Mama Zola went back into the kitchen and I grabbed the folder and followed behind into the Books side.

"We have any customers while I was at lunch?" I asked Pete.

"One. But they just looked."

"Okay," I said, and stuck the folder down into my shoulder bag.

"The box of books came."

"Oh. Good," I said. "Gives us something to do."

But we didn't get through half of the box of books, inventorying and putting them out, when foot traffic in the store picked up.

The smells from Koby and Mama Zola's kitchen must have leaked through the bricks and oozed through the framing of the door and windows, because people started to pile in.

And once she got those ribs started out back, that aroma was like the pied piper's flute. Everyone wanted some.

"Looks like you'll have to sell these," Mama Zola said after we'd told a few of the customers the ribs weren't on the menu at the restaurant.

And lucky for me, as the customers wandered through, dazed by the smell of the food from Biscuits, a few even bought books.

I was definitely getting on board with Mama Zola coming to work for us. With her, we might not need social media. Her cooking was all the advertising we needed.

After the buzz of activity while the ribs smoked up our corner of downtown, there was a lull in customers around a little after four. I decided to take that opportunity to go and get the papers copied that Brian, the lawyer, had brought over for Koby.

"I'm going to run over to the library," I told Pete. "Do you mind being here by yourself?"

"No problem, boss."

"Thanks." I went around the counter and grabbed my

shoulder bag. "I shouldn't be more than fifteen minutes, tops."

The library was only a three-minute walk, and there were quite a few papers in the folders, but I figured I could put the stack in the loader and press start. Shouldn't take more than a couple of minutes.

I'd have to avoid Liz, though. She'd want to talk. Come to think of it, I hadn't seen anyone since I'd left. They'd probably all want some kind of conversation.

The copiers were off to the right of the main entrance. I was able to get through the door and past checkout with a wave and a smile. People might not be buying books, but they were definitely borrowing them. There were a few patrons waiting with armloads of books.

I forgot all about that the machine had to be fed coins in order to do what I needed to do.

I dug down in my purse and found $3.73. I dropped the three cents back in my purse and put in half of what I'd found.

Placing the folder on the counter next to the copiers, I opened it, careful not to make the key come off. It was taped on, and the tape seemed old and not sticky enough anymore. I ran my fingers across it to try and secure it better.

YALE. The word was printed across the front of it on both sides, and I thought, *Another key we don't know what to do with*. Hmm. Probably should have asked Brian.

The first couple sheets I'd seen when Brian took them out of the folder. The survivorship deed. Something that was titled *Judgment Entry*, and examining it, I saw that it was for the quiet title action he said he had to file to make the boat legally Koby's. And then there was Reef's death certificate. I stared at it for a long time—not reading it, didn't think I could stomach that.

I got those copied and put them in a pile. I'd keep it separate. It was the stuff Historia needed to see to prove Koby had the right to go into Reef's storage unit.

Next were a few sheets of invoices. Payment for the slip fee to a company named East End Pacific. I scanned the pages through the copier. From the number of them, it seemed like Reef had been paying for them even before the title to the houseboat was in his name. After I copied them, I put them in the pile with the other things for Historia. They would show he was paid up to date.

Even though I didn't see Historia's name on the invoices, I thought that must be why her name was familiar to Brian. East End Pacific must be her company. Brian had been sending payments there, so her name must have come up.

The next thing in the folder looked legal to me. It had *Timber Lake Court* across the top. There were a few pages stapled together. I started reading through them, and when I got to the last page, there was an exhibit. Exhibit A, as such. Across the top was *Title Search* and listed below were names. If I was reading it right, Reef had purchased the boat from EEP, LLP. *Weird name*, I thought. But then, the next name surprised me. It was Isabella Ramirez.

Why was her name on there? Brian had said that a title search showed a list of previous owners.

She had owned the boat before? Weird. Maybe she bought it before she bought the one she lived in now?

I checked to see whom she had bought it from.

EEP, LLP. Again. What kind of name was that?

That didn't seem right. She bought the boat from one person and then sold it back to them?

Was something wrong with the boat, and she returned it? Or was she the reason that there had been a problem with the boat?

What exactly had been wrong with the title?

I shook my head to clear it. I didn't know enough about titles and quiet actions, or whatever, to understand it, and my brain was filling up with bad thoughts. Like what if the reason Reef was dead was because of him purchasing the boat.

That would be awful, seeing as we found out that he bought it for Koby.

If he never bought it, would he still be alive?

I'd have to go through the paperwork and see if I could figure it out. Later. I couldn't do it now. I thumbed through the file. If I read all the twenty pages or so that were still left in the folder, I could easily be gone from the bookshop for longer than the fifteen minutes I told Pete I would be.

I'd take time later and do it. For now, I'd just get the copying done.

I did a good job of hurrying along until I got near the end of the pile. Turning around to get the staple remover off the counter, out the corner of my eye, I saw Jason Holiday. He had a cart of books going to the shelves to restack. And the sight of him made me angry.

I'd forgotten he might be here.

Then I remembered how Koby and I thought he and Tessa might have told the detective about who was at the houseboat. Jason might be a troublemaker if he was a nosy neighbor. Not that Koby would do anything illegal, but while a murder investigation was going on, it could make the police even more suspicious of my brother. Especially if Jason was trying to cover his own tracks. And if he was telling the police things, he might just tell Historia. After all, he was catching a ride to work with her. The marina was where my brother was going to live. He didn't need any trouble. And it really wasn't any of Jason's business what went on there.

Why would he tell anyway? What difference did it make to him what went on on the boat next door if it didn't concern him or hurt the property?

I pushed the last pages through the copier, keeping an eye on Jason, even walking away from the copier while the papers went through so to keep up with him when he ventured out of my sight. I put the papers of the original file and the copies into the folder, making it kind of bulky. Worrying

about the taped key inside, I took it out and tucked it in the
zipper part of my wallet and stuffed it inside my bag.

Then I decided to get a closer look at Jason.

I'd only seen him close up on the train. The next couple of
times—on the houseboat he shared with Tessa and going
into the library—he was farther away from me.

Folder tucked in arm, bag slung over shoulder, I walked
toward the stacks to take a look at him.

I didn't know what I was expecting to get from that look.
I surely wouldn't find out anything. He wasn't doing anything at the time but his job. I positioned myself opposite
him, noticing a regular paperback mystery in with the large-
print mysteries.

Muttering, "This doesn't belong here," I pulled it out so I
could get a better look at Jason. But just as I did, he was pok-
ing his nose through an opening to get a look at me.

"Are you following me?" His voice was a strained whisper, but I could hear the agitation even through the books.

I still knew how to wield a good library voice. "Why?
Should someone be following you?" I whispered back.

"Why are you following me?" His whisper seemed harsh.

"To see what you're up to!"

His face scrunched up. His brows furrowed.

I saw him stick something on the bottom shelf of the cart
with the books.

"Is that a candy bar?" I asked. It looked just like a Her-
shey's with almonds. "You can't have that. Chocolate will
make a mess all over the books."

"What the he—heck are you talking about?"

I think he was about to use a swear word, which definitely
was not library appropriate, even if it did come out in a low
voice. But he turned it around.

I was talking about the chocolate but wasn't sure what *he*
was talking about—telling on himself about something relat-
ing to the murder, perhaps? Like already knowing Reef?

Pointing the paperback I was holding at him, I said instead, "Stop telling Historia about things that are none of your business."

"Historia?" He looked even more perplexed.

"Don't play dumb with me," I said in my most heated whisper. I knew he knew her. I saw him get out of her blue Mercedes the first day I spotted him at the library. "You're telling her things about my brother. Why? Why are you trying to get him in trouble?"

"Are you crazy?" he said in a voice much louder than allowed in a library.

"Shhh!" someone said from somewhere in the stacks.

"Look, you"—his voice back down at a whisper—"I don't know what you're talking about."

"I know why you don't want the police around." His reason could be twofold—murder and desecrating books with smudgy chocolate. The worst nightmare of any librarian. "I have a good mind to tell on you, too."

"Tell who what?" He shook his head. "You sound bonkers," he said. "And if you don't leave me alone, I'm going to get someone to throw you out of here."

"Hi, Keaton." It was Liz. "Is everything okay?" She looked through the stack to where Jason was standing. He immediately removed his face from the other side of the books and acted like he was working.

"Hi, Liz," I said. "Yes, everything is okay." I made my voice pleasant. "I was just telling this guy that this book is shelved wrong." I handed over the paperback to her. "Sorry. Gotta go." I gave her an innocent smile. "I have to get back to the bookshop."

I didn't know how upset, and yes *bonkers*, I could get over someone doing my brother wrong. Or at least my perception of doing him that way.

And him eating that candy bar bothered me, too. Didn't he know there was no food around the books? Okay, so I was one to talk. I'd just opened a bookstore with a café as part of it. But libraries were different. Those books were on loan and

needed to go out to other people. We sold the books at
Books & Biscuits. People could do what they wanted with
their own things.

I blew out a breath as I left the library and shook off whatever it was I was starting to feel. I couldn't believe I just
confronted that guy with little proof of anything he'd done. I
couldn't ever remember acting so bold. So unlike me.

Lost in thought, I didn't see Koby until he was practically
right next to me.

"Hey," he said.

"Aagh!" My knees buckled and I nearly fell down. "Where
did you come from?"

"Books & Biscuits." He made a face, telling me I was acting crazy. If he only knew. "You didn't see me coming toward you?"

"No." I didn't want to tell him I'd been lost in thought,
because he'd want to know what I'd been thinking about. And
I didn't want to tell him how I'd been accusing Jason, in a
whisper no less, of things I wasn't completely sure he'd done.
"What are you doing here?" I said instead.

"You make the copies?"

I held up the folder.

"I thought I'd meet you and we could go and give Historia
Krol the paperwork so we could get into Reef's storage unit.
See what's in there."

"You want to go now?"

"Yeah. I have to take Mama Zola home after we close. I
know she'll be so tired by the end of the day."

"I'm sure she will." I didn't mean to sound sarcastic, but
she was cooking up a storm.

"And I was thinking," he said, "that most offices don't stay
open past five o'clock. I don't want to miss being able to show
her the paperwork. Then when I get back from taking Mama
Zola home, we can open up the storage unit. See what's in it."

I was curious about what was in that thing. And why another lock had been put on it and couldn't be opened with just the one key that Reef had left.

Sam was silently hounding us to get in it. Historia Krol didn't know why it had been secured by an additional lock, and Old Man Walker didn't either. He had even said he didn't think Reef was past due with his slip fees, and according to Brian's invoices, he was right.

I glanced at my watch. It was just past four forty. It would take less than ten minutes to walk over to the marina. We'd just have time. "Okay," I said. "Let's go."

Chapter Thirty

"I DON'T WANT any trouble around here." Historia Krol didn't even look up at us from her desk. "So, you need to hurry and settle your friend's affairs and vacate my property."

"Sorry?" I said. Out of breath from trying to beat the clock, we soon learned all that hustling to get there didn't do us any good. It didn't accomplish anything more than to make me dizzy.

We'd only just walked into her office, if that was what she was calling it. The room was a mess. Much like her property, but unlike her and her car. Both of them were always shiny and looking sharp.

There were yard signs and flyers and stickers lying around that read HISTORIA KROL FOR MAYOR. There wasn't even an election going on. And then there were papers and file folders stacked everywhere. I couldn't see how she'd even fit the desk and file cabinet in. And then the office reeked of old coffee, Mrs. Grayson's yard and mint. I looked at the coffeemaker splashed with stains, sitting on a two-drawer file cabinet—it smelled as if she was fond of flavored creamers. I didn't even want to smell the coffee in this room. It was such a mess. And an empty glass ashtray, wiped clean. She must be a closet smoker, I thought, maybe why she wore so much perfume and ate mints—to mask the smell of cigarettes.

I scrunched up my nose and squinted my eyes. The place was giving me a headache.

"You two are trouble," she said. "And I don't like—or need—any trouble. I have a reputation to maintain."

"What have we done?" I asked.

"I heard the police were here. For you two. Asking questions. Knocking on houseboat doors. All to do with something you've done, I presume."

I frowned. Maybe she didn't know Reef had been murdered.

"Well, you presume wrong. It was about Reef," I said. "Not us."

"Is he still causing trouble?" she asked, and for the first time looked at us. "I thought helping you was going to be an end to that."

I was going to say, *Reef hadn't caused trouble*, but Koby spoke up before I could.

"We have the paperwork you requested to show ownership." He pushed the brown envelope toward her. She didn't even reach for it.

"You'll have to come back when Walker is here. He's in charge of the bolt cutters."

"He isn't here now?" I asked.

"No," she said, and put her attention back onto that piece of paper she was writing on. "That's why I said you'd have to come back. The law does require I give him days off."

"When will he be back?" Koby asked.

"Tomorrow," she said. "Then once you get his things, I want you off my property."

Koby and I just stood there and looked at each other. She was throwing a wrench in his plans to live on the houseboat and for no good, apparent reason.

"What are you waiting on? I'm busy, and you are taking up space and my time." It was obvious she was done talking to us. "Thanks for stopping by."

"HOW DID SHE know the police had been here." Koby said as we stepped outside into the fresh air. It wasn't a question, he just seemed to be thinking out loud.

I gulped in a huge amount of air and swallowed, clearing my nasal passages from all the dust in Historia's office before I answered. "She owns the place," I said. "He probably talked to her. Except, I'd avoid the police if I kept my place in such disrepair."

"Her car wasn't here this morning, and she just told us that Walker has the day off."

"How do you know her car wasn't here?" I asked.

"It wasn't in the parking lot," Koby said. "You didn't notice that?"

I didn't answer that. I was, in my defense, though, trying to hone my observation skills. But keeping up with Koby was going to take a lot of training.

But that didn't matter because he was already on to something else. "Speaking of who was around this morning. Maybe it was Tessa who told her."

"Why would she do that?" I tried to think of a reason. "Did Tessa even know *we* were around?"

"We're going to find out." Koby pulled his cell phone out of his pocket. "We still have time."

"Not to talk to Tessa," I said.

"Yes. To talk to Tessa," he said. "We thought we were going to go through Reef's storage space, but we didn't. So we've got time."

"I don't like the idea of confronting killers," I said. "Seems counterintuitive."

"True, but necessary if we're going to figure out this whodunit."

I was of the mind that we should just tell Detective Chow and not necessarily try to solve anything.

I thought of all kinds of arguments in my head as we waited for Tessa to come to the door. It seemed as if it took her an eternity. How large was the houseboat that it was taking her so long?

"You two," she said when she finally made it to the door. She didn't seem surprised.

She'd wrapped herself in a silk kimono-like robe, and underneath was a T-shirt and thin cottony pajama pants. Her hair mussy, her face undressed—no eyeliner, no lipstick, no foundation.

But what struck me most, other than it was the middle of the day and she looked like we'd woken her up at some ungodly hour, was how young she looked close up.

"Hello, Tessa," Koby said. "We thought we'd come by and talk to you."

"About what?" she said. She leaned forward and looked outside around us, perhaps thinking that we hadn't come alone.

"Well. For one thing, you don't seem surprised to see us. Why is that?"

"Timber Lake isn't that big."

That was true, but I hadn't ever seen her.

"Why didn't you say that when we saw you on the train?" I asked.

"Why would I?" she asked a question back. "Ugh. Is that what you want to talk about?"

"No," I said.

"What then?"

"Reef," Koby answered.

"He's dead. I have nothing to say about him." She started to close the door, but Koby stuck his hand out, keeping her from shutting it.

"Do you have anything to say about his phone?"

Her face went white. And for a long moment, she didn't

say anything. I could see the hand she held on to the door with start to shake.

"What are you talking about?" She tried to keep her voice from trembling as well.

"You took Reef's phone from the train," I said.

"No." She made a face, telling us we were mistaken. "I did not."

"You did." I wanted to say, *I saw you*, but I really hadn't actually seen her pick up the phone. And I didn't want to stretch the truth like my brother does either.

"She saw you," Koby said, nodding toward me.

Exactly what I meant. He just couldn't help himself.

"I saw you come and stoop next to me," I said, trying to get some truth into the conversation. "That phone had been on the floor then, I'm sure of it. But it disappeared before the police got there."

"I don't know what you mean," Tessa said, letting go of the door and tugging her robe tighter around her. Her body language said she was closing down.

"What were you doing on that train with Reef?" Koby asked. "How was it that you were there on the day he died?"

"I don't have to talk to you."

"You might want to," I said, having more courage than I thought I would. "Before I tell Detective Chow what I know."

"You're not scaring me," Tessa said. "And you can tell that detective anything you want. Doesn't matter to me."

"If you weren't trying to hide something," Koby said, "you wouldn't have taken the phone in the first place."

"You don't know anything," she said, which wasn't a denial.

Koby glanced around the room behind her. It seemed to make her nervous, and she shifted to stand in front of him.

"Where's your boyfriend?" Koby asked.

"Boyfriend? I don't have a boyfriend." Tessa sputtered the words out.

"Jason Holiday isn't your boyfriend?" I asked.

"No." Her frown said that it was a ludicrous question. "I don't even know who that is."

She couldn't be serious, I thought. They had acted as if they didn't know each other on the train the day Reef died, but my goodness, they were living on the same houseboat. She really couldn't think we didn't know.

"Look," Tessa said, moving past my Jason Holiday questions. "You can tell that detective whatever you want and do whatever you like. I'll be long gone before he can get to me or you can cause problems."

"Long gone?" Koby gave a sly smile. "I don't think so." He pulled out his phone. "We'll just call him and then wait here with you until he gets here."

"No you won't!" she said. She balled up her fists at her side, and I had thought she was going to stomp a foot. "What do you want!" Tears were welling in her eyes. "Oh my God! Why can't you just go away?"

"We want to know why you killed Reef."

"What! I did not kill Reef," she said, but to me, her eyes said something different.

"What are you hiding?" Koby asked. "Why did you take the phone?"

She stretched her eyes like she was trying to keep the tears from falling. Opening her mouth, she let out what seemed to be a chuckle. "I'm not telling you anything," she said.

"How old are you?" Koby asked.

"What? Why?"

"I didn't notice before," he said. "All that makeup you had on." He cocked his head to one side. "Who are you running from?"

Where did that question come from? We were talking about her being a killer. Now he was questioning her like she was the victim.

"I don't know what you're talking about," she said.

"I think you do."

Koby put his phone back in his pants pocket, then reached in another one and pulled out Reef's second phone. The one Koby'd gotten when he picked up his property.

"Reef had two phones," he said as he unlocked it and clicked on it a few times. He stretched out what he'd found and held it up to her. "We've got more pictures of you hanging out at the jazz club. Pictures with Reef. All showing you knew Reef and didn't tell the detective any of it the day Reef died."

Her gasp was audible.

Her eyes showed that she was trying to calculate something to say, and just when her shoulders relaxed, seemingly figuring out her next move, Koby spoke again. "Maybe instead of sharing this information with the homicide detective, we'll show your picture to somebody in the missing persons department."

That turned her attitude around.

"Why are you doing this?" she said.

"I just want to know if you killed Reef."

"No. It wasn't me," she said. Again, I thought she was going to stomp a foot. "Here," she said. Turning around, she disappeared back into the house, leaving the door open and us standing there.

"What is this missing person thing you're talking about?" I asked.

"Do you see how young she is?"

"I thought that, too," I said. "Without her makeup, she looks like a teenager."

"I bet she is," Koby said just as she came back.

She shoved the phone into Koby's chest. "Take it."

"Why did you take it?" Koby asked, not reaching for the phone.

"Take it," she said again.

I took it out of her hands. It really seemed to be upsetting her. And now that I was thinking she was possibly just a kid, I didn't want to do that.

"I'd rather not tell anyone you're here," Koby said.

"Then don't," she said. "My birthday is in two weeks anyway."

Which birthday, I wasn't sure. I also wasn't sure what difference that made.

"It would be terrible to be locked up until then," Koby said.

"Okay. Fine," she said. "I took it because I don't want anybody seeing those pictures of me with Sam."

"Sam?" I said. She said it like we would know who that was. I only knew one Sam. "Sam Anderson?"

"Yeah. Who else?"

I thought I saw her roll her eyes. Then I figured Sam must've been in the picture Koby had shown her.

"Why didn't you want to be in a picture with Sam?" I asked.

"Because he killed Reef."

Chapter Thirty-One

TESSA CHAIKEN HAD no concrete proof of her accusation of Sam Anderson as Reef's murderer. Heck, at the time she took the phone, no one even knew Reef *had* been murdered. But then again, we were going around questioning people, and we didn't either. And Sam had made me feel uncomfortable, too, just by hanging around.

"How did you know Reef was even dead when he fell over on the train?"

"I didn't know for sure," Tessa said. "But I knew the police and an ambulance would be coming to get him. I didn't want anyone in law enforcement to see me in the pictures Reef had on his phone. *Any* of the pictures." She bounced her head back and forth, weighing what she was going to say next. "I only figured Sam might have something to do with it later."

"Why did you think that?"

Then she told us that she'd heard Sam and Reef arguing the night before.

"So when you first took it, you really weren't worried about anyone seeing you with Sam, were you?"

"I said I didn't want anyone to see pictures of me. And now that I know Sam is the murderer, I really don't want anyone to see me with him."

I started to wonder if we should believe anything this girl said. She seemed to make up stuff as she went along. I started thinking maybe she took the phone just to have it.

"What were they arguing about?" Koby asked. It seemed he was going to take her at her word.

"I don't know," Tessa said.

"What did they say?" he asked.

"I don't know that either."

After a bevy of questions, we'd gotten nothing more than that the two of them were shouting at each other, ready to box it out. Reef pushed Sam off the boat onto the dock, and Sam left.

Koby seemed to be getting exasperated, but I couldn't be mad at Tessa. The same thing had happened to me. I'd watched her and Jason talk that day I followed her to the marina, but I hadn't been able to determine what they talked about. At least she knew it had been an argument.

"Then what?" Koby asked.

"I don't know," she said again.

She was exasperating.

"Then why do you think Sam did it?" I asked.

"Because the next day, Reef was dead."

I wanted to suck my teeth and roll my eyes from that pronouncement of deductive reasoning, but she wasn't doing anything we weren't doing—concocting suspicion on threads of thin air.

And it was the same thing that Detective Chow was doing.

"How do you think Sam did it?" I asked. "He wasn't even on the train."

"By poisoning one of those peppermints Reef was always

sucking on and putting it somewhere Reef would be sure to pick it up," had been her answer.

It seemed like the perfect murder. Anyone who knew Reef could have done it and not have been anywhere around him when it happened.

But then it popped into my head, if she hadn't talked to the detective, how could she know that was how Reef died? That made me nervous.

Was she the killer after all? I took a step back.

But while I was wondering how she knew, my brother was asking.

"Because," she answered him, "he put one in his mouth just as you were getting on the train."

WE HEADED BACK to the bookstore café. We'd been gone long enough. But even with Books & Biscuits business in front of us, Koby was still asking questions about the murder—though, this time they were directed to me.

"Maybe that's why Sam hadn't gotten his equipment, tools or whatever from Reef, huh?" Koby said. "Because they'd been beefing."

"And maybe that's why he wants to get that stuff out, to move any evidence."

But what was the reason, if he was the killer, he was lurking outside our business door every morning?

Koby bit his lip—he was thinking about something, and that look he had usually meant it wasn't exactly what we were talking about.

"I wonder what Jason is to her?" he said.

"Definitely not her grandfather," I said. "That's for sure."

"Which means she's trying to cover up where she's living, which makes me think he's not a relative."

"You think he's holding her against her will?"

"When I was coming up, kids would run away all the time."

"From the group home?"

He shrugged. "From their homes, too. They either stayed on the streets or some nice person would let them crash with them."

"Maybe that's why they acted like they didn't know each other on the train," I said. "Wouldn't look too cool for him to let a juvenile stay with him. Especially one of the opposite sex."

"Right," Koby said.

"But she might be acting suspicious because she's a runaway," I said. "Or she might be acting that way because she had something to do with Reef's death."

"True," Koby said. "Maybe she's trying to throw us off her scent by saying someone else did it."

"But why tell us that? That's something she should tell the police."

"So, I'm thinking," Koby said, "that Detective Chow hadn't talked to her before he saw us this morning."

"Why don't you think that?"

"Because she didn't ask us anything about him," Koby said. "I would want to know what a policeman knew about me."

"So you'd ask someone the policeman talked to what he said?"

"Yeah. I would. Wouldn't you?"

I shrugged. "I guess." I nodded. "Yeah. I probably would." I thought about that for a second. "So you think he maybe talked to Jason?"

"That's what I'm thinking," Koby said, and smiled. "See? We think alike." I smiled back at him. "What made you think that?"

"Because Jason was probably leaving for work if he worked the morning shift, like we were thinking when the detective showed up at the boat. That made me remember the day I saw Jason at the library."

He just started chuckling.

"What?" I said, laughing with him just because I knew it was something I must've done.

"Is this going to be something else you forgot to tell me?"

"No," I said, and frowned. "Well. I guess kind of." I flapped my arms. "I only remember stuff when I see a connection to them. And I don't always make the connection right away."

"It's okay, sis. What did you see?"

"Hmpf." I blew out first before I continued my, albeit late, observation. "I remember seeing Jason get out of a blue car."

"Whose blue car?"

"I can't say for certain, but I'm pretty sure it was Historia's car."

"Jason saw the detective this morning and taking his usual ride to work by Historia, told her so?"

I hunched my shoulders. "It's a theory. She didn't necessarily sound like she'd talked to him. She wasn't there when we first got there, and I watched him leave."

"I agree with it," he said. "And with him not telling her why—or that detective may have been looking for him as well, it made Historia suspicious of us and want us gone."

"In a hurry," I said.

"Exactly."

"And I may as well tell you this, too, just in case it has some connection to something else later on."

"What?" He put up a hand. "Don't tell me. You saw the peppermints that killed Reef?"

I cocked my head and thought about that. "I did see a bag of peppermints in the marina store."

"I bet you did."

"I did. When you were talking to Old Man Walker. I'm sure that's not that bag used to kill Reef, though. They weren't even opened yet."

"And you were hiding behind the shelves?"

I should have known he'd noticed that.

"I wasn't hiding. I was staying out of the way. But that's not what I want to tell you," I said.

"There's more?"

"Today," I said, not paying any attention to his goading, "when I was copying the papers at the library . . ."

"Yeah?"

"I kind of confronted Jason Holiday."

He started laughing.

"It wasn't funny," I said. "I was almost thrown out of there."

"What the heck, Keaton? What did you do?"

"I didn't do anything." I held out my hands. It was like I was pleading for understanding from him. Only I didn't even understand why I'd done it. "He and I just kind of had a whisper-shouting match."

He was still laughing. It made me laugh, too.

"What the heck is whisper-shouting?" He shook his head. "What is that about?"

"I don't know what it's about." I closed my eyes and shook my head. "He made me mad. For some reason I don't understand, him telling Historia that Detective Chow was at the houseboat this morning got my goat."

"Aww, sis"—he wrapped an arm around me and gave me a hug—"I didn't even know you had a goat."

I pushed away. "Neither did I."

We got back to the store and found everything had quieted down. No Sam lurking around. Pete was dusting, a pile of books in the crook of his arm. I could still smell the charcoal, but there was an overlying scent of nicely charred meat.

There was only a little less than two hours before the store closed at seven. I was glad Koby was going to Seattle and we wouldn't be able to get into the storage closet later. I didn't have enough energy to sleuth or snoop tonight. I just wanted to curl up with a cup of hot tea and Roo.

Chapter Thirty-Two

KOBY SHOWED UP at my house Thursday morning way too early. Again. I didn't fuss as much as I had the day before, keeping my roar to a low grumble in anticipation of him cooking breakfast. He didn't disappoint.

We had big, fluffy waffles. I didn't even know I had a waffle iron. Chicken breast—breaded and fried—and he made a hot sauce for dipping and powdered sugar sprinkled overtop. (I definitely didn't have powdered sugar—he made that from scratch.)

"We're not going to do this every day, are we?" I asked.

"You don't like my cooking?"

I stuffed a chunk of waffle in my mouth and let my smacking answer that question.

We left the house and thought ahead about how much food we'd have in the kitchen. The day before had turned out well—we'd sold some of it. But that just made me think Mama Zola would try to cook up even more food.

But my thoughts were soon diverted because Koby had plans on our morning trek to work.

"Let's stop by the marina," he said.

I glanced at my watch. I hadn't noticed that we'd left earlier than we needed to, to get to Books & Biscuits for our ten o'clock opening.

"Why?"

"I want to see what's in Reef's locker."

"You still looking for clues?" I asked.

"Maybe."

When we got to the store, it was locked tight. No sign of Mr. Walker and no sign on the door saying when he'd be back. I cupped my hands to see inside. I thought about that bag of peppermints and wondered if they were still there.

"What time does the store open?" Koby asked.

"I don't have a clue," I said, turning back to him.

He stood for a moment, thinking. "You think Historia had him take the lock off yet?"

"Well, we know he wasn't here yesterday, so he would have had to do it this morning. If he's here." Koby watched me as I pondered. "I do sometimes see him when I walk past here on the way to the bookshop. So he may be here already."

"So, let's go see," he said, stopping me from continuing my assessment.

He started walking around the building to the back.

"We don't have the code to get in the gate," I said.

"I do," he said.

"You do? How did you get it?" I didn't remember seeing it in the folder the lawyer had brought us. Neither did I remember Koby ever looking through the folder.

"How do you know it?"

"I watched him put it in," he said. "Then I remembered it."

"Figures," I mumbled.

Sure enough, he tapped the code in and the metal gate slid open.

"Fourteen. Thirty-one. Seven. Star," he said.

"Star?"

"Some people call it an asterisk."

I chuckled. "Oh, okay."

"The point is, you know the code now, too. Say it so you'll remember it."

"Fourteen. Thirty-one. Seven. Star."

"Now if anything ever happens to me, you'll be able to get in."

"Don't say that."

He pulled open the metal door to the building and let me through first. "Nothing *is* going to happen to me." He gave a comforting smile. "But just in case."

"Moving on," I said. "You remember which one is his?"

"Easy to remember. It's fourteen, just like the first number in the code."

We arrived in front of Reef's storage unit, and there were still two locks on it.

"So nope. Old Man Walker hasn't been here," I said.

"I wonder, did she even tell him?" Koby said, and examined the locks.

"I wouldn't be surprised if she didn't." I watched as he fiddled and yanked at them. "Maybe the one key fits both locks," I offered.

"I don't think so," he said, and pulled the set of keys out of his pocket. "This top one with the long hook is a Yale lock. See." He rubbed his finger along the bottom of it. "This one doesn't have any markings." He picked that lock up, the first one on, and stuck the third key on the ring in it. It popped right open.

"Just try," I said.

He did, but it didn't fit.

"We'll have to come back later," I said.

"Okay," he said. "Probably not today. We've got the memorial tonight."

"I've already been thinking about that," I said.

He chuckled. "Worried about how much food we have."

He knew me well.

We left the storage building. Koby reentered the code,

saying it out loud as he punched in the numbers on the keypad, closing the gate back. He started to go across the crumbling parking lot.

"Let's go this way," I said, and tugged his arm.

"Through the woods?"

"It's just like the one we take when we leave my house. It'll lead us right over to the ravine, and we'll come out in the same place."

"Alright."

As soon as we got into the wooded area, I started smelling gasoline again.

"You smell that?" I asked. "Gasoline again."

"No," he said. "Don't smell a thing." He grinned at me. "You have such a sensitive sense of smell."

"It shouldn't smell like that back here. These are protected lands."

"They are?" Koby looked around. "It's just the woods."

"Green space. Specially designated to stay this way. By law," I said. "So is the area by the ravine."

We walked along the path, which led us to the ravine area. Coming from the way we had, we were already on the right side of it and followed on through the wooded area until we came out the other side. We stepped onto the paved sidewalk and turned onto Eighth. Koby stopped in front of the same house he had the day before.

"I wonder they didn't call me back." He pointed to the FOR RENT sign.

"You called them? I didn't even know you took down the phone number."

"Yeah. Yesterday. I got a voice mail. Some corporation. EP or something like that. Some kind of partnership company, not a person. I left a message."

"Maybe they'll call you back today," I said.

"I hope so. I wanna get Mama Zola situated." He glanced back up at the house. "I like this place."

I hunched my shoulders. "Go knock on the door."

It was clear to see that only one half of the duplex was unoccupied. There was a gray pickup truck in the driveway, which hadn't been there the day before, if I remembered correctly. Meaning, I guessed, that the renter on the other side might be at home. But before Koby could decide to knock to speak to the occupant, the door opened.

Darius Anderson was standing in it.

"Hi, Darius," I said. He was the least suspicious person we'd met so far who had known Reef. He and Maya. I liked her and she had made my brother happy, including him in the memorial at the Hemlock Jazz Club.

"Hi," Darius said, and came down from the porch. "How are you guys?"

"Good, brother," Koby said. "We wanted to let you know about Reef's memorial."

Leave it to Koby to come up with something off the cuff about why we were staking out a house.

"Oh right. Thanks, man." He walked down the driveway toward us. "When is it?"

"Tonight. Around seven thirty at the Hemlock."

"Wow. That was quick. I'm glad you stopped by." Then he frowned up. "How did you know where I lived?"

"We were wondering about the empty unit." Koby pointed to the opposite side of the house from where Darius had come.

"You thinking about renting it?"

"I'm going to live in Reef's houseboat," Koby said. "I wanted to rent it out for my foster mother."

"Oh." Darius nodded thoughtfully.

"We're going to hire her at the restaurant."

"She's a good cook, huh?"

"Best," Koby said. "Taught me everything I know."

"And you're a good cook, too?"

"He is an excellent cook," I said, and rubbed my full belly. "It's how I get people to come into the bookstore. They have to go through it to get to the restaurant."

"My foster mother is cooking for the memorial," Koby

said. "We're having chicken. Ribs. Mac and cheese. You don't want to miss that. And you can, you know, pay your last respects to Reef."

"Sounds good, man," Darius said. "I'll be there. I'll see if my brother is free. I'm sure he'd want to come, too. He and Reef were close."

Koby and I looked at each other.

If you listened to Tessa, Sam was the reason Reef needed a memorial.

"Sure." Koby smiled. "That'll be good." He licked his lips. "So, your brother was telling us that he does the same kind of work that Reef did."

"Yeah. I told you." He narrowed one eye, trying to remember. "Didn't I tell you? They worked together."

"So why were you looking to work with Reef and not your brother?"

"My brother isn't as easy to get along with, and people don't call him back like they did Reef. Reef was good at what he did."

"Are you saying that your brother isn't good?" I asked.

"Naw"—he chuckled—"I'm not saying that. He does okay work. Good work." He scratched his head. "Reef was just more reliable. You know, he had more steady work. My brother is the one who told me to go and see Reef for work."

"He did?" Koby said, and smiled. I knew it wasn't genuine.

"Yeah. Just that morning I came by. I guess he hadn't known yet what had happened to him."

"Yep. He must not have known yet." Koby was warming him up for more questions. I checked my watch. "Are you going to work with your brother now?"

"I don't know. I might just pick up a couple of gigs later on with him."

"You guys get along?"

"He ain't the easiest person to work with." He gave an embarrassed chuckle. "Not trying to drop any family drama on you or anything."

"No, I understand." Koby winked at me. "My sister and I had to do a lot of talking before we went into a business together. And we had just met. It was a huge decision."

"Right. Family aren't always the ones to work with." He wagged his head back and forth like he was weighing the idea. "I might eventually, you know," Darius said. "I just can't now."

Koby nodded like he understood. "We're trying to get his tools out of Reef's storage now."

"Tools?"

"Equipment," Koby said.

Darius seemed confused.

Koby let him stay that way.

"So back to seeing about renting this place. You got the landlord's number?"

"Oh. You don't want to rent from this lady."

"No?"

"She's a terrible landlord. Doesn't take care of the property. Won't get things fixed. I'm trying to move out."

I could see Mrs. Grayson pointing her shears at me, telling me, *I told you so*. She was all about not letting the slum landlords ruin our town.

"Oh yeah, I don't want any trouble."

"You might have some, though. The lady who owns this place is the same one who owns the marina."

"Historia Krol?" I asked.

"Yeah. And she doesn't care when you complain about what needs to be done. All she wants is the rent money."

"Yeah," Koby said. "I've already found that out about her."

"There's another place right down the street." He went to the curb and pointed. "That little bungalow. The white one with the yellow shutters."

Koby stood next to Darius and shielded the sun from his eyes with his hand.

"Looks nice."

"It is. Matter of fact, I think Reef may have done some

work on that house. Not sure. I'd have to ask Sam. Anyway. It's all on one floor, which would be good if she's an older lady."

"I think that would be perfect for her," Koby said.

"Okay. Well, I know the guy who owns it. I can tell him about you, if you want."

"That'll be good," Koby said. "I'd appreciate that."

"Sure, no problem." Darius cleared his throat. "How about if I get you the info tonight when I see you at the memorial?"

"Cool," Koby said. "I'll see you tonight."

THE MORNING AT Books & Biscuits was slow. It seemed like what drew customers in was free stuff, like the first day we'd opened, or the wafts of Mama Zola's and Koby's food going up the noses of passersby when they were cooking outside. By midmorning, not one person had come through the door.

I was definitely going to have to do something more about marketing. And I thought, as Pete and I shelved books that had come through the mail, something about Sam Anderson, too.

He was back again that morning. Standing around outside the door. Loitering, like he was up to something. If he had something to say to us, why didn't he just come in and say it? He had the first day. Did he think we'd move a little faster in getting him his stuff just because we were seeing his face all the time? Or did he think my brother was going to do something with his stuff?

That upset me. Then I stopped to take an accounting of myself. I stood up straight and got real still. I was feeling the same way I'd felt the day before when I accosted Jason Holiday, at his job, no less. That should have given me pause. But it didn't.

Was it because I was bored? I had nothing to do and I was

letting out-of-the-way thoughts fill my head? Or maybe upset
that we didn't have any customers? All of that didn't seem to
matter.

Even my mother in my ear saying to channel whatever it
was I was feeling into something constructive didn't help.

And even as I pushed around the counter, I realized how
much this was not like me.

I wondered what my mother would say about my recent
aggressive behavior. Did it stem from me being under suspicion for murder?

"Hello," I said, sticking my head out of the door. Not waiting for an answer, I told him what I had on my mind. "You
can stop hanging around here. We see you. And we should
be able to get into Reef's storage sometime today. You can
get your stuff then and stop coming around here bothering
us." I punctuated my word to let him know I wasn't putting
up with his shenanigans. I didn't wait around for a response.
I pulled my head back inside. And even with just an unlocked
door between us, I wasn't worried about him coming in and
trying anything.

(Something else I probably needed to speak to my mother
about, this newfound bravery.)

I did wonder, though, how I was going to back up all that
bold talk if he did decide to come and confront me.

I retreated back behind the counter.

I needed to find something to do.

Tessa said he was a killer. Sam thoughts still filling my
head as I sat down. I crossed my hands and set them on the
counter in front of me. Even his brother didn't want to work
with him.

I looked through the window. He was gone. Well, that
worked. I blew out a breath.

I wondered what exactly was in that storage unit that he
wanted to get his hands on so bad that he had taken to standing around outside our door.

I tried to take my mind off Sam by keeping busy around

the store. But without customers, there wasn't much to do. Maybe Koby and I could go back over to the marina to see if Old Man Walker had gotten in yet. Get into that storage.

Pete could keep an eye on things. I looked around the empty store. Heck, Remy could keep an eye on it. And with Pete helping, things got done twice as fast. And with him following behind me redoing the things I did, everything was done twice.

Pete finally wandered out back to say hello to Remy. He'd kind of turned into the guard dog, I guess. I wondered if Koby would still bring him to work when he officially moved into the boat.

And with that thought, I pulled out my phone and Googled property titles.

Attorney Brian Jenkins had said that was the problem with Reef acquiring the boat without getting his legal expertise. And I had seen Izzy's name on the paperwork. I wanted to understand what all of that meant.

I found a site: 10 Common Title Problems.

Hopefully, it would help me understand what it meant and if it gave anyone a motive to kill Reef.

I clicked on it and read it through.

It seemed that the title was the record of all the people who had ever owned a piece of property. Recorded at the county, it could go back hundreds of years. The title on Reef's houseboat went back thirteen years.

The website listed ways that a title might not have been handled properly. Some wouldn't matter on a houseboat, but some did. Like liens not being paid and so someone is owed money if the property was sold. Or people illegally obtaining a property and not being able to pass good title—by forgery or a legal heir not getting it. In that case, the rightful owner could come and take it even if you paid good money for it and didn't know about the earlier theft.

Then I looked up to see what a quiet title action was. I found it was a lawsuit to "quiet" any challenges that may come up from a title dispute—someone coming later saying they have a legal right to the property. If they hadn't answered the lawsuit, then they lost the right to claim the property later.

Well, that was good to know that no one could take the houseboat from Koby. But had Izzy really owned the boat at one point? I remembered her name hadn't been the one right before Reef's, so that meant he hadn't bought it from her, but somehow, she had been in the mix.

I had to find out why, only on this one, even though he'd complain. I didn't want Koby to know. He'd feel bad if Reef was killed over the boat he'd bought for him.

I needed to talk to Izzy.

I thought about the memorial. It was happening tonight. Maybe she'd be there.

Then thinking about the memorial made me hungry. I could smell our contribution to the event wafting over from the kitchen. Maybe I'd grab some lunch, and Koby and I would go back to the marina afterward.

I put down my phone and followed my nose.

We'd certainly done our part in helping with the memorial, even though I had not cooked one morsel of food. And I knew we had cooked more than enough.

Koby had invited people that he and Reef had grown up with, but that didn't stop me from worrying about all that food they had cooked up in our little kitchen. Koby and Mama Zola had cooked enough food to feed the entire city of Timber Lake. I didn't want any of it to go to waste. I'd even called my mother, inviting her to come, as if one more mouth would make a difference.

And it showed. When I got over to the Biscuits side, I found Mama Zola sitting out in the empty restaurant at one of the tables with her feet up in a chair. Georgie was staring out of a window.

"You okay?" I asked.

"Just catching my breath," she said.

"Mama Zola, you are doing too much."

"I'm done now," she said, and swiped a napkin across her forehead to get rid of the sweat.

"Maybe I should help Koby in the kitchen," I said. I glanced back over to my side of the store and could see Pete had come back inside and was keeping himself busy straightening the already neat stacks of books. He'd done a good job while I played hooky the day before, I knew he'd be okay.

"He's got help," Mama Zola said as I started for the kitchen.

"He does?" Georgie was still behind the counter. She had taken to filing her nails with an emery board. I thought, *She could at least be reading a book, that would be good advertising.* But, as it was, no one was in the store anyway. "Who?"

But before she could answer, I heard giggling and knew immediately who it was.

Izzy.

Speak of the devil.

What was she doing hanging around? What in the world was she up to? First claiming she was Reef's girl, then chasing after Koby. (Or was it the other way around?) Now I find out she had her hand in some misdealing around the boat. Even though I was clearer on what had happened with the boat title, I wasn't sure what it meant as it pertained to her or if any of it tied into Reef's death.

I was going to have to watch her.

Chapter Thirty-Three

AN ENTIRE MIGRATION of butterflies took flight in my stomach when Avery Moran walked through the door of Books & Biscuits.

The last time he was there, he'd given the news that Detective Chow was gunning for us. Koby took that as a cue to ratchet up our investigation into Reef's death and try to figure out what happened and who did it.

I didn't mind doing the investigation. Even confronting Tessa hadn't been bad. But leaving it up to the good detective to solve by giving him the information we'd found was good enough for me.

But with Moran visiting again, I wasn't sure we'd be able to do anything. Maybe he was coming to tell us that Detective Chow had decided to arrest us.

"He doesn't have anything on you," Moran said when I voiced what my gut was telling me might happen. "On either one of you."

I'd come around the corner of the counter on the Books

side and led him to the Biscuits side to find Koby as soon as he'd walked through the door.

We had a few customers at the tables and Koby didn't want to talk in the restaurant. We stood next to the back door of the kitchen.

"Did you get the information?" Koby asked.

"Information?" I was sure my face showed my confusion. "What information?"

"Koby asked me to look and see what I could find out about some people who might actually be involved in Reef's death."

I narrowed my eyes. "You didn't tell me."

I couldn't believe it. Wasn't he the one always chiding me about not sharing information?

"I don't know anything you don't know," he said. "Capt'n Hook is telling us now."

"You know that's not what I meant," I said.

"You know how Reef was killed, right?"

"Yeah," Koby said. "Chow told us."

"Cyanide," I added.

"Right. And guess what Jason Holiday's family business is?"

"Producing cyanide," I said. It was the only thing I could think of.

"No." Moran chuckled. "They're jewelers."

I nodded thoughtfully, then it hit me. "Oh! Potassium cyanide is used in electroplating."

"And for cleaning jewelry," he said.

"Oh, then he could've gotten it easily," I said. "Brushed it onto some peppermints, went into the houseboat and left them for Reef."

"Only we didn't see any peppermints in Reef's house," Koby said.

"Because he had them in his pocket," I said.

Koby had his arm crossed over his torso, his legs spread

apart, and I could tell by his face, he was thinking. "What else did you find out?"

"The Holidays are loaded," Moran said.

I frowned. "Then why is he working as a page at the library? They pay like minimum wage."

"I don't know," Moran said. "But the Holidays have money. Probably no reason for him to work at all."

"Interesting," Koby said.

He was being so calm. My head was buzzing like it was a beehive.

"And the girl," Moran continued. "That name doesn't come up for her."

"I thought it might be fake."

"The only instance I found of that name was for a girl who died five years ago."

"Who?" I said. They were having a conversation all around me.

"Tessa," Koby said, answering me, then turned to Moran. "Any missing persons matching her description?"

"A couple of maybes," Moran said. "And on that one, you'd better be glad I'm retired. You know I'd have to follow up on it. Probably haul her in and put in a call to her parents."

"She's got a birthday coming up, remember."

"So she says," Moran said. "Looking at the birthdates for the ones that came up, she may still have a year or two before she's legal."

"What about those Anderson brothers?" Koby asked. He didn't seem to have anything else to say about Tessa. I still had lots of questions.

They were moving along and I thought, *Wow, Koby had been thorough*. I smiled at Moran. Must be nice to have an ex–law enforcement officer on your side. And a good one. He didn't have anything written down. He was doing it all from memory.

"Couldn't find anything on the youngest one."

"Darius," Koby confirmed.

"Right. Samuel Anderson did come up, though. About the same age as you. Lived in Seattle and, from what I could tell, moved here around the same time as Reef. Now, unlike his brother, he has had a few run-ins. Nothing enough for anything more than a night in jail. Traffic tickets, disorderly conduct. He had one misdemeanor theft that was dismissed, and he had a juvie record that was sealed."

"You couldn't get in it?" Koby asked.

"Could have"—Moran nodded—"but I would have had to call in a favor." He put a hand on Koby's shoulder. "Thought I'd better hold on to those in case I need to save your behind. On the chance you can't get yourself out of this."

"Thanks," Koby said. They both seemed to find that funny—there was a look of amusement on their faces. It made me wonder how many things my brother had had to get himself out of in the years before he found me.

"Okay. Give me the last one," Koby said.

"Now that one seems to be fond of getting herself all tangled up."

"Who?" I asked.

"Isabella Ramirez," Moran said.

And I thought, *Don't I know it.*

Chapter Thirty-Four

I HAD HEARD that it was a thing for girls, on a night out, to go to the bathroom together. I hadn't ever had the opportunity to know if that was true. Not until the night of Reef's memorial.

We'd gotten to the Hemlock Jazz Club, name taken after our state tree, and it looked just how I'd pictured it.

The club was located on the other side of the marina. Past it, as I had told Koby, was a beach area, but beyond was another boardwalk and a couple of bars and restaurants—nothing fancy, but our representation of nightlife in Timber Lake—and the Hemlock.

It had outside seating on the patio, where there were steps that led down to the beach. Although I didn't really have to use my imagination, thanks to the pictures in Reef's phone, I did have an idea. (Unlike the plant, the tree wasn't poisonous, but what a coincidence that Reef had made that place a fixture in his life. A place named after a poison.)

Inside, there was one big room. In the front was an elevated platform for a band, on an adjacent wall a bar that ran nearly the entire length of it. Lights gave the place a smoky atmosphere—not from cigarettes, they, of course, were not allowed—they were dim, hung low, they were sparse and cast a cloudy glow.

Wasn't long after we came in the door, we hadn't even had the time to set out Reef's picture, that people started spilling in, coming to pay their respects to Reef. Nothing was set up. The bar hadn't even opened yet.

Koby and Mama Zola had to mingle—couldn't ignore the guests, seeing they couldn't yet get food or drinks. Mama Zola seemed to know everyone my brother did, which seemed liked everybody. That left me to do the food and, for the most part, the memorial table. Mama Zola did come by a few times to rearrange something and put her touch on it.

Thankfully, Maya had gotten there even before we had and, without hesitation, helped out. She met us at the door and grabbed trays of food, took one end of the six-foot banquet tables we rented, carried them in and got them adorned with tablecloths and chafing dishes.

Just as I'd feared, Mama Zola had cooked the whole two days, in between cooking at our restaurant. When it came to preparing food, she was a whiz. No wonder Koby was such a good cook. But it made Maya laugh.

"How many people do you guys think we're feeding?" she'd asked when we brought the last bag in.

I threw up my hands. "They don't let me in the kitchen," I said.

"For good reason," Mama Zola said.

Maya chuckled. "Look at Mama Zola throwing shade."

"She just means there'd be too many cooks in our small kitchen," Koby said.

It was nice for my brother to take up for me, but I couldn't cook—no need having my feelings hurt about that.

There was roasted chicken, fried chicken, baked butter crumb cod and barbecued ribs. (I was surprised there were any left. I thought we'd sold out of them the day before.)

Green beans with white potatoes, collard greens with ham hocks, fried corn, macaroni and cheese, sliced onions and tomatoes, pinto beans and corn bread. My mouth started watering just thinking about it. Koby said it was a holiday meal. I didn't ever remember having that much food at once at any time in my life.

And don't get me started on the dessert—peach cobbler, banana pudding, a 7 Up and red velvet cake and a sweet potato pie. I could feel my blood glucose going up as I got them all onto the table and cut them into slices.

Once we got the buffet set up, Maya and I took one of the square tables scattered in the club and pulled it to the side. We spread a black tablecloth over it and set in the center of it a picture we'd blown up and framed of Reef that Mama Zola had.

When Izzy came through the door, Maya had just come back from getting flowers for the table. She and I had talked and laughed the entire time. It was, so I thought, what having a girlfriend must be like. But Izzy's presence changed Maya's whole demeanor.

She came in grinning, belly shirt, capri pants and sandals— a bit scant for the cooler spring evening. But the way she slithered up to my brother, it was clear all she wanted to keep her warm was him.

"Ugh!" Maya had no shame in letting her feelings be known. "Are they dating?" she leaned in to ask. The music had started playing, and with the crowd growing, we couldn't speak normally any longer.

I hunched my shoulders. "I don't know. I don't think so."

"I thought you two were close."

"We are. But he's giving me mixed messages about her."

"Like what?"

"He says she might not always tell the truth."

Maya's mouth dropped open, but before a word came from her mouth, Koby and Izzy came over.

"Keaton, you guys nearly finished setting up?" Koby asked.

"Yep," I said, and looked around. We had unwrapped all the food and set out the plates, forks and napkins.

"Okay," Koby said. "I'm going to say a few words, and then we'll let them know the food is ready."

"I want to say something, too," Izzy said.

I couldn't help but feel the glare shooting from Maya's eyes.

"I have to go the restroom," Maya said, a sickly sweet smile on her face. "Koby, can you hold on a minute until you get started?"

"Sure," Koby said. "Can't start without you. Plus, we're still waiting on the bartender to get here."

"He'll be here." Maya flashed a smile. "Keaton." She grabbed me by my wrist and pulled. "Come go with me."

I raised my eyebrows in question, but before I could lower them again, she was dragging me along, and I came stumbling behind her.

"What did he say about her?" Maya asked.

Picking right back up on our conversation, I wasn't sure what her expression was. Jealousy? Hate? And I didn't know what to say. I couldn't very well say that in our discussion of who may have murdered Reef, we had discussed her as a suspect.

Should I include Maya as a suspect? Because the grip she still had on my wrist was disturbing.

"Uhm . . ."

"She is a liar," Maya said. Her face wasn't as tight, but I still didn't have a clue as to what was going on with her—or her feelings. "She wasn't dating Reef, if that's what she said."

"She did say that," I said. Then I was the one getting jittery. Was she next going to tell me that *she* was the one dating Reef?

"I warned him not to go there."

"Go where?" Maya seemed pretty angry at Reef.

"Entertain her thoughts about the two of them as a thing." She snorted. "Because they weren't. And now look at her. All over your brother and talking about she wants to say something."

"You don't want her to speak?"

"We don't need all of her phoniness," she said. She crossed her arms and huffed. "This is to honor Reef, not to put a spotlight on her. She always wants to be the center of attention. She is a typical Leo."

I wouldn't have guessed Maya could get so angry. Or that she was into zodiac signs.

"Reef did not like her." She punctuated each word with *umph*. "She isn't anything but trouble. I should have stopped *her*."

"Stopped her?" I asked. And then wondered, stopped Izzy as opposed to whom? I wasn't sure if I wanted to hear the answer to that. I backed up closer to the door in case I needed to make a run for it.

So much for finally having a girlfriend to hang out with.

She must have seen my reaction because she calmed down. Her face relaxed and her eyes softened. "Reef liked you."

That made me smile.

"But Izzy went around telling people she was going out with him because she helped him with that boat."

"Helped with the boat?" I asked. How did that make sense?

"He'd been trying to find one for Koby. A gift for his brother." She smiled at the memory. "That's how he put it. And she said she knew about one for sale."

"Reef told you all of that?"

"Yeah." I could see her blush. "We'd gotten to be close." She frowned. "Close friends." She seemed to want to emphasize that point to me. "He told me about you, too. Said he had to be careful. Take it slow, you know, because he didn't want Koby being upset about it."

That made me sad. Happy, but sad, too. I was hoping no tears would come. I'd never had a boyfriend before. Yes. I know. Midtwenties and never dated. I was shy, into my books and hanging with my dad. Nope. No men in my life other than my father and then Koby. Being with Reef would have been something I would have liked. I was sure of that. After meeting my brother, I'd become less of an introvert and, it seemed, no longer wanted to be a loner.

"But she messed up."

"Huh?" I was only half paying attention. Didn't she know she couldn't tell me about how Reef felt and then keep talking about something else?

"Izzy," she explained. "Getting that boat gave Reef so much trouble. At first, he was super happy. It was the right price. The right size. But then the title was all messed up." She shook her head in disgust. She turned toward the door, pointed to it like she could see through it. "And Izzy was to blame. She had to know. She's to blame for what happened to Reef."

"Wait!" I said, and held up a hand. I swiped a tear from my cheek with the other one. I hadn't been able to keep it from falling. "You think Izzy had something to do with his murder?"

Her head jerked like a switch had just flipped inside. "Murder?" She groaned. I could see her chest moving up and down, her eyes fixed and glossed over. "That's the question you should be asking yourself," she said. "The question that should make your brother really cautious."

I stared at her. Was she trying to deflect some guilt she was feeling onto someone else? Was she doing a Tessa? But why? Maya hadn't even come into my mind as a suspect. Why would she point a finger at someone else unless there was something she was trying to hide? Someone I already thought suspicious. But Maya wouldn't have known that.

Or was I just thinking like Koby? Maybe she was, like we were, trying to figure out who had killed Reef.

"We'd better get back," Maya said, opening the restroom door. "I want to be out there in case I need to stop Izzy from killing Reef again."

Chapter Thirty-Five

WHEN I CAME out of the bathroom, Koby was on the stage talking to a couple of people setting up instruments. Maya went up there with them. I slid onto a barstool to wait until Koby let me know what he needed me to do next.

The place was starting to fill up. A lot of people cared about Reef, which warmed my heart. People were mingling around, and there was music coming from a DJ set up in one of the corners of the bar. There was going to be a lot of music going on.

I saw a couple people with drinks in their hands and figured the bar was open. I swung around on my stool to get some nonalcoholic drink to nurse while I waited for everything to get started.

The first thing I saw on top of the bar was a bowl of peppermints.

My heart took off like a jackhammer in my chest.

What the hey . . .

I didn't know who else knew exactly how Reef had died. But this sight gave me more than pause.

"Oh my goodness!" I choked out the words. It was all I could manage, my breath caught in the back of my throat.

Turning my back on the peppermints, I let my eyes wander around the room, trying to see if anyone else was looking at them, and that was when I nearly fell off the barstool backward.

"Crap!"

It was Detective Chow.

What if he thought I had brought them here? That I put them on the bar? Like I was getting rid of evidence.

But why would I put them there? I was trying to think this through before I hyperventilated and passed out. He wouldn't think that, I reasoned. But the rest of me wasn't going with that thinking. I felt guilty. I felt like I needed to hide them.

Geesh! Why was I feeling guilty?

Who knew? Who cared? I'd discuss those feelings with my mother later. For right now, I swiped the bowl from the countertop. Then I picked up my shoulder bag and started to dump the peppermints into my purse.

No, my crazy, guilt-ridden conscious screamed at me. *That would be crazy!*

What if they were laced with cyanide, and now I was carrying them around? In my purse!

I decided I would flush them down the toilet, but thought, if they had been poisoned, I'd be putting cyanide in the water. I might kill someone. Then I really would be a murderer. (Not sure why I thought that since I had nothing to do with them in the first place—another conversation for my mother.)

Holding them in my hand, I gulped in some air to try to calm myself, steady my hand (it was shaking uncontrollably) and clear my head. This was not supposed to be a stressful event.

That was when I noticed who was behind the bar.

Sam Anderson.

Oh Lord.

Had he put them there?

I didn't have to think about that. I ducked out of his sight, used my purse to shield sight of the bowl and stood up. Before I retreated from the bar, I quickly scanned the top of it to make sure there weren't any other bowls and went to get my brother.

With the tight knot in my stomach that had expanded into my chest and throat, I could only hope that I'd have enough air to breathe long enough to make it to him. I could just see myself falling out in the middle of the floor, needing CPR. And the evidence needed to convict me of Reef's death sprawled out right next to me.

"Look at this," I said, leaning into Koby. I could hardly get my words out.

"Where'd you get those?"

"Bar." I pointed back toward it. "Bowls of nuts, popcorn and"—I thrust the bowl into him—"peppermints." I gulped in more air. "Do people really put peppermints on a bar?"

"I think we're the only ones who know how Reef was killed," he said, raking his hand through the bowl of candy.

"And the killer," I reminded him. "They know."

Koby looked around the room. "You think they're here?"

"I don't know." I sidled up next to him. "But one other person knows, too, and he's here."

"Who?"

I jerked my head toward him. "Four o'clock."

Koby followed my direction.

His eyes widened. "Chow."

"Chow," I confirmed. "And Sam is the bartender."

"Yeah, I know that." Koby moved to stand between me and the bowl of peppermints.

I appreciated him shielding me, but he didn't seem to get what that meant. At least what it meant to me. So I shook the bowl, rustling the candy around. "Sam *is* here," I said again, then stretched my eyes so he could get my drift. "Remember what Tessa said."

"I don't know." Koby shook his head. "I don't know that

he'd put a bowl of poisoned candy right on the bar where he's working."

Out the corner of my eye, I saw Chow go on the move. "Oh my goodness! Can you just get rid of these?" I said. "I don't know what to do with them, and Chow is going to put me in jail if he sees this." My whole body was shaking.

Koby put a hand on my shoulder and his eyes met mine. It seemed he was using them to try and hypnotize me to keep me calm. "Throw them away," he said slowly and softly.

"Where?" I sputtered the word out louder than I intended.

"Come on," he said, finally understanding that, clearly, I couldn't do anything on my own. As we passed the tables, he grabbed a plastic bag from where we'd brought the food in and led me out back. "Here." He held the bag open. "Dump them in here."

I did and he tied up the bag with the handles, then double-tied it and tossed it over in the garbage dumpsters lined up by the door.

"Good?" he asked.

"Good." I nodded. Just knowing they were gone was returning my adrenaline secretions to normal levels.

"Before we go back in, guess what I found out?" he said.

"Who killed Reef so I can stop being scared of a bowl of candy?"

He chuckled at that. "No." He looked behind him as if he didn't want to be overheard. "I found out that Tessa would come here and sing sometimes with the little group Reef played with. She's supposed to be here tonight."

"I thought about those pictures on Reef's phone," I admitted, "and wondered how she was able to get into the bar after we learned she was probably a juvenile."

"That's nothing," he said. "Fake ID. Like the one that I had." He answered that without thinking about it. That was not a common occurrence in the world I grew up in. "We know Tessa," he continued, "is not her real name. Heck, Reef might have even helped her get it."

I nodded.

"What it made me think about was how unaffected she seemed when we found Reef. She didn't cry or scream." He turned and looked at me. "Did she scream?"

I hunched my shoulders. "I don't think so." I pressed my lips together and tried to remember. Nothing. "Not sure, Koby. I was so busy screaming myself. But I really don't remember anyone having any kind of emotional reaction. Not the kind that showed they knew Reef and were sad he was lying there like that."

"And, what? If they did know him, they weren't surprised?" he said.

"Yep." I nodded. "That's what I mean."

"I didn't notice that either," he said. "But that could also be said about us."

"I just said I screamed."

"Anyone would if they came up on a dead body. But the rest of the time, while they packed him up, hauled him out and we waited to be questioned, we sat there mostly quiet, unaffected with no grief evident."

I thought about that. It was true. We hadn't been beside ourselves with any angst over the situation. No boohooing, and I was known for that.

"My mother would say everyone deals with grief differently," I said.

"Good," Koby said, a smirk on his face. "We'll have her testify on the witness stand for us at our trial for murder."

"Not funny," I said.

"But that flies in the face of us judging the reaction of the people on the train."

"No, it doesn't," I said, not agreeing with his logic. "We may have reacted differently than others think we should have, but we know we didn't kill him."

"Okay, sis, if you say so." He patted my arm. "The same goes for Tessa and Jason, if that's your reasoning. If they were the killers, they wouldn't have reacted either. Not only because they knew he was dead, but they would also be too concerned with covering it up to get emotional."

"Do you think they gave the detective the wrong address?" My question was kind of off topic, but it still was about Koby's new neighbors. "I mean, why isn't he stopping on their boat to talk?"

"We already talked about that. Remember? He may have talked to them. But if he hád, I'm sure she would have deflected his accusations against her onto Sam."

"Right. Because she said Sam killed him."

"Do you believe that?" I asked.

"I don't have enough information to know for sure who did it."

"But from what you know, do you think he could have?"

"I only know they argued. People kill for that. But then again, people will kill on little or nothing. Even a perceived wrong, if it upsets them enough."

I rubbed my fingers across my forehead. "But then if Tessa really thinks Sam is the killer and doesn't want to be around him, why is she coming tonight?"

"*If* she comes," he said. "I said she's supposed to be here."

"Maybe she doesn't know Sam will be here," I suggested.

"He's the bartender. She would know he'd be here," Koby said. "And get this: Reef got him the job."

Koby was amazing. He was able to find out so much about these people. How did he do it? Here I was following them around, accosting them in libraries and on the sidewalk in front of our store, and I had nothing.

"Reef is nice enough—enough of a friend to help Sam get a job but locks up his tools in his storage?" I said, after me being in awe of my brother had waned somewhat. "How does that make sense? Was Reef trying to stop Sam from getting his own tools? Why? Maybe the things that were in there weren't even Sam's."

"Or maybe that was what the argument was about."

Chapter Thirty-Six

AS KOBY REACHED the handle to the back door, it swung open.

"I thought you two were the hosts."

It was Daniel Chow. Homicide detective.

I almost peed on myself.

Koby acted as if he'd invited him.

"Thanks for coming, Detective Chow," he said.

"What are you doing back here?" he asked, and pivoted from his hip, taking in the area.

"Keaton isn't handling Reef's death too well."

That was true. I'd been acting like a different person as of late.

"Her father died not too long ago, too. It's hard to lose people you love."

"Sorry for your loss, Miss Rutledge," he said.

I didn't know if I could speak, but I figured I needed to try. "Thank you."

"Why are you here?" Koby asked.

"A few people I want to keep an eye on," he said.

"Try not to cause any trouble during the memorial," Koby said.

The detective thought that was funny.

"I'm going to the restroom," I told Koby as we went back inside. I did have to go, but I wasn't sure if my legs could hold me up. They were shaking so bad.

"Steer clear of the detective," Koby said, whispering in my ear from behind me. "Your face back there looked like we'd just buried a body. He'll be suspicious of us for sure."

God, I hope there weren't any dead bodies in that dumpster, was all I could think of.

It didn't matter, I figured. Those innocuous-looking peppermints might just be enough to incriminate me.

I sat there on the toilet for as long as I could, taking deep breaths and trying to talk myself into not being nervous because the detective was there.

You haven't done anything, Keaton.

But even though I knew that was true, I found it quite nerve-racking to have someone "gunning for" me, as Koby had put it. It's makes you feel guilty regardless.

Eventually, I thought that Koby wouldn't want to start the memorial, for whatever that consisted of, without me present.

I left the stall and, standing at the sink, ran warm water and splashed it over my face. I didn't want to use cold water, because I needed some comfort.

I wished my mother would come. I'd definitely get a hug from her. Hugs are always a good thing and can give anyone courage. Especially one from their mother.

Instead, I got Historia Krol.

Yep. While I was standing there, staring at myself in the mirror, trying to look less like "I've been up to something," I saw her come out from the other stall.

She had on a business suit, this one navy. Heels, but smaller than the ones she'd worn that first day we'd seen her in the parking lot.

"Hello," I said. I thought that was only polite. Plus, I didn't want to make anything harder for my brother.

She didn't say a word. She leaned in closer. Wiped a pinky at each edge of her lips, fixing the lipstick she had on that was the same color as her hair. She gave it a few fluffs and walked out.

"Well," I said out loud. "That was rude."

"What was?"

I looked up to see my mother.

"I'm so glad you're here," I said, wrapping my arms around her and squeezing tight. "I think I'm having some kind of mental breakdown."

WE HAD TO serve the food, even though it was being placed out as a buffet. Because, as Mama Zola explained, when you let people get their own food, they don't seem to remember there're others in line behind them who have to eat, too. *They pile up their plates like they got twelve kids at home to feed*, was how she put it.

The "we" included my mother, Mama Zola and me. But the "me" part came only after many assurances to my mother that I was okay. She finally said okay, but if she knew anything about my recent outbreaks or that I was a murder suspect, she probably would have had me admitted for a three-day evaluation.

Koby had decided that we'd let everyone get their plates, then while they were eating, the band would play, and then people could come on the stage and give their reflections on Reef.

That's how I ended up at the end of the table dipping up candied yams and string beans with potatoes. The last two chafing dishes on the two long tables. Even though I'd never done it before, I did most of my job with a smile plastered across my face and a genuine "Thank you for coming" as each person came through the line. Until *he* came and stood across from me.

"You!" I spat my whisper across the foil pans I was serving from, leaning in close enough for him to hear me over the music and noise.

He narrowed his eyes at me and leaned in to meet me. "Are we doing this whispering thing again?" He had a smirk on his face.

It was Jason Holiday. I don't know why I had such animosity for this man, but I did. He was standing in front of me with two plates.

"What are you doing here?" I hissed out.

"Aren't you supposed to be serving food? Not asking personal questions." He pushed one plate toward me.

"Hey, bae, are you coming?" A woman walked up to him and spoke. She had a phone in her hand and a dress that was a little too tight around her middle. When I pulled my eyes off him to look at her, I almost fell face-first into the string beans.

"Isn't that Aubriol Meijer?" I asked him, continuing with my strained whisper.

"I'm just trying to get the rest of the food. Last thing," he said, and smiled at the girl next to him. "I'm coming."

"What are you doing here with Aubriol?" I asked as soon as he turned back.

"That's none of your business." His smile fell from his face, and his whispers were starting to get louder, just as they'd done in the library. "Just give me my food."

Oh my goodness. Where was Detective Chow when I needed him? I tried to look through the crowd for him. Was he seeing this?

All this stuff going on. I knew Koby wouldn't want me to tell Chow anything, but this had to be told. All these people from the train the day Reef died knowing each other. There had to be some connection.

It really was turning out just like *Murder on the Orient Express*. Nearly everyone from that day was here: Aubriol, Jason, Chow, Tessa was supposed to be coming, and then Koby and me. Were they all involved somehow? I was finding out that we all knew Reef. Heck, all that was needed was for the Pussetts to walk in. I glanced toward the door. It didn't swing open, but I spotted Izzy near it.

And yes. I'd like to introduce Detective Chow to Izzy. Something was up with Izzy, too. I was sure of that. Maybe he could find out what. Maybe then he'd have someone other than me and Koby to accuse. But what was in front of me right now was more pressing.

"Why didn't you say you knew Tessa?" I leaned in to make sure my surly tone came across with my whisper. I wanted him to know I was onto him.

"Say what to who? When? When was I supposed to tell somebody?"

"She was on that train."

"I know."

He was making me so mad.

"Aren't you with Historia?"

"What?" he choked out, his face stiff. I thought he might be having some cardiovascular accident.

But I was on a roll.

"Did you kill Reef?" I whispered—angrily.

"What? No! Crazy lady." He looked down the row at my mother, then past her at Mama Zola, like he was looking for help.

"Who helped you do it?" I turned his attention back to me. "Was it you and Tessa? You and Aubriol? All three of you?"

"Like I said yesterday." He leaned across the pan of food to be right in my face. "You. Are. Bonkers."

"Come on, Jason. All the tables will be full." Aubriol was tugging on his arm. Then she looked up, I guess for the first time, at me. "Oh, hi." She squinted at me. "Don't I know you?"

"Hi," I said, using my regular voice. She didn't get a smile from me like everyone else had, but boy was I going to have some questions for her. I needed all the information I could get before I made *the* call.

I'd decided, against the wishes of my brother I was sure, to tell Detective Chow everything I knew. It might be the only way to keep my sanity. This whole thing was so stressful.

Chapter Thirty-Seven

THE ROOM HAD been abuzz with noise before everyone got their plates of food. But not after.

"You hear that?" Mama Zola said.

Koby, my mother and I looked up from our food.

"What?" my mother said.

"You could hear a pin drop in here," she said, a grin on her face. "That means the food is good."

We all laughed. "Better than good, Mama," Koby said.

"Even the band can't play," I said. "The DJ had to put on another record."

"They too busy lickin' their fingers," Mama Zola said, laughing. She was really proud of herself.

She should be, I thought. She had been cooking for two days. But I shouldn't have worried. I didn't think there'd be any left. I saw people going back to get more.

Good. Less food for us to have to pack up when it was time to go home.

The band didn't play long once they started. They finished eating and were just getting started when Koby went onstage to introduce himself and thank everyone for coming. He got a round of applause when he asked if they had enjoyed the food and then told them who cooked it.

"Stand up, Zola Jackson!"

She popped out of her chair, waved at the crowd and took a bow. You'd think she was the star at a celebrity dinner in Hollywood.

"And she will be cooking, alongside me, on the restaurant side of the new Books & Biscuits on the corner of Second and Park. I'm running it with my former librarian twin sister, Keaton." He pointed to me and I waved my hand. Mama Zola tried to get me to imitate her and take a bow. I didn't.

"Make sure you stop by," Koby said. "Give our bookshop and café some love."

That got another round of applause.

"Now we are going to have whoever wants to, to come up and say a few words about Reef. Please keep your remarks to under two minutes." Koby held up his phone. "And I will be timing you."

That got a laugh from all.

"I'll go first," he said. I could see him swallow, and I knew speaking about his lifelong friend was going to be hard.

"Reef was my brother. Not *from another mother* as people like to say. Group homes and foster homes, the people in them, were the only mothers we knew, so that made us family. He took care of me, helped me navigate the system that kids like us got lost in. And he gave me my sister." Koby looked over at me and smiled. "He didn't deserve to go like he did. He deserved the best in everything, because he was the best. I love you, man"—Koby looked up—"and I'll see you on the other side."

Koby swiped the tears that had started streaming down his face. He came down from the stage and sat at the table with us and let the tributes run themselves. People stood behind one another to wait their turn, the line snaking around the entire place.

A few people came up to speak. Darius. Tessa, who seemed to have appeared just in time to go up onstage, then disappeared again.

"I may have not always admitted to it," Tessa said, tears streaming down her cheeks, "but Reef was a good friend to me. He was a support and a shoulder that I needed. I probably wouldn't have made it this far without him." And then she broke out in song. A capella. And she was good.

She sang the first verse and the chorus of "One Sweet Day" by Mariah Carey. Then she kissed two fingers, held them up to the ceiling and walked offstage.

Tears started welling up in my eyes as she sang, but the floodgates opened when she got to the line, *"And I know you're shining down on me from heaven . . ."*

Next was Brian Jenkins. Reef's attorney. I hadn't seen him get any food either. His remarks were warm and kind and not lawyerly at all. After he finished, he came and sat at the table with us.

Thereafter came lots of people from "the old neighborhood," as Koby put it. And with each one who spoke, Koby leaned in and told me who they were.

We laughed, and tears sprang up as we listened to them tell us about Reef Jeffries. A friend to all, it seemed.

Although I could think of at least one person who didn't share that opinion . . .

Koby and Mama Zola nodded, clapped and agreed with everything everyone said.

I wished I'd known him that well.

But the one I couldn't figure out what facial expression or emotion to have in response to was the tribute by Historia.

I had thought she'd only had a vague, just-in-passing sort of acquaintance with him. Not that she really knew who he was.

Then again, she could have, because her words seemed only to echo the things that had already been said.

"There's no place like a small town," she started. "People

are neighborly, and we look out for each other. That was Reef. Homing in on things, finding a perceived problem and jumping in to help. It amazed me how many pots he was stirring." She folded her hands in front of her and gave a sweet smile. "Tessa Chaiken sang it right. The ones we love are never far." She placed a hand over her heart. "Just look over your shoulder, I'm closer than you think." She held up a glass. "To Reef."

The audience held up their glasses, too. "To Reef."

Maya closed out the memorial. She didn't make any personal remarks. I guess she didn't want to tear up onstage. She didn't seem the type of person to wear her emotions outside of her shell. She read a poem.

Notably absent from making remarks were Aubriol Meijer, Izzy Ramirez and Detective Daniel Chow.

I WAS KEEPING my eye on Aubriol. She hadn't seemed concerned at all that Detective Chow was at the memorial, or that she was there with Jason.

She was smiling and giggling every time my eyes landed on her. But I wanted to stop all of that because I had some serious questions to ask her.

I'd learned from Maya about having a meeting in the ladies' room. And it was the quietest place in Hemlock. So when I spotted Aubriol going in, I put my shoulder bag over my head and put one shoulder through and followed her.

I was standing at the mirror, where I'd positioned myself after she disappeared behind the stall door. I wasn't wearing any makeup, and my hair was in a topknot. I couldn't primp, so I just stood, staring at my reflection until she came out. Then I pretended I needed to wash my hands.

"Hi, Aubriol," I said.

"Hi," she said. She leaned into the sink and turned on the water. "Where do I know you from? Are you a friend of Jason's?"

"The train," I said. "The day Reef died."

"Oh," she said. "Seems like a lot of people from the train that day are here."

My thoughts exactly.

"I didn't know you knew Reef," I said.

"I didn't know *you* knew him."

That wasn't true, I thought. When I got on the train, I went right to him.

"He and I were close." I didn't want to say he was my foster brother (technically he wasn't) because that would seem strange, seeing I'd discovered he liked me.

"I didn't really know him." She threw the water off her hands and got a paper towel from the dispenser.

"How do you know Jason?" I said. "I couldn't even tell you two were friends that day."

"Oh. We weren't." She looked in the mirror at herself and must have thought she looked perfect. She didn't make one adjustment. "We got to talking after we got off the train and had to wait for another one. Then we rode that one together. He seemed nice, so I gave him my number."

"Oh, that was nice," I said.

I don't know if I believed that either. I remembered how Tessa and Aubriol rolled their eyes at each other when passing on the train. I hadn't thought that maybe there was animosity between them then, but now seeing Aubriol with Jason, I wasn't sure.

"Yeah," she said in a dreamy voice. "It was nice." She giggled. "At first I thought he was dating Tessa. She hadn't said anything to him while we were on the train, but on the platform, she started yelling at him."

"About what?" I asked.

She shrugged. "Just that that was a dumb thing to do. And that people were going to find out."

"Oh." I turned to her to let her know she'd gotten my attention. "What were people going to find out?"

"I don't know. I know I was trying to find out if I'd made a mistake by giving him my number."

"I can understand that."

"But he told me he was just doing her a favor."

"What kind of favor?"

"She's like his cousin or something. I think he said she was like two times removed."

"A distant relative."

"Yeah, like a real distant relative. Her place had caught on fire and she needed a place to crash." She shrugged. "He's just really nice. You know, like everyone was saying Reef was."

I didn't like her comparing Jason to Reef.

And I didn't know what Jason was up to. He seemed to have her fooled, though. I wondered just what it was he had fooled her into doing.

WHEN I CAME from the bathroom interrogation, I found my mother waiting for me.

"You're going to the bathroom a lot," she said. "Are you sure you're okay?"

"I'm fine," I said.

"I have to leave," she said. "I have an early appointment tomorrow. Then I'm going to drive to Portland for a conference this weekend."

"Okay, Mommy. Thanks for coming." I gave her a hug. "Did you let Koby and Mama Zola know you're leaving?"

"Oh yeah. I'm taking Zola with me. Save Koby the trip."

I smiled. "Aww. That's nice."

"I'm nice," she said.

"Yes. I know you are."

"Seems like Reef was a nice guy, too."

"He was," I said.

I hadn't told her anything about me and Reef, because, technically, there wasn't anything to tell.

"You want me to walk you out to your car?"

"No. I just wanted to come and let you know. Zola is saying her good-byes."

"Oh. Okay."

"She's been saying them for the last ten minutes."

I laughed.

My mother went to try and pry Zola away from fan and friend, and I thought maybe I'd better start packing things up. Looked like I was going to be doing it on my own. Thank goodness most of the food was gone.

Then I remembered the memorial table, as I called it. We'd put a black tablecloth on a round table and set an eleven-by-fourteen framed picture of Reef on it. Maya said she was going to put flowers around it. I grabbed a box from under the buffet table and headed over to it.

"Aaah!" I squealed when I got to it. "Who keeps putting this peppermint candy everywhere?" I turned from the table and ran right into Maya.

"What is going on with you?"

"Peppermints." I pointed to the table.

"They were Reef's favorite."

"Not ones laced with cyanide."

"Those aren't," she said.

I looked at them. They looked innocent enough. I just didn't know if I'd ever feel the same about that red and white swirly candy.

"Wait," I said, and narrowed an eye at Maya. "How do you know they aren't laced with cyanide?"

"Because who would do that?" She smiled. "Sounds crazy."

"You do know that's how Reef died, right?" I asked.

"How did Reef die?" she asked, and eyed me.

Did she know? She was still staring at me. No emotion in her face, just waiting for me to answer. I shook my head. She didn't know. How would she know? And maybe I wasn't supposed to tell her. I decided to change the subject.

"I liked the poem you read."

"Thanks," she said. "I wrote it."

"For Reef?"

"No. I wrote it a long time ago. I just thought it fit the occasion."

"It did," I said.

"Izzy's been pouting all night," she said, leaning into me and lowering her voice.

"She has?" I asked. "Why?"

"Probably upset because she hasn't been able to spend time with Koby all night."

"Oh," I said, and nodded.

"He didn't even sit with her to eat."

She hadn't sat at our table. I hadn't thought about that. I guess Koby hadn't either, or else he would have invited her over. I wasn't too keen on her, but I would have been cordial. He knew that, and I knew things were okay between them. She had been at Books & Biscuits earlier in the day, and they seemed fine then.

"She's been drinking a lot," Maya said.

Standing with Maya, we watched Izzy. Maya didn't trust her, although I didn't quite know why.

I had wanted to question her about the houseboat. But if she had been drinking, maybe now wasn't a good time.

Then I saw her pull a peppermint out of her purse and start to unwrap it.

That sent me into a panic.

Chapter Thirty-Eight

"PLEASE DON'T EAT that," I said. I had walked away from Maya and went over to Izzy, standing over her where she sat, alone with her drink and a piece of peppermint.

"What?" she said, looking up at me. She frowned. I could smell the alcohol on her.

"The peppermint." I pointed to it, wanting to take it out of her hand. I didn't want anyone else to die. "I'm worried that Reef died because of a poisoned peppermint. Who knows if those are safe?"

"That's ridiculous. Leave me alone," she said. She struggled to stand up, it seemed, but when she did, she took her drink and purse and headed for the front door. "I've had enough of this. You do nice things for people, and they just mistreat you."

I didn't know what that was about. Someone had upset her, but it wasn't me. I followed her.

It had gotten dark out and cooler. I folded my arms and rubbed them to warm up.

"Are you talking about my brother?" I asked, following her outside onto the patio. She went toward one of the tables.

"Why are you following me?" she asked. She turned around, walked past me and down the steps to the beach.

"How did you use to own Reef's boat?" I followed her. As I walked back past the door, Maya stuck her head out. It seemed she wanted to check on me, make sure I was okay. I gave her a smile, letting her know that I was good.

"What are you talking about? I never *owned* Reef's boat. I just told him about it. He saw mine and wanted to buy one."

I gave her a look that said I knew differently.

"Reef talked to you about it."

"No he didn't."

"Your name was on the title search his lawyer did."

"It was not," she said, and waved a hand. "Somebody we knew owned it."

"Who?"

"None of your business."

"It's Koby's business, because he owns it now."

"You said you have a title search. You should know," she said. "But my name couldn't be on it because I never owned Reef's boat." She pointed back at the Hemlock. "Don't you have some sweet potatoes or something to pass out to people?"

"Is that why you killed Reef? Because of the mix-up with the boat?"

"What?" She squinted her eyes at me.

"He got that all fixed. But what?" I persisted. "Did he come to you first? Tell you he knew that you were trying to scam him? Is that why you killed him?"

"Go away. You messin' up my buzz," she said. She saw I wasn't retreating. "Can you just leave me alone? I didn't kill anyone." She turned and started walking back toward the bar. "And don't tell your brother any of that stuff either." She spoke over her shoulder. "Everybody's always trying to get into my business."

"Don't try to put my brother in your stuff," I said. "You're not getting anything from him."

"I don't want anything from him!" she yelled. "What are you talking about? OMG. What have I done to deserve all of this? I probably should be the one dead!"

Izzy took off running. Where that outburst had come from, I didn't know, but I had hurt her feelings.

This aggressiveness was so not me, and I felt bad. I didn't like Chow accusing me of things, and here I was doing the same exact thing to everyone else.

What was wrong with me?

And I had just found out how wrong I could be about situations. I had to stop.

I went after Izzy. I wanted to apologize. I hoped I could say that I was fine with it if she liked my brother. Wasn't sure if I could do that, but I could say that I shouldn't have jumped to the conclusion that she was nefarious. I'd come up with making amends on my own, but I was sure my actions were mother-approved.

"Izzy. Wait."

She turned around to swipe at me like she was a wounded bear, and when she turned back, her foot twisted. Those slide-in sandals and sand didn't mix.

"Ugh!" was what I heard as she went down.

"You okay?" I asked as I made it over to her.

Trying to get up, she swiped at me again before she plopped back down into the sand with another grunt.

"My ankle," she said. "I twisted my ankle." Her complaint, though, was voiced with a failed second attempt to get up.

"Don't try to get up," I said, stooping down next to her. "I'll go get somebody to help."

"Don't try to be nice to me now," she said.

That made me feel worse.

"I just want to help," I said. I blew out a breath and sat in the sand. "Sorry about accusing you of doing anything to Reef."

"What about using your brother?" She wiped tears away

from her eyes. I was worried she'd get sand in them and be in more pain. "Are you sorry you said that, too?"

I hadn't used those words, but I guess they meant the same thing. And now I didn't want to hurt her feelings and lie to her, too.

"I just got my brother back," I said, feeling that warmth in my eyes when tears are about to materialize. "And I think that I am afraid of losing him again."

"Oh, because I killed Reef," she said, the sarcasm dripping from her voice, "you think I'm going to kill Koby, too."

"No wait. Just wait." I grabbed her arm. "I apologize. I didn't mean that." She pulled away from me, and I raised my hands in surrender. "I just want to keep my brother. Maybe because we had once been womb-mates"—that brought a flicker of a smile to her face—"or because we were separated for so long, but I have a fear"—I put a fist over my heart—"a real fear of losing him again."

"You wouldn't *lose* him because I dated him."

"*I* know that. But I don't think my psyche does."

She gave me a look that said I was talking sideways.

"Bear with me," I said. "My mother is a psychologist."

"Your *mother*?"

"My adoptive mother."

"Oh." She nodded her understanding.

"She would call it 'emotional quicksand.'" I grabbed a fistful of the sand we were resting on and let it sift through my fingers. "Revisiting old hurt and clinging to it."

"That sounds deep," Izzy said, although I could've sworn I heard a touch of skepticism in her voice.

"Something I have to work through," I said.

"Maybe your mother can help you."

I chuckled. "She'd be happy to. But I just wanted to explain that I need to get past our past—when we were separated. And to be honest, I didn't know I felt like that, because I hadn't been around other people vying for his attention or who I thought might want to hurt him."

"I'm in the vying category," she said. "Not the one that wants to hurt him."

"Okay," I said.

I wanted to say, *I believe you*, but I hadn't exactly ruled her out.

"I seem to have that effect on other girls."

"What?" I asked.

"They like to protect guys from me."

"Why?"

"I don't know," she said. "Maya used to do the same thing about Reef. Heck. She was still shooting daggers at me tonight, and Reef isn't even around anymore." She scrunched her nose. "I didn't mean for that to sound callous."

"It's okay." I patted her arm. "Was she trying to date Reef?"

Maya and I had just had this conversation, and her words, although she didn't say the exact words, told me she hadn't had feelings for Reef.

"No," Izzy said, making a face. "Like you, she didn't like him, just thought he needed protecting from me."

I wanted to giggle at that, but I knew it would hurt her feelings. "Sorry that that happened to you."

"It's hard for someone as pretty as me."

I felt an eyebrow go up, just like Koby's does.

"Is it?" I queried.

"Yes. Girls hate me, and boys think I wouldn't date them because I look so good."

"Sad place to be." I hoped I didn't sound mocking.

"That's why I go after the ones I want."

"Like Reef and Koby?"

"Yes."

To have her problems . . .

I looked at her as she sat rubbing her ankle. I guess I'd rather struggle with being too pretty than to have a phobia of a made-up, unfounded future loss based on something that happened in my past.

Yep. I *was* turning into my mother.

"Now let me go and get you some help."

A man's voice startled me. "I can help. What's going on?"

"Hi, Sam," Izzy said, looking up above my head. "I fell. Twisted my ankle."

Sam?

I slowly turned around, and there he was, standing right behind me.

Chapter Thirty-Nine

"YOU WANT TO go back inside?" Sam asked Izzy.

I sat there frozen. I didn't have the cover of my brother or the store in this encounter with him. Everything here worked against me—a dark night where it would be hard for people to see what he was doing and only the help of a girl with an inoperable ankle.

"I'd rather go home." She pointed down the boardwalk. "If you could help me get up."

"Sure," he said, and walked around me.

"I can go get my brother," I said. The first words coming out of my mouth were shaky.

"No need," Sam said. "I got her."

"Hold on," Izzy said when he went to pull her up. "I'm feeling a little dizzy."

"Oh yeah," he said. "Take your time." Then he looked at me. *Uh-oh.*

"That was a really nice memorial you guys gave for Reef."

"Thank you," I said, which came out more like a question. I didn't know what to say to him. What happened to all that boldness I'd been exhibiting over the past couple of days? I think my confession and apology to Izzy had weakened me.

"And the food was on point."

I raised both eyebrows. I wasn't sure I knew what that meant, but he had a smile on his face, so I took it to mean a good thing.

"If it's that good at you guys' restaurant, I'll be there." He rubbed his hands together. "Have you been there, Izzy?"

"Yeah, I've eaten there." She smacked her lips like she was eating it then. "All the food is really good," she said, showing no fear of Sam at all.

"Darius told me that Koby's foster mom helped cook?"

"Yep." My answer showed no enthusiasm.

"Was that her there tonight?" Sam asked. "Helping to serve food?"

"Yeah." I swallowed hard. I was thinking how I was going to make my getaway from him. But I didn't want to leave Izzy. "Mama Zola. She'll probably be working with us."

"Oh, that was Mama Zola? Oh wow. I finally get to see her." His head swayed to the side and back. "Sorry it was under such bad circumstances, you know."

"You know Mama Zola?"

She sure knew him. And she didn't like him. She'd called him a knucklehead.

"Reef talked about her a lot." His eyes drifted out across the water. "He said she was the best foster mom he'd had."

I didn't say anything. How do you wax sentimental with a possible killer?

"Hey, you said something to me this morning." He turned his eyes toward me. "I didn't quite hear what you were saying. I had been trying to catch up with you all evening to see what it was."

Well, I wasn't going to repeat now how I told him to stop lurking around our store, I thought. I wasn't feeling as brave as I did earlier. Especially since now I wasn't standing on the other side of a door from him.

"I didn't expect to see you." He was still talking.

I just bet you didn't.

"I was waiting for my ride."

Wait. What?

"They're late every morning," he said, and shook his head. "But just like Reef said, it's my own fault."

"Your ride?" I asked.

I couldn't see his eyes. I didn't know if he was telling the truth or not. But the way he said it, it sounded sincere. And why would he say it if it wasn't true?

"Yeah. For work," he said.

"Where were you waiting for it?" I asked.

"Right outside your place. On Second Street. Like I do every day. That's why I stopped in that first morning."

"Every day?" I squeaked the words out.

"Yeah. You've probably seen me," he said. "I'm there every day. Gotta get my truck fixed. I've been just wasting my money doing stupid stuff. And what makes it so bad, Reef had just yelled at me the night before he died. Told me to get it together." I saw him tug on the corner of his eye. "Now I want to do it when he's not around to see me."

"Were you on the houseboat?"

"What?" he said and sniffed.

"When Reef yelled at you. Were you on his houseboat?"

"Oh yeah. He pushed me off of it, too." He chuckled. "Told me to go and get it together."

Exactly what Tessa had described.

"What was he talking about?" I asked.

"I needed to get bonded and licensed, you know, for construction. Especially if I was going to be working with him." He licked his lips. It seemed it was hard for him to talk about it. "But it cost money, you know. So Reef helped me get this job bartending"—he jerked a finger toward the Hemlock—"and let me work with him sometimes."

"Sounds just like Reef," Izzy said. Her words came out jumbled together. "Gotta love that guy."

"I did." Sam dug his hands down in his pockets. "Told me to put my money up, save it, so I could do what I need to do. Be self-sufficient. Be responsible."

"He told me the same thing," Izzy said.

"I got in some trouble when I was younger"—Sam was feeling cathartic—"and I just let that get the best of me."

"I'm always in trouble," Izzy said, echoing his thoughts. His were more sober than hers.

Sam chuckled. He seemed to agree with her but kept talking about himself. "My past indiscretions had me thinking I couldn't accomplish anything worthwhile. Still in that mindset, I went and did something stupid to get the money back that I'd wasted. Man, I'm glad Reef didn't know about that. If he had, he probably wouldn't have said what he did."

"What did he say?" Izzy asked.

She was good to have along on this interrogation.

"Reef told me I was better than what I thought. To give myself some credit for the good things I'd done. Said we all make mistakes."

"We do," Izzy said. She leaned back on her hands and shook her head.

"That's why I wanted to get my stuff out of his storage," Sam said. "So I could get on the right track. Reef told me I had a good head on my shoulders and I could do a lot with it. And he'd help me as much as he could."

"Aww. He said that?" Izzy said.

"Yeah. You know Reef. Always doing something nice. Always trying to help people."

"That was Reef," Izzy said. "He was good through and through."

"That's why I sent my brother to him." He shook his head. "I wanted Reef to help Darius. He's a better listener than I am." His chuckle came out in a cough. I could tell he was getting choked up. "Yep. Reef was good through and through, just like you say, Izzy. I hate he's gone. I would have taken that bullet for him."

"He wasn't shot," I said, in shock of this revelatory information from Sam.

Sam laughed. "It's just a turn of phrase. I'm just saying that I would have died in his place if I could have. He was doing too much good for us to lose him at such a young age."

"Who put out the bowl of peppermints?" I asked.

"Peppermints?" he repeated. It seemed I'd caught him off guard, changing the subject like that.

"Probably Maya," Izzy said. "In honor of Reef, I'm sure. He was always stuffing one in his mouth."

"You didn't do it, Sam?" I asked.

"No," he said.

"So, I guess that means you didn't kill him either," I said.

"Huh?" Sam's eyes widened and his mouth dropped open. Even in the moonlight I could see the confusion on his face.

"Don't pay any attention to her," Izzy said. "She's been accusing everybody." She waved a dismissive hand. "She's going through some psychotic episode from being separated from her twin for so long."

"Oh," Sam said. "I'm sorry to hear that. I hope she'll be okay."

I hate when people talk about me in the third person when I'm standing right there.

Chapter Forty

AND THAT'S WHEN the connection came together.

I don't know why things don't trigger in my brain right away like Koby's. My response just isn't as fast.

Maybe that means I was the second one born . . .

"I can get you into Reef's storage space now," I said. It seemed now I wanted to help him do good, too—show his potential.

"You can?" Sam said. "I'd appreciate that. I've been waiting for your brother to call me."

I dug down in my purse and found my wallet. Opening the zipper compartment, I pulled out that key I'd taken from the folder we'd gotten from Reef's lawyer.

I held it up. There on both sides was the word YALE. The same as the word on the bottom of the second lock on the door of Reef's storage space.

It had been in a folder about the boat—it only made sense the key was for something concerning it.

"Cool," he said. "And this will be perfect. I have Darius' truck. I could put it in there for now."

"Let's get it," I said.

If Reef wanted him to succeed, so did I. I no longer thought he was the killer. I looked over at Izzy, her head bobbing, and thought she probably wasn't the one who'd done it either. But even if she was, she was too far into the sheets to do anything to me now.

I stood up. "You ready?"

"Yes," he said. "You know, I really don't want to let him down." He paused. "I don't want to let myself down anymore."

"Hey, you guys can't leave me here." Izzy held up both her hands like we were going to pick her up.

I took one hand, Sam took the other and we pulled her up. She didn't even try to put any weight on her foot, she hopped on the other one a couple of times until Sam took ahold of her arm and wrapped it around his neck. I stood on the other side of her and did the same. As we headed down the boardwalk, I thought I should have let my brother know where I was going . . .

But I had noticed Maya peeking out the door a few times. I was sure she'd let him know I'd left with Izzy and Sam.

WE GOT IZZY to her houseboat. She had mostly stopped helping us transport her by the time we got there. We were practically dragging her.

"Where's the key, Izzy?" Sam said. "To the door."

"Oh," she said, and looked around.

"We're here," Sam said, commenting on her actions. "At your place."

"Okay," she said. She seemed groggier than she had while we were at the beach. But then again, we'd been arguing. Anger may have pumped more adrenaline into her veins. After Sam came, she'd been more subdued.

"It's open."

I shook my head. People leaving their doors open was dangerous. It might have been how the killer, whoever that turned out to be, had gotten into Reef's place and left the tainted candy.

We got her inside and to her couch.

Izzy's furniture had a modern vibe. The couch was mustard color, and she had it accented with brick-colored throw pillows. She had one of those chairs that was shaped like a hand. Like Reef's boat, there was an open concept, and the kitchen was connected to the living space. It was shiny and new-looking. Her place mirrored her. Beautiful.

"You going to be okay?" I asked. "If we leave you right here?"

"I'm fine," she said, and let her neck roll onto the back of the couch.

"Put that under her foot," I said to Sam, and pointed to a black cloth footstool. "I'm going to get some ice for her ankle."

I put ice in a baggie, grabbed a tea towel she had hanging on the handle of the fridge and we got her settled in before we left.

"I'll go get my brother's truck," he said. "And pull it up closer to the storage building."

"Okay," I said. "Be careful. That parking lot is so raggedy. You don't want to mess up his tires and frame."

"Alright," he said. "I'll be careful." He stopped walking. "I'll meet you over there, unless you want to come with me and we drive over together."

It would take all of thirty seconds to drive from one end of the parking lot to the other, although I knew he'd have to walk to it, and that would take a few extra minutes. Still, he wouldn't be long.

"No. I can go on over and get it open."

"You're not afraid?" he asked.

"Afraid?"

"Of the dark. Of the woods."

I chuckled. "No. I'm good."

"Okay," he said. "I won't be long."

We parted ways. I walked back down the pier the way we'd just come. He went the opposite way.

I cut between the buildings and carefully made my way across the parking lot, avoiding potholes so my ankle wouldn't end up being iced like Izzy's.

I saw a big truck parked, the front of it tucked behind the building. **THE PACIFIC WEST RESCUE ROOTER** was printed on the side with their green and yellow logo. Their services listed were:

HEATING & FURNACE
HVAC
PLUMBING AND GAS LINE
COMMERCIAL & RESIDENTIAL

"That wasn't there earlier," I said to myself. "And who works at night?" But thinking about it, I realized it was probably a good thing. I had smelled gasoline earlier, and Old Man Walker had said the pumps weren't even working.

It had to be some kind of federal offense to have that smell emanating from the protected wooded property behind the storage building.

"Figures," I said. "Mrs. Grayson was right. Slum landlords are not good for Timber Lake."

"Fourteen. Thirty-one. Seven. Star," I said as I punched in the code to open the gate, renaming the asterisk. I chuckled. "Good thing Koby had me memorize that."

The gate slid open. "Great," I said. I hadn't really paid attention to it before, but I remembered the gate stayed open until you put the code in again. "I won't have to come back out and let Sam in." The metal door to the building was heavy, and I had to give it a good push to prop it open. "Stay," I said, and gave it a pat.

Chapter Forty-One

THE VOICES STARTLED me at first, but then that surprise grew into alarm.

The voices were muffled. But the cadence was quick. The tone angry. The volume—a sustained crescendo.

The Yale key had worked on the second lock. I got them both off the door and opened it. I had turned my flashlight on and started to survey the room when I heard them.

One male. One female.

Sam, I figured. But who was the other voice? I knew it couldn't be Izzy. She wouldn't have been able to make it over here with that ankle and all the potholes.

I went back toward the door to see who it was. But when I got close, their words were so heated, I didn't want to get in the middle of it.

"Why are you here?" It was the woman's voice. "Get out of here! Now!"

"Oh. I am," Sam answered her back. "I know you don't want anyone around during your after-dark criminal activity."

"Who do you think you are?" she hissed.

"Back up, lady. Don't walk up on me like that. Pointing your finger at me. You know I know what you got going on over here."

"You don't know a blasted thing about me or my business."

Sam chuckled. "Oh, yes I do. Didn't you get my note?"

"What?" she said, her voice changed. She seemed confused now instead of angry.

"If you don't get it together," he said, "and take care of your property like you should, I'm going to report you."

"You?" she shouted. "You left that message?"

"Yeah. I probably shouldn't have. But I needed money. That just ain't how to get it."

"But you weren't the one . . ." The woman sputtered out her words. "Someone came to my office, told me they knew what I'd done."

"What? What are you talking about, lady? I don't know who you're talking about. This is about what you're trying to do to my family. You putting my little brother in danger."

"What are you talking about?" She spat out the words.

"That furnace you put in that house wasn't even installed right. And then you got these trucks coming in here at night."

"Brother? What brother?"

"Darius. And I can't let that happen. I don't want no money. You can forget I said that, but I will report this. All of this."

"Get. Off. My. Property." She shouted each word louder than the last one, and I realized whom Sam was talking to.

Historia. He was arguing with Historia.

"You ain't said nothing but a word," Sam said. "As soon as I get my stuff, I'm outta here."

"You're not getting anything. You. Are. Gone," she said.

"How you going to stop me?" he asked, and laughed. "And I know you're not calling the police. Ha! Wouldn't they love to know what's going on."

"You have no idea what is happening on my property." Historia's voice was filling up with anger again.

"You're right," Sam said. "But I'm sure they could figure it out."

Then there was quiet. No more shouting. No more nothing. I didn't know what happened until Sam walked through the open door and right into me.

"Aaaah!" I tried to muffle my scream. "You scared me!"

"Shouldn't have been eavesdropping."

"You two were shouting," I said. "Probably everybody back at Hemlock's heard it."

He laughed. "Yeah, shouldn't have let her get to me like that. I'm moving on. I'm better than that," he said.

"What was that about?" I asked.

"She's a slum landlord. That's what it was about." He clucked his tongue. "She put in a bad furnace over where my brother lives."

"I saw the house," I said.

"Yeah. So, I left her this note saying she better get her properties up to par, or I was reporting her. That I knew what she was doing."

"Oh," I said.

"C'mon," he said. "Let's get a cart to load my stuff up on. Can't have you carrying stuff out to the truck." He squeezed my upper arm like he was checking for muscle. "I think there's one at the other end."

"You've been in here before?" I asked, following behind him, the lights popping on as we made our way down the hallway.

"Yeah," Sam said.

I turned and looked behind me. It seemed I heard the door shut at the other end.

"With Reef. How you think my stuff got in here?" He laughed. But one thing he said brought my attention back to him.

Reef.

When Sam said his name, I got another connection.

Connection. Sheesh. I was acting like they were some psychic revelation.

"She said she thought someone else had left it," I said. "What if that someone else was Reef?"

"Who?"

"Historia," I said.

"Did what?" he asked.

"I don't know." My voice drifted off. "But I think . . ."

"She's crazy." He made circles with a finger next to his temple. "I don't know what she's talking about. Don't let her get to you."

"Koby said *EP*. A partnership. That was who he said was on the voice mail when he called about that rental property."

"Don't rent anything from her. Didn't you hear me when I said she's a bad landlord?"

"He got it wrong. He missed a letter."

"Huh?" Sam said, then, "Oh, here's that cart. I knew it had to still be back here. No one uses this storage."

"Maybe Koby meant EEP, LLP."

"What are you talking about?" he said, and glanced up at me. "Watch out! I don't want to run into you with this."

The trolley cart was a flat board about two feet off the ground with a handle on one end and rickety—it seemed, hence the warning—wheels underneath it.

I was talking out loud, but mostly I was talking to myself. It seemed like there was something . . . "LLP stands for limited liability *partnership*," I said.

"What?" he said, pushing the cart back to the storage unit.

"If Historia's company is EEP"—I rubbed trembling fingers across my forehead—"and that stands for East End Pacific, the place where Brian paid the slip fees . . . That means Historia is the one who owned Reef's boat."

"Keaton." Sam stopped at the door. "Yes. That's her company. It's who my brother pays his rent to every month. EEP, LLP. I don't know what you're talking about. But you shouldn't give that woman a second thought or a penny to rent one of her houses."

He dug in his pocket and pulled out a cell phone and

swiped it. "Here. Hold up this light for me so I can see what's what. That light from the hall is not enough, and it won't last. Once we stop moving, they'll go out." He looked at me. "Are you alright?"

"Brian said that Reef knew the previous owner of his boat and that he had confronted that person."

"Who is Brian?" Sam said.

"And Izzy said he didn't confront her."

"Izzy might have said anything tonight." He chuckled. "She took advantage of the bar."

"He was talking about the boat. When he confronted her."

"Who," Sam said. He wasn't really paying attention to me. His response wasn't even a question. It was more like an obligatory response.

"Reef. To Historia. When he said to her he knew what she'd done, he meant about the boat. That's what she just said to you out there." I pointed toward the outside door. "He was saying he knew how she sold it and bought it back. But wait . . ." I turned my head on an angle. "Izzy said she never owned the boat."

"Uh-huh." He walked past me and put something on the cart.

"There's gasoline leaking into the woods behind here." I made the proclamation. Because I realized that meant something, too. These things all were related. Somehow . . .

Oh my.

Sam stopped. "Gasoline?"

"I smelled gasoline around the gas pumps in front of the store and behind here when we walked through there this morning."

"You did?" Sam asked. "I've never smelled gasoline around here."

"Koby didn't smell it either," I said, puzzled why no one else could. "But then"—I shrugged—"he can't smell the almonds on Mrs. Grayson's tree."

"Almonds don't have a smell," he said.

"Yes, they do," I said.

And then a big connection came. I remembered how I smelled Mrs. Grayson's yard. It wasn't just the floral fragrance of her plants. It was her tree. Mrs. Grayson's almond tree. That's what I had smelled in Historia's office. Almonds. And mints.

"And that was an empty candy dish," I said out loud. "Not an ashtray."

"What?" he said absently.

"She must have had him come to her office after he told her he'd tell what she'd done. Lured him there. That's how he got the candy. She knew he couldn't resist it."

"Oh good," Sam said, picking up some large tool, "I've been looking for this."

Hadn't I read that cyanide gives off the scent of almonds . . . ?

"Hey," he said. "Watch the light. You have to shine it over here. Keaton." He called my name. "Over here. So I can see."

"Historia killed Reef," I said. It just popped out. Suddenly, I knew. The almond and mint scent in her office was cyanide and peppermint.

"What?" Sam was paying attention to me that time. His reaction was from disbelief, not some rote response.

I cocked my head to the side. "You smell that?"

"How do you tell me that revelation and then change the subject? Why did you say Historia killed Reef?"

"You don't smell that?" My heart started racing.

"What now?" he said, holding up his hands, realizing he wasn't going to get an answer from me about Historia.

"Smoke," I said. "Something's on fire."

Chapter Forty-Two

THAT SOMETHING WAS the dilapidated structure at the back of the marina that had a room full of flammable liquids—turpentine, paint, varnishes right at the only exit. The structure that had me and Sam locked inside of it.

"Oh my God!" I said, and ran down the hallway toward the flames.

It might not have seemed like a good idea to anyone *hearing* about my actions, but as far as I knew, it was the only way out. If there *was* a way out.

I handed Sam his phone and pulled out mine, my hands shaking so bad I could hardly hold on to it, let alone dial it. I started to punch in 911, but I didn't have a signal. This place was all closed in, sitting next to protected lands, where no towers were allowed, and lined with metal doors.

"Check your phone," I said, breathless. "Do you have a signal?"

He shook his head. I could see the Adam's apple in his throat bobbing up and down.

"Historia did this," I said, out of breath and sweating with fear. "She used her storage contents as an accelerant."

"What are you talking about?" he said. I noted the same desperation in his voice that I felt throughout my whole body. "Why would she do this?"

I pointed to the open storage unit. The flames were spilling out of it and followed a trail of paper products—perhaps wallpaper, cloth tarps, cardboard boxes—strewn past the front door over to the other side. The unit that Old Man Walker told me was hers. And then she had apparently locked the door behind her.

"I hope nothing in there is combustible."

Sam ran toward the fire and tried to kick some of the paper out of the way. The flames had already fully covered our only exit.

"That won't work," I yelled. The crackling of the fire and thickness of the smoke were making it hard for my normal voice to carry. I swung around and pointed down the hallway. "There's trash everywhere, this place is made out of wood. The smoke will get us probably before the fire anyway."

He pointed up to the windows. Vertical windows, two together, were lined up at the right at the curve of the roof of the building. "We need to try to get up there," he said.

I nodded. I'd forgotten about those windows. They were so dingy, they looked the same color as the walls. The smoke was getting to me. I started coughing. We couldn't stand here much longer. I held up a hand to shield my face from the heat of the flames. "We need to pick a window further down." I pointed down the hallway. "We need to find something to climb on."

I really didn't give much hope to us being able find anything tall enough that we could climb high enough on.

I could feel the tears welling up in my eyes. I was scared, but I knew I needed a clear mind because there was no one to come to my rescue.

My mother had gone back to Seattle. Izzy knew Sam and I had come over to the storage space. Maybe. She'd been drinking and hadn't even realized she had made it home when we'd gone to drop her off. Plus, she wouldn't know of any reason we'd be in danger.

And Koby. My twin.

We might have radar, but nothing like what I needed now. I'd have to have one where the beeps were being broadcast over an amplified loudspeaker.

He had none of the clues I had to figure out that Historia was the killer. He couldn't pick up the almond smell in her office. He didn't know that it was her company that was in the title search, or that she was probably the reason Reef's lawyer had to do a lawsuit. And he hadn't heard her say to Sam that she thought it was Reef who'd left an *I Know What You Did Last Summer* kind of note for her. I was the only one to know all of that.

Even with his keen ability to notice things, he'd never figure out I was here. About to die.

Even Historia, I believe, didn't know I was in here. I think she was aiming to get only Sam. But I'd be willing to bet that wouldn't matter to her at all.

"I can't find anything to stand on," Sam yelled out to me. "Nothing that'll get me high enough."

I looked up. I didn't know how to estimate the height, but aren't ceilings ten feet high? Twelve feet?

I coughed before I could talk. "Maybe if I stand on your shoulders," I said.

I was short. Five feet five inches. But together . . . It was worth a try.

"Here," he said. "I'll stand on this." He pointed to the trolley cart he had started to put his things on. "Help me take this stuff off of it."

We worked quickly. I could feel the heat on my back as the flames made their way down the long corridor.

"The wheels have a lock on them," Sam said. He got on

his knees and leaned the top part of his body down so he could see. "So, they won't move when we climb on."

I saw him fidget with it. Hit it. Move the cart slightly back and forth to realign the wheels. He sat up on his legs, blew out a breath and took the tail of his T-shirt to wipe the sweat off his forehead.

"I don't know," he said. He peeked around me to gauge the movement of the fire. "Maybe they're locked." He hit the handle with a hand. "This darn thing is so old."

"We have to try," I said.

"We die from a fall or from the fire, huh?" His voice said we didn't have much of a choice.

"It might work," I said, tears in my eyes.

"Okay," he said, and stood up. He moved the cart parallel with a piece of wall between the metal doors. "You ever done anything like this before?"

I shook my head, too nervous to speak.

He climbed up on the cart slowly, testing it to see how steady it was. He seemed satisfied it would hold, if the relaxed muscles on his face were any indication.

"C'mon." He beckoned me with his hands.

He stooped down. I stepped up on the cart and gave a slight jump when it creaked.

"It's good," he said. "We're good. C'mon."

I held on to the wall and, one foot at a time, stepped onto his shoulders.

He held on to my hands. "I'm going to stand up. You ready?"

"Ready," I said.

He stood up. Taking his time. Making sure I was steady. But my knees were shaking. My hands were sweaty. And all I could think of was that I wasn't going to ever see my twin brother again.

I don't know how, but I made it up to those windows. The layer of dust and grime was so thick and the smoke from the fire was starting to rise. I had to hold back a sneeze that was trying to come out of my sensitive nose and a cough that wanted to clear my throat.

I placed one hand on the wall next to the window to steady myself and pulled on the lever to the window.

It didn't budge.

"You got it?" Sam asked. I could tell he was trying not to cough, too. We both knew that that would be disastrous.

"It's tight," I said. "Probably hasn't ever been opened."

"Pull harder."

"I'm trying."

I didn't know how hard I could pull. I had no leverage. I was keeping coughs internalized, and the ensuing dust from trying to jar the window was killing my nose.

"I don't know if I can."

"Come down," he said, and started lowering me. "Maybe we can break the window."

I climbed off his shoulders.

He picked up the cart and moved it down. "The fire is catching up with us," he said. "We'll do it down here."

He left me, went back down to Reef's storage and grabbed a cloth and a hammer. He coughed all the way there and back.

"Wrap this around your hand. You don't want to get glass in your hand." He passed me the hammer. "Put this in your waistband. Pull it out when you get up there."

"Okay," I said, coughing out the word.

"It'll be okay," he said. "Someone should be able to see the fire soon."

"Or smell it," I said.

He smiled. "Right. Even if they don't have the nose you have."

I nodded. Tears tumbling down my cheek.

"And when you break through, you get out. Go get help."

"What about you?"

"I can't get out there. I'll go to the back, try to cover my face." He nodded. "The air from the broken window will help with all the smoke. I should be okay."

"Okay," I said. I blew out a breath. I could do this. I adjusted the hammer to make sure it was secure.

"Cough, get the smoke out."

"Does that work?" I asked.

He hunched his shoulders. So I did it. So did he.

"Okay," he said. "Let's do this."

I made it back up. And with tears mixing with the sweat on my face, I broke the window. It was a small hole. But a hole. And I managed to get most of the glass to fall outside.

"Make the hole bigger," he called out to me. With his words I felt his body tremble. Talking, moving air around made him take in more of the smoke.

I pulled my arm back, and as the head of the hammer hit the window, Sam let out a cough that moved his shoulders, made my foot slip from it. I went down. Sam tried to catch me, and he twisted a foot, falling, hitting his head, and he was out.

I fell on top of him. I heard a *thud* coming from him as I landed, pushing air out of his chest. Then everything went black.

Epilogue

"KEATON!"

Koby was there. Calling out to me. That made me smile. How did he get to heaven with me?

I wondered, was my father here? I'd have to look for him. It would be good to see him again.

Or my biological mother? Koby was always looking in the obituaries for her.

"Keaton!"

Drops of water splashed in my face. I opened my eyes and blinked several times to clear them. I was still in the storage center. I looked up at the ceiling. Water was coming through the broken window.

"Keaton!"

I tried to sit up. Koby was calling me. But how?

"Keaton, where are you?"

"Koby?"

"I'm here, Keaton. I'm coming."

The firefighters had drenched the building in water and had had a hard time keeping Koby from coming through the door before the fire was doused. At least, that's what the paramedic told me as I sat in the back of the ambulance and breathed in oxygen from the tank I'd been hooked up to.

"And he hasn't left your side since," the EMS guy said, and gave a nod toward my twin, who was standing five feet away.

"It was Historia who did this," I said to Koby. He came over next to me after the EMT left.

"I know," Koby said.

"She had a gas leak going into the protected lands, I think." I rubbed my temple, trying to collect my thoughts. "It must have been from the broken pumps out front."

"You smelled it," he said, nodding, a smile forming on his face. "I'll learn to trust your nose."

I smiled. "Reef talked to her about the bad title on the boat. It's in the file," I said. "She'd bought the boat, then somehow put it in Izzy's name, then changed it again."

"Brian told me that at the memorial tonight. It's called a strawman transaction," Koby said.

"Yeah, I've heard of that," I said, holding my head up with my hand. "It's when a third-party person purchases something on behalf of another person."

"It's a legal term. Versed in legalese?" Koby asked.

I shrugged. "Must have read it somewhere. Makes sense for Historia to have done that, though, if she didn't want her name on it."

"Yeah," Koby said. "But she didn't think about how her name would be associated with her company name. If someone took the time to look into it. That's how Brian remembered where he'd heard the name Historia Krol." Koby nodded. "I knew then Historia had killed Reef," Koby said.

"How did you know?" I asked.

"Twin radar," he said, and smiled. "When you got it, so did I."

I tried not to laugh. My head was already hurting enough.

"It was more than radar." Chow stepped up next to Koby. "He put it all together from a few words in a remark at the memorial."

"You knew the words, too," Koby said.

"True, but I wouldn't have figured it out quick enough to save Keaton."

"What words?" I asked.

"Historia's," Koby said. "She said, *Just look over your shoulder, I'm closer than you think*."

"I remember that," I said. "What does it mean?"

"The Happy Face Killer, Keith Jesperson, wrote that in a letter to a paper in Oregon back in the nineties," Detective Chow said.

I looked at Koby. "And you knew that?"

"Yeah. And then I remembered you said cyanide is used to clean jewelry."

"Jason?"

"I went and found him and asked if he had given any of the solution they used to Historia. He said she'd told them there was an infestation of mice at one of her properties."

"Why didn't he tell her to go buy rat poison?" I asked.

"He didn't want it told that he had an underage runaway living with him," Koby said.

"He told you that?" I asked.

"Yep. He didn't know she was going to use it to kill anyone."

"I don't know if that'll matter," Detective Chow said. "I'm taking him over to the station." He turned and looked at a black-and-white. Following his eyes, I could see Jason sitting in the back of one. Facing the window, he was looking out at all the activity. Then I saw Historia. Sitting in the back of another police car. She had no interest in what was happening. Her face was stoic, eyes straight ahead.

"But how did you know I was in the storage facility?"

"Izzy," Koby said. "I wanted to tell you what I found out,

but I couldn't find you. Maya told me she'd seen you leave with Sam and Izzy. I knew you weren't too fond of her—that made me curious."

"When we got to her houseboat," Detective Chow said, "she said that you two had come over here."

"You went with Koby to help find me?" I asked.

"He wouldn't leave me alone," Chow said. "Kept telling me all these things he'd found out." He gave Koby a smirk. "But I was really following the smoke."

"Right," Koby said. "The smoke I was making or from the building burning?"

"Still, you wouldn't know that I was inside of it," I said.

"I knew that's where you'd gone," Koby said. "I saw Darius' truck parked outside."

"And he saw the glass on the ground outside," Chow said, clearly impressed. "He knew, somehow, that that meant you were in there. And after that, there was no stopping him."

"SO, WE'LL ALL be living in Timber Lake," Mama Zola said.

"Everyone but me," my mother said.

"Well, Imogene, you'll just have to move, too," Mama Zola said.

I looked at my mother. I didn't think there was any way she'd leave the house she'd shared with my father and where she'd raised me.

It was Sunday. Books & Biscuits was closed, but we were all there. Koby, Mama Zola, my mother, Avery Moran—Koby's Capt'n Hook—and me. We'd been talking about everything that had happened just over the past week. Whew! It seemed so much longer.

"Such a whirlwind," Mama Zola said. "But an adventure, too." She grinned. "You opened a bookstore and soul food café, and you solved a murder."

"An adventure?" Koby seemed to mull that over. "I'm just happy to have the store open. Have a place to live near my sister and my job. We caught Reef's killer. And"—he looked at Moran—"I've got a better landlord," he said.

"I'm not a landlord," Moran said. "But you'd better get those marina fees in on time, or you'll be outta there faster than the Space Needle ascends."

We all laughed. The Space Needle traveled at only about ten miles per hour. A snail's pace in a car, but it was able to reach the top in about forty-one seconds. Less than a minute.

Avery Moran had bought the marina with his retirement money from the Seattle Police Department. He wouldn't tell us the exact purchase price, but he did tell us it was dirt cheap.

I guessed so, seeing that the owner was in jail.

He made a vow to us, as we sat around the table eating a full Sunday meal of meat loaf, mashed potatoes and succotash with okra and corn.

My mother, so proud she'd made the corn bread from scratch, said at least a dozen times that she hoped he would restore the marina to its former glory.

"I remember how nice it was," my mother said. "Keaton's father and I used to bring her down here. Take her out on a boat, eat at the restaurant. He took fishing trips from there. It was really a fun place to come."

"Good you remember it, Imogene," Moran said. "Maybe you'll be able to help me get it back to how it used to be."

"I'd be happy to," my mother said.

"I'll come down, too," Mama Zola said.

"Do you remember it, too?" my mother asked.

"Never been there," Mama Zola said. "But I am not one to miss the fun."

"You'll be working," Koby said. "Not much time to goof off."

"Don't I get vacation days?" she asked.

"You have to work for a while to get vacation days."

"Well, I'm going to need moving days. I can't wait to move into that little bungalow. It is so cute."

"When are you moving, Zola?" Moran asked.

"It's gotta be painted first. I don't like the colors on the walls, and Koby's going to get the carpet in the bedrooms steam-cleaned for me." She patted Koby's hand. "And I have to wait on Sam to get that bum ankle to heal."

"Was nice of him to offer to help you move," Moran said.

"Yes. It was. Both of the Anderson boys are going to help. Good boys. Men," she said with a firm nod. She'd changed her opinion about Sam after the fire. "And Darius has that nice truck," she continued, "which should move all my things."

"They'd have to make a hundred trips in that truck, Mama," Koby said, "to get all your stuff."

"I don't have that much stuff," she countered.

"Yep. Only thirty years of things. Are you throwing any of it out?"

"Why in the world would I throw any of my things out? Those are my memories."

"Exactly," Koby said. "We're renting a moving van. The biggest one they have."

That brought a chuckle from everyone but Mama Zola.

"Anyway, smart talking or not, I'll be happy to be close to my boy." Mama Zola nodded at Koby. "I've lost one now. Reef. He'd always come by, help me out, spend time with me."

"I heard you had him hooked on the soap operas," Koby said.

"That's because they're good. You should watch them, too," she said.

"I'll give them a try," Koby said earnestly. He was eager to make her happy.

But in my shoulder bag was something that might make him even happier. It was an envelope with a return address of the King County Adoptions Department of Family Court Services. Inside, perhaps, was information on Morie Hill, our biological mother—maybe even where we could find her. I hadn't opened it yet. I wanted to wait and do it with my twin brother. And maybe that would take us on an adventure more exciting and compelling than any we'd taken so far.

Acknowledgments

As I always do, I want to thank God for all the blessings I've found through writing—good friends and good times. And I always include my mother, Leslie Vandiver, in this, who made me believe in being able to do big things and good things. A little of her will always be in my books and all of her remains in my heart.

In my own family there has been adoption and kinship care for generations, and initially, without notice, I oftentimes added those elements into my stories. My maternal grandmother died when my mother was two. Afterwards, my grandfather took his six children and split them up between his sisters and one of his wife's sisters to be raised. It meant a lot to my mother to keep her family close, even seeking out relatives of a mother she didn't remember. I think she passed that down to me. My books are usually filled with families who are close and caring. Keaton and Koby have all the elements of family and extended family that I have. I hope you enjoy their story.

I want to thank my fearless writing crew, the Friday #am-writing authors—Rose Fairman, Nicole Clarkson, Natassha Ricks, Brandi Larsen, Cheryl Fields, Molly Perry, LaBena Fleming, Maura Weiler, and Constance Harris, who have helped me every step of the way. You are the best! And of course, my favorite librarian, Laura Kincer, and my writing partner extraordinaire, Kathryn Dionne.

A big thank-you to my agent, who puts up with my messiness and still sticks by me, giving me the encouragement and help I need to reach for all my writing aspirations. And to my literary family at BookEnds—agents and authors, I'm so happy to be a part of it all.

And to the best editor ever, Jessica Wade, whose patience and literary smarts help me and my books to become so much better. And to my publisher, Berkley, and the great team behind the scenes that whips my book into shape, I am forever grateful.

And to the relatives I've found in my own genealogical search and have included in this book: Hey, family . . .

Recipes

Soul food is typically referred to as ethnic cuisine—prepared and eaten by Blacks. But of course, anyone can enjoy it, and certainly a lot of dishes that fit the soul-food description are cooked by Southerners everywhere, regardless of race or ethnicity. And the good thing about soul food? You can make it your own!

There is no exact way to cook some things. Say, for instance, collard greens. In writing this recipe, I asked several people, "Do you measure what you put in your greens?" (I already knew the answer, but I asked anyway), and they said, "No! You have to taste it!" Most soul food recipes that are handed down don't come with anything written in stone (or on paper). You put in some of this and a little of that and you taste it to see if it's right. Tasting is the key. If it doesn't taste good, you need more of something. Of course, there are certain things that must go in . . .

Mama Zola's Collard Greens

- 1 or 2 ham hock(s) (or some other smoked meat—smoked turkey neck or turkey wing will work)
- Lawry's Seasoned Salt (to taste)
- Black pepper (to taste)
- Garlic powder (to taste)
- Vidalia onions (if you like them), onion powder (if you don't)
- 7 to 10 bundles of collard greens
- 1 teaspoon sugar (to take the bitterness away—optional)
- Red pepper flakes (if you like it spicy)
- Juice from a jar of banana peppers (not too much)

Cooking greens is very time consuming. (You might get tired just reading what you need to do!)

Before you start with the greens, you'll have to first put on your meat. Put one or two ham hock(s) in the pot you'll cook the greens in (4 or 5 quart pot) and fill it up with water, covering the meat. Add seasoning salt, pepper, garlic powder (do you prefer garlic gloves? You can put two or three of those in) and Vidalia onions (or onion powder) to the water. Sprinkle a good amount—I usually have enough seasoning to create a film across the top of the pot. Let the ham hock(s) cook until it's nearly done (meat close to falling off the bone). You may have to add water as it cooks. Keep it submersed. Cook time is an hour or more. Taste to see if it is done.

While your meat is cooking, you can get started on your greens. First you have to pick them. (Not from the garden, you can get them at the store.) The stems (stalks) have to be removed. No one likes stems in their greens. Even if you buy prepackaged greens, you'll have to get rid of the big, stalky stems (smaller, vein-like ones are okay to leave in). I use two plastic grocery store bags—one to put the discarded stalks in, one to put the picked greens in.

The most important thing about cooking greens is cleaning them properly.

Next you clean them in running water. (You do not soak them. You soak beans, not greens.) Some people add a little baking soda to the first wash. (I don't.) If you decide to use some, just sprinkle a little over the greens while they're in the sink. And, yes, even if you buy prepackaged collard greens, you still have to wash them. At least three times. Otherwise, they will taste gritty. Like dirt in your mouth. (It will actually be dirt in your mouth.)

HOW TO WASH GREENS:

After they have been destemmed, put them in one side of a double sink. Single sink only? No problem. Use a dishpan as the other sink. Turn on the water and rinse off each leaf. Each. One. (If they are small leaves, you can do a couple at a time.) Run your hand over the leaf to clean it. Take off any stems you may have missed or you notice are larger sized. Put each leaf you clean in the other side of the sink (or in the dishpan). Repeat. Then repeat again.

Now you are ready to cook them. You only need about half a pot of water to cook them in.

Stuff all the greens into the pot with your meat. It will seem like they won't fit. They will. Don't wait until some cook down. Put them all in at once. You can put a top on the pot if you can't get them all to stay in on their own. Push them down! Stuff them in! Don't be shy!

Add another round of seasoning salt, black pepper, garlic powder (not cloves this time) and onion powder to season the greens. Not as much as before. Just sprinkle a little in. You can add more later after you taste it. If you decided to add the sugar, do that now, too. (I don't add sugar.)

Now you let the greens cook for about an hour or so on medium heat. With the top on. Checking on them and adding water to the pot when necessary. Not a lot. You just want to make sure they don't burn. You have to keep an eye on them.

After an hour or so, if you like onions, dice a medium-size one and put it in now. You can add the red pepper flakes now, too. Not too much. Greens are not a spicy dish. And now is the time to add about a third of the juice from the jar of banana peppers. Pour it right out of the jar. You have to eyeball it. Taste it. If it needs something from the list of ingredients, add some more. Then taste again.

The collard greens are done when the leaves have cooked down and are tender and taste good. (Remember, tasting while you cook is the key.) About an hour and a half. It's okay to let them cook a little longer if they're not tender enough. But you have to eyeball it . . .

Serve with sliced tomatoes and onions and, of course, cornbread and hot sauce.

Enjoy!

Koby's Soul Rolls

- 2 cups cooked greens
- ½ cup diced ham
- Sprinkle of diced pimento
- 1 package eggroll wrappers

Take leftover collard greens and add the ham and pimento to them. Warm in a pot.

Fill each wrapper with a teaspoon of the warmed mixture. Fold wrapper according to manufacturer's instructions. Deep fry until the wrappers are golden and crispy.

Serve with a dipping sauce made with hot sauce or mustard.

Books & Biscuits' Signature Biscuits

(There *is* a recipe for biscuits!)

- 6 tablespoons unsalted butter (not margarine)
- 2 cups all-purpose flour
- 1 tablespoon baking powder
- 1 tablespoon sugar
- ¾ tablespoon salt
- ¾ cup buttermilk (or whole milk will do)

Preheat oven to 425°F.

Chill butter in freezer before using. About 15 to 20 minutes. Butter should be firm and not frozen for light, flaky biscuits.

Combine dry ingredients into a large mixing bowl.

Cut butter into parts (or use grater), and mix into flour mixture. Combine until mixture is crumbly.

Add milk. Stir until combined. Do not overwork dough.

Put dough on floured surface and knead the dough, folding it over and flattening together. Repeat 4 to 6 times. If dough is sticky, lightly sprinkle more flour.

Press down dough to 1-inch thickness.

Use the mouth of a glass or a biscuit cutter to cut out biscuits, and place on sheet pan.

Fold over leftover dough, repeat previous two steps.

Repeat until not enough dough is left for another biscuit.

Bake on 425°F for 10 minutes or until tops turn a light golden brown.

While hot, cut down the middle and put a pat of butter inside. (If you like, brush outside with melted butter.)

TODAY I WAS going to touch the stars.

Lying on my back, I stared up at my bedroom ceiling. When I'd moved to my own place, the only things I'd taken from my childhood home were the star-shaped glittered cardboard cutouts my grandmother and I had made when I was seven. I hung them as a reminder of what she'd told me—always shoot for the stars.

She'd also told me, on days I had to make ice cream for the store, don't sleep past five a.m.

I sat up in bed and looked over at the red glow of my digital alarm clock.

Four thirty-nine.

Up ahead of time. Already, the day seemed promising.

A smile escaping my lips, I pulled back the covers and stood on the bed. On my toes, I reached up and felt the coarse bumps from the glue on the gold-glittered star that hung the lowest. Closing my eyes, I walked the length of the bed, socked feet sinking into the mattress, and ran my fingertips along the points. Inhaling happily, I jumped off the bed and padded down the hall into the bathroom, humming a tune.

Yes, today was the day that I was going to realize my dream.

As I brushed my teeth, I stared back at my reflection in the mirror and could almost see all the excitement oozing out of me. Running my family's ice cream shop hadn't *always* been my dream, surely not the one I'd left for college and earned a degree in marketing and an MBA for. But when my dad's sister, Aunt Jack, had moved to North Carolina and left our little business without a manager, my grandfather had chosen me, his only granddaughter, to run it. He'd put the key to the shop in a box with a key ring that said "Manager" and a card that said "Carte Blanche" and placed it under the Christmas tree. Tearing into the red-and-gold Ho-Ho-Ho wrapping paper that holiday morning, I'd felt just like a kid—wide smile, nervous giggle and my insides squealing with delight.

That had been nearly a year ago.

I let out a long sigh as I put away my toothbrush and closed the medicine cabinet. I pulled a plastic cap over my short-cropped black hair and stepped into the shower.

Yep, today I was confident about opening the shop, but that confidence had been born out of trouble. After the baton had been passed to me and I came up with the plan to turn our little shop around, I found out the hard way just how quickly plans could go wrong.

I closed my eyes and let the hot water from my brand-new luxury spa showerhead—the only modern amenity in the old Victorian rental—fall down on me.

I had opted to revamp the store, modernizing it with what I deemed strategic, moneymaking renovations. It had a full glass wall at the back of the dining area, a 1950-ish soda shop motif (complete with a black-and-white checkered floor), an open-view kitchen where customers could see their ice cream being made and a menu based on the recipes my grandparents, Aloysius Zephyr Crewse and Kaylene Brewster Crewse, had used when they opened shop in 1965.

I didn't have my grandmother's original recipe box—no one seemed to know what had happened to it. But I did have photocopies of some of the recipe cards she'd used, and, having worked alongside her for my entire childhood tugging at her apron strings, I was pretty sure, for the recipes I didn't have, I could remember most of the ingredients and churn out her bestsellers, or at least be pretty close.

Known for being the methodical and analytical one, I had carefully mapped out a blueprint to restore the business to what I called its glory days—when all we sold was ice cream—but all my planning and practical graduate coursework had gone straight out of the window by week two. I learned firsthand about real-world time delays.

I'd never worried so much in my life. My plan had been to relaunch the shop at the Chagrin Falls Annual Memorial Day Blossom Festival. But between the wrong glass shipping for my partition wall, a prolonged crop of rainstorms and an overbooked contractor, it would be closer to our little village's October Pumpkin Roll before I could flip the sign on the shop door to OPEN.

I say "closer" because my vision still hadn't been actualized. The plexiglass wall needed to partition off the kitchen still hadn't arrived. And the supplier of our fair-trade cane sugar had gotten into a ten-car pileup—no casualties, but tons of the white grains had been overturned across the highway, making me have to wait to get the first batches started until another truck could be loaded. It turned out to be only a two-day delay. Thank goodness it had arrived in time.

I reached over and flipped the showerhead to pulsating, letting the water beat down and wash away those thoughts of all the hiccups that had tried to give my ice cream dream a meltdown.

I basked in the spray for a few more minutes before I turned off the water, stepped out of the shower and wrapped a towel around me. I slid my hand across the condensation on the mirror and grabbed a bottle of face moisturizer.

Smearing the liquid under my eyes and across my fore-head, I couldn't help but grin, thinking about how our little business, with me at the helm, was going to come full circle today. We were back to selling ice cream and *only* ice cream.

I pulled off my shower cap, ran a comb through my hair and felt the first of the butterflies flapping around in my stomach. I whispered a little prayer and headed back to my bedroom to get dressed.

My grandfather had often reminisced about how hard it had been for him and my Grandma Kay to start that little shop. Just relocating to the village of Chagrin Falls, a suburb of Cleveland, from the South, had been an ordeal. My grandma hadn't gotten used to the snow and cold when they took on the business of digging in a frosty freezer every time she served a customer. But then she'd made it her own. Over the years, she came up with flavors that captured everyone's fancy—smooth and lemony luscious ice box pie, sprinkle-splattered cake batter and, my grandfather's favorite, pralines and cream—folds of gooey sweet caramel and salty praline pecans swirled into her homemade vanilla bean ice cream.

But selling ice cream in a place where four seasons some-times slid into two—either hot or cold—meant our family business had hit more bumps than the almond-filled rocky road ice cream my Grandma Kay used to whip up for her fa-mous cakes. So, to keep up, other family members had stuffed the shop shelves with non–ice cream items in an attempt to keep it viable all year round.

Crewse Creamery had become more of a novelty shop—T-shirts, Chagrin Falls memorabilia, hot dogs, lemonade and candy. "No one wants ice cream in the wintertime, Bronwyn," my aunt Jack had said, calling me by my full name, something no one did, while setting up an Ohio lottery machine she'd purchased. "We have to follow the money. Diversify."

With Aunt Jack's changes, our family business had been teetering on the point of no return, especially after she stopped making ice cream by hand. She ordered mix for soft serve and frozen tubs all the way from Arizona. Homemade ice cream had been what set us apart from all the other ice cream shops. But she said it made no economical sense to continue to make it half the year when she could get a year-long contract to supply ice cream to cover the late spring and summer months. Luckily, she'd found love on the internet and moved to follow her man to the Tar Heel State before the first shipment arrived.

My radio alarm clock had popped on at five and was issuing a weather alert when I got back to my room. *Cold. Wet. Dreary.*

Pulling back the sheer curtains at the window, I took a peek outside. I couldn't read the still-dark sky, and the dry ground illuminated by the yellow glow of the streetlight didn't give a hint of what the forecaster warned.

I pulled out a sweater as the old radiator clanked and hissed, held it up and thought better of it.

"Cold weather may be blowing in," I said, folding the sweater up, "but churning ice cream and waiting on customers is gonna make me work up a sweat." I smiled. "Yeah, lots of customers. Lots of sweat."

I stuffed the sweater back into the drawer and, opening another one, pulled out one of the shop's custom T-shirts. I layered it with a button-down flannel shirt—always best to be prepared—and snaked my way into a pair of jeans. On my knees, I rustled through the floor of my closet. I pushed work shoes down into my knapsack and dug my UGG boots out of the back.

I was ready to start my day—*the* day—the first day of our family's new and improved ice cream shop.

First stop, though, my parents' house.

I grabbed my puffy coat and a hat from the coat rack, picked up last year's Christmas gift from PopPop and stuffed it in my jeans pocket and plodded across the old wooden floor and down the back stairs that led out from my second-story apartment.

The sky spit down droplets of rain on me as I walked

outside. Right now it was hit or miss, but something was brewing, I could tell. The wind let out a low howl, blew the autumn leaves across my path and gave me a shiver up my spine. I pulled the hood up on my coat, shoved my hands into my pockets looking for gloves. Nothing. I balled my fists up and tried to keep my fingertips from freezing. The weather forecast was rarely right, at least for Cleveland and its surrounding areas, and—fingers crossed—I hoped the wintery forecast for the day would be a miss.

Around my hometown, snowfall could come with the daffodils in April and not so much for sleigh rides and decorated trees in December. It wasn't odd anymore for Christmas to arrive with sixty-five-degree weather, which was what I was wishing for today.

Ready to find
your next great read?

Let us help.

Visit prh.com/nextread